Praise for Homecoming: A Soldier's Story of Loyalty, Courage, and Redemption

A meticulously researched look not at politics or strategy, but at the men who fought the war in Vietnam, whose stories we risk forgetting.

- Jon Marcus - Award Winning Writer/Editor, Journalism Instructor, Boston College

In thoughtful detail, *Homecoming*, delves into the mental and the physical struggles experienced by two aviators who served in Vietnam. The story makes us pause to see the person behind the uniform. As a member of the generation who watched the war unfold nightly on the news, it brought back a flood of memories of friends who were faced with a similar circumstance. David has given us insight into the life-altering decisions of these soldiers by blending their personal family upbringing, military training, and primal fears - choices that will ultimately affect their survival and future lot in life.

- Linda Valentino, Maine State Senator

The writing in this novel shows that combat is the ultimate crucible and will always separate the wheat from the chaff. War is the forge that creates this unbreakable bond between warriors. This bond is for a lifetime and will persevere, no matter how long between encounters. I salute Arenstam for his efforts and his accomplishments. What a terrific ride it took me on as I recalled my own odyssey as a Huey pilot in many of the same locations and combat areas described in this book.

- Mark Steven, Lt. Col. - U.S. Army (ret)

David Arenstam understands that we should not just honor veterans on Veterans day. This story is not just historical fiction, it is a tribute to Vietnam veterans, everywhere, and this debut novel is making a difference by honoring all those who served.

- Kim Block – Reporter/Anchor – WGME, Portland, Maine

From the streets of quintessential small town America to the battlefields of Southeast Asia, Arenstam's debut is a poignant look back at the Vietnam war through the eyes of those who served. –

- Bruce Robert Coffin, Author of Among the Shadows

This might be historical fiction, but the vivid details the author describes transports you to the real-life situations of our brave men in uniform. Based on interviews with Veterans, **HOMECOMING**, is by far the must-read novel of the year. It's easy to forget about the selfless sacrifice of those who went off to war. It's easy to take the freedoms we enjoy for granted.

This story makes us search inward to appreciate life. It's a firm reminder that there are people who made our lives possible; made it possible for us to carry on with the daily care-free hustle and bustle. History has come alive through the eyes of *A SOLDIER'S STORY OF LOYALTY, COURAGE, AND REDEMPTION.*

- Justin Chenette, Maine State Senator

Homecoming: A Soldier's Story of Loyalty, Courage, and Redemption

A novel by
David Arenstam

A MANAGEMENT & PUBLISHING COMPANY
199 NEW COUNTY ROAD SACO, ME 04072

www.BrysonTaylorPublishing.com

Written by: **David Arenstam**

ISBN-10: 09983867-0-
ISBN-13: 978-0-9983867-0-6
LOCN: 2016959769

Author Photo by: Don Wiggin
Cover Photography by: Fran Osborne

Copyright 2016 © All rights reserved

Homecoming: A Soldier's Story of Loyalty, Courage, and Redemption is a work of fiction. Any references to real people, events, establishments, organizations, or locales are intended to only give the fiction a sense of reality and authenticity, and are used fictitiously. All other names, characters, and places, and all dialogue and incidents portrayed in this book are the product of the author's imagination.

Homecoming: A Soldier's Story of Loyalty, Courage, and Redemption. Copyright © 2016 by Bryson Taylor Publishing and David Arenstam. All rights reserved. Printed in the United States of America. No part of this book may be used or reproduced in any manner without written permission except in the case of brief quotations embodied in critical articles and reviews. For more information, contact Bryson Taylor Publishing, 199 New County Road, Saco, ME 04072.

DEDICATION

To Teri - nothing makes me feel better than seeing you smile and laugh. Thanks for sharing the ride and making me the luckiest man in the world. I couldn't have done this without you.

To my family and friends – thank you. For more years than I like to think about, you've had to listen to my stories. I'll admit here that not all of those tales were always filled with the truth, but all were told from the heart and with only one goal in mind, to entertain and inform anyone who was listening.

To Sergeant Russ Warriner – This work would not have been possible without his help and guidance. For more hours than I can recall, Russ spoke patiently with me about his experiences in Vietnam and what it took to become a crew chief at the tender age of 19. His stories and his advice will never leave me. So to my friend, let me simply say thank you for your service, and I hope you have nothing but gentle days and following winds.

CONTENTS

Prologue

Book I – A World Apart

1. Battle Wounds
2. Birds of a Feather
3. The Boy From the Berkshires
4. Changing Habits
5. Death has a Name

Book II – 365 and a Wake Up

6. Meeting the Family
7. Looking Back at the World
8. Leaving the Nest
9. Too Many Candles for the Cake
10. The Valley of The Living

Book III – The Only Road Home

11. Cages for the Dead
12. My Brother's Keeper
13. The Man in the Mirror
14. Watching the Count
15. Final Days

Epilogue

Foreword

When you have lived well into your seventh decade, you often spend time looking back at your life and the events that shaped the path you followed. For me, and many of my generation, that path was directly influenced by the actions of our government toward a small country in southeast Asia - Vietnam. I am proud to say I served my country and was one of thousands of young men who enlisted in the armed services as we were faced with the overwhelming question of whether or not our number was going to come up in the annual draft. School, politics, or a deferment of any kind was not an option and thinking about it now, I guess I thought that if I kept my head down and my hands busy, I'd be home and unaffected at the end of my 12-month tour. Besides, the recruiter told me that if I became a helicopter mechanic, most likely I would be at a base camp. I had no idea then how wrong I was to believe him.

I served in the U.S. Army from March 1967 until November 1975 and worked as a mechanic on helicopters. Along the way, I completed an extended tour in Vietnam with Charlie Battery, 2nd Battalion, in the 20th Artillery, and I'm proud to say I was a member of 1st Cavalry's Aerial Rocket Artillery Division from November 1967 - June 1969. Looking at those months of service, it's safe to say they shaped the rest of my life.

This novel is based on historical events and facts as I remember them. Initially, I came to know the author when he was working for a local newspaper and was assigned to write a story about a POW/MIA event I was organizing in Maine. The event was dedicated to a friend of mine, a pilot who happened to be the only surviving crew-member who flew on a mission that I was pulled from. I should have been with him. I should have been with the others. More than 44 years after he went missing, together with three other men from Charlie Battery, I waited to see him again, to close the circle. David Arenstam was there too. He wanted to document the final chapter of that story, to see how the drama of that flight ended. In many ways, that's how this tale begins.

After writing the newspaper stories and witnessing our reunion, he asked me if it would be all right to continue talking. He wanted to find out more about my time in Vietnam and the effects it had on me and the other men in my unit. What I came to learn was that at the time we started meeting and discussing my time in the service, his son was in the Army and had been deployed to Afghanistan. We had something to talk about.

For nearly two years, David Arenstam and I spent many hours talking about my experiences and the missions I flew. I introduced him to some of the men who served with me as well as others who were stationed in Vietnam at about the same time. His research and the time we spent together has helped give the novel an accurate feel for how things were, not only for the soldiers caught in a daily fight for survival and sanity, but for our families back in the world. In an almost eerie way, reading the book brings me back, and it helps me understand again why the men I served with are my brothers.

      I hope you enjoy this story as much as I do. At this stage of my life, and given what our country has been through recently in Iraq, Afghanistan, and other combat areas around the world, it's an important book for everyone to read. It will help you better understand one of the more turbulent times in our nation's history and some of the facts surrounding the lives of those who served with me. Like me, many of them, and really soldiers from any era, still feel the effects of their days in a combat environment.

      Russell Warriner, SSG – U.S. Army (ret)

"In war, you win or lose, live or die - and the difference is just an eyelash."

Douglas MacArthur

Prologue – Portland, Maine

September 2012

Rolling across the concrete surface without making a sound, the spotless silver Cadillac with veteran's plates came to a stop at the end of the short-term parking lot at the Portland International Jetport. The license plate read "NAM67" and the magnetic AMVETS sign on the driver and passenger doors almost made the large American sedan appear as if it were an official government vehicle.

The car carried four men and each was dressed for a cold September night in Maine. Jeans, sneakers, t-shirts, and golf jackets were the uniform of the day. Russ Warriner, the owner of the car, was driving and that was unusual for this former helicopter crew chief. Most of the time when he was in the company of these other men, they piloted the vehicles and he rode along.

Patrick Walsh, Billy Braxton, and Michael Francis McCarthy, the other men with Warriner, were all Army helicopter pilots during the Vietnam War and along with Warriner they served in the 1st Cavalry as members of the Aerial Rocket Artillery division. This night, their mission was simple and safe. They were picking up a friend and fellow veteran who was flying to Maine from his home in California, a place he had returned to after the end of the Vietnam War. Most of them hadn't seen him for 44 years, since they were together at Camp Evans in South Vietnam, and in a little less than an hour they would all be together again.

It had been decades since the men in the vehicle had been together in the same part of the world, and as they stepped away from the car and moved toward the main entrance, they lowered their heads, pulled on ball caps, leaned into the night wind and followed one another toward the door that had a sign above it indicating arriving flights could be met here. McCarthy (Lt. Colonel) was the most senior among them, but tonight Warriner, the former Staff Sergeant, was on point.

They made their way through a sliding circular door and immediately scanned overhead for the automated computer screens that displayed the status of arriving aircraft.

"I think he's supposed to be here at 9:05," Warriner said. He was the last man through the doorway after holding the door for the former officers and letting them enter first, a habit he'd learned long ago.

All of the men were in their 60s and some pulled out eyeglasses or squinted as they tried to decipher and decode the messages on the oversized computer displays.

"Is he coming from Atlanta or San Diego?" Billy Braxton asked with a southern drawl.

His words spilled from his mouth as if they were some thick syrupy concoction trying to make its way forward on a cold winter morning. And yet, even though he was waiting and unfamiliar with the airport or the region, the former pilot kept moving, he kept looking for his friend. His eyes, dulled by age and the hour of the night, were focused on the only navigational instruments he had that day, the words on the large computer screen.

He didn't turn his head or remove his hands from his pockets as he waited for an answer. They had all come so far, and the experiences they shared together when they were barely out of their teens forged a bond that drove them to stand by one another, no matter where or when. Braxton was known to his friends as a joker and he was the most light-hearted member of the group, but this night, with these men, the laughter was left behind. He still had work to do and missions to fly.

Bobby Connelly, the man they were waiting for, was shot down on February 4, 1968, during a mission near the city of Hue. Of the four men flying that day, he was the only one who survived the crash. After evading the North Vietnamese Army for more than 36 hours, he was captured and taken prisoner. He spent the next five years as a prisoner of war in Hanoi and was ultimately released in 1973 with nearly 600 other American prisoners. In a matter of minutes, they would meet again.

"Atlanta," Patrick Walsh said. He knew these procedures well.

After retiring from the Army, Walsh flew jets for Continental airlines for 20 years and spent most of that time shuttling passengers up and down the eastern seaboard. As he spoke to the others, the computer screen changed and now displayed a map of the United States. In the lower right corner, the image of a small plane moved from state to state on its way to Maine.

Above the image, in bright red digits, was the flight

number of the plane carrying their friend, Bobby Connelly.

"There's no way his flight will be here on time," said Walsh.

Within seconds, the computer screen that displayed arrival and departure information changed, and Connelly's flight was now listed as delayed, with a new arrival time of 9:28 p.m. The other men watched Walsh as he adjusted his dark blue 1st Calvary cap and unconsciously smoothed his bristly white mustache. It was as if touching the space above his lips had a calming effect on him.

"Braxton, what are you doing with yourself now that you're out?" McCarthy asked.

The two men hadn't seen each other for decades and yet, like siblings, they shared a bond unaffected by time or distance.

"Just about anything I can think of," Braxton said, ending with a smile and small chuckle. "You don't really want to know."

Time passed quickly for the men, and as the small plane on the screen got closer and closer to the map of Maine, their familiar banter and jokes slowed and then stopped. The computer display indicating a flight's status changed again and next to the number that represented the Delta flight from Atlanta, the word "ARRIVED" magically appeared.

Without speaking to on another, the men formed a rough semi-circle at the bottom of an escalator to watch the passengers arrive. Conversations swirled around them as wives met husbands, fathers greeted their children, and boyfriends and girlfriends smiled at the arrival of their loved ones. The men waiting for Connelly stood and the conversations between the former soldiers ended. They were on watch. Over the years they all had practiced waiting to see a friend or loved one. They knew the drill. With heads tilted up at an angle, they hoped to see someone with gray hair, possibly a limp, a man in his 60s, a soldier like them.

After several minutes, a young soldier made his way through the maze of security gates. He had closely cropped hair, a dark tan, and creases in the corners of his eyes that made his face appear weathered, older. The words U.S. Army adorned a badge on his chest and the military insignia below the words indicated he was a sergeant.

Moving as if he had a purpose toward the stairs that led to the parking lot, he carried three small packs made with the same camouflage pattern as his uniform. An older woman standing close to the door, waiting for another passenger, had been watching the soldier, and as he got closer to her, she hesitated for a moment and then approached him. With wrinkled hands and watery eyes, she touched his sleeve.

"Thank you," she said.

The nearly silent exchange between the young soldier and the older woman happened in a little less than 30 seconds.

Walsh shifted his focus and turned once again to his friends and said, "Things are different now. That's good."

He smiled in the direction of his old crew chief,

nodded once more to the woman and said, "Did I ever tell you about my mom, what happened while we were over there – why we had an unlisted number?"

Warriner didn't answer. Instead of speaking, he simply kept his focus on his old friend and raised his eyebrows.

"I went to see her when she was dying of cancer. I never knew it," Walsh said.

"I came from a small town near Stockton, and every time I was promoted or something, the Army would send a press notice to the local paper. My name would be in it."

Warriner nodded. He too was a small town boy.

"People were protesting the war and they thought it would be a good idea to call her and pretend to be from the Army," Walsh smoothed his mustache again and continued. "They'd tell her I'd been killed in action."

His story was interrupted by a quick announcement – Connelly's plane was pulling up to the gate.

"Things are different now," Warriner said, more to himself than any of the other men, and he turned his attention back toward the top of the escalator.

Book I − A World Apart

1 – Battle Wounds

October 1945

Not many people are able to point to a specific date or time and say that's the moment their life changed; that's the moment they became connected with their present, past, and future. Bobby Connelly is one of them. Connelly grew up 30 miles northeast of San Diego in the small town of Escondido, California. Jimmy Connelly, his dad, and a Navy veteran arrived in San Diego at the end of World War II. Not on a ship or a Navy transport plane, but on a train from Seattle, Washington.

The destroyer he served on, the U.S.S. Thatcher, limped into the Bremerton harbor two weeks after the bombs were dropped on Hiroshima and Nagasaki, its battle scars clear for all to see. Jimmy, a machinist's mate first class, served on the destroyer from 1942 until 1945 and at the end of the war, he stood alone on the stern of the ship as it sailed into the secluded harbor. He had money in his pocket, luck in his hand, and no idea what to do with his life.

Jimmy's family lived outside of Los Angeles in the hills of Pasadena, and his father, Francis, ruled the Connelly clan with an iron fist, often quoting the bible and John Quincy Adams in the same breath. He wasn't shy about reminding those at the dinner table that their family had once helped settle the Massachusetts Bay Colony, and to his way of thinking, the values and temperament that proved so successful then were certainly good enough for the world today.

Jimmy had not heard those sentiments for more than three years, and truth be told, that was one thing from home he didn't miss. After surviving typhoons, torpedo runs, and kamikaze attacks, the decorated and battle-weary sailor had no intention of living under his father's roof. He wasn't sure how long it would take to clear the shipyard or what his future might be. He only heard a singular voice that told him not to settle near his parents in Pasadena.

The men who worked at the Bremerton Shipyard spent two weeks climbing in and around every inch of the deeply wounded destroyer. They took photographs, drew illustrations, and completed countless pages of the Navy's official survey form. Within two days after the 263-page document was delivered, the survey report received a large, ornate red stamp on the top of the first page indicating the ship was a total loss. The vessel was to be decommissioned.

Scrawled beneath the stamp, in a typically formal fashion, was the base commander's signature and a date – 22 October 1945. As far as the Navy was concerned, the government was better off selling the ship for scrap than trying to rebuild it and put it back into service.

That was fine with Jimmy. Most of the crew had been on the ship for a while and when the skipper, Commander Fowler, called him to his cabin, he had an idea that he wanted to talk to him about his discharge. Fowler had once been an enlisted sailor, like Jimmy, but shortly after Pearl Harbor, the exceptional chief boatswain's mate was plucked from the enlisted ranks and sent to Officer Candidate School. Because of his experience and the needs of the service, 90 days later he came out the other side a freshly-pressed lieutenant, and by the end of the war, he had his own command.

Fowler was in for life and he wanted Jimmy to stay with him.

"Come!" he barked at the closed cabin door.

"Sir, you sent for me?" Jimmy asked, standing for the first time inside the captain's cabin. It was smaller than he expected, and the only sound in the room came from the portable rotary fan that stood on the skipper's filing cabinet. The captain turned slightly toward the petty officer and without raising his head more than an inch, he got right to the point.

"Relax, Connelly. I wanted to ask you something. Most of the crew will be getting their final orders in a day or so. I'd like you to consider staying in. The Navy's going to lose a lot of men, but I think you should give some thought to making a career out of the Navy." For a few seconds, both men remained silent. Only the sound of the fan pushing the stale, cabin air filled the room. Captain Fowler looked as if he wanted to say more, but either he couldn't find the words, or wouldn't let them leave his lips. He drew a second, deep breath and continued. "The war may be finished, but we're not done. I have a chance to send someone to OCS and I want to send you. You've proven yourself more than once."

Jimmy stared past his captain and saw the blades of the fan spinning slowly, almost like a plane's propeller. Without warning, the sound from the tiny electrical motor changed, increased, and became deeper. He thought he heard the violent hum of the Japanese aircraft engines that had once threatened their lives. The cabin was hot and with the door shut behind him, the only ventilation came from a small porthole that opened to the starboard side of the ship. As the noise of the phantom aircraft engines raced through his head, he focused on the damaged steel plates outside the small hole. The strips of rust covered steel looked as if the deck crew had dumped a five-gallon bucket of primer over the side of the ship. Jimmy could almost see the burned and buckled deck plates where the last Zero hit their ship.

It flew low toward the ship at more than 200 miles per hour and no matter where he fired the deck gun, it just kept coming. He remembered that when it was no more than 100 yards away from its target, Jimmy started screaming and the combination of his voice and the whine from the dying aircraft engines drowned out any other sounds, all other thoughts. He was sure the stricken plane was going to crash into the rail below his seat.

The enemy aircraft shifted its path in the last three seconds of flight, and the Zero missed the main deck by no more than 10 feet and Jimmy was sure he had seen the bloody face of the pilot as the plane plunged into the sea and exploded. What was left of the plane's canopy contained at least a dozen holes from the American shells and a white ceremonial ribbon, stained with blood and brains, encircled the dead pilot's head. It almost appeared as if the dead pilot was leaning to one side, or slumped forward to check one of his instruments. From the size of the blast, and the force of the shock wave that hit them, Jimmy's gun crew thought the aircraft must have been nearly full of fuel and bombs. The sound of the aircraft engines disappeared in seconds as the waters of the Pacific swallowed the doomed plane. The memory faded almost as quickly as it came and Jimmy again focused on the captain in front of him.

The old man was sweating. Stains circled his neck and a long dark line ran straight from his shoulders to the edge of his uniform web belt. Jimmy knew it was hot, but by now he was used to the feeling of water running down his back. He hardly noticed. Deep wrinkles sullied the edge of the skipper's face, and the corners of his steel-gray eyes were marked with small black dots. It was as if someone had taken a sharp knife and created a crisp patchwork of thin incisions on the side of his skull. His always skin-tight crew cut only accentuated the netlike lines near his temples. He wasn't more than 10 years older than Jimmy, but there was a lifetime of difference between them. He had been in the service when the war broke out and he'd stay in after the Thatcher was sold for scrap, but not Jimmy. He couldn't stay. He didn't want to stay.

"Sir, ... I really can't," he said. "I've already written to my folks and they think I'm getting out."

The captain picked up his black, government-issue pen and sat back in his steel chair. He tapped the side of his head with the pen and drew a deep breath as he gazed at the sailor in front of him. Methodically, the fan shifted direction from one side of the cabin to the other and as the warm air brushed against the skipper's cheek, he lowered the pen and wrote three quick words on the form in front of him and asked Jimmy to sign and date the bottom of the page. The discussion was over. Within 30 days he'd leave the ship and the service behind.

The meeting with Captain Fowler lasted no more than 15 minutes, but in that time, Petty Officer First Class James Connelly charted the course for the next portion of his life. He was leaving the Navy, heading away from the sea and trying to live a normal life. With a little luck, he might find a wife and have a family. He wasn't the only guy in the Navy with these hopes and dreams.

A general buzz of excitement and anticipation rolled through the ship as sailors who served together packed their belonging and made arrangements for discharge, liberty, and leave. Jimmy had a few hours before his watch was supposed to start and he thought he might try to get in touch with his Mom and Dad. It was strange; he wanted to talk to them, for them to know he was safe and back in the U.S., but he didn't want to go home. He pulled his cap and coat from his locker and headed for the gangway connected to the dock. The yardbirds had set up a bank of phones in the cafeteria and as he headed toward the brick building near the front gate, he smiled a little more with each step he took on firm soil. He was still swaying a little bit with the roll of the sea, but the land didn't move. It was only his head.

Once inside the cafeteria, he was directed by a cook toward the phones with instructions that each sailor had five minutes, no more. Jimmy didn't respond; he took a seat in front of the first idle phone. He almost laughed when he noticed the back wall of the cafeteria and saw a yellowing poster with large blue, block lettering with the now familiar words, "Remember, silence means security!"

The telephones were black, government-issued, and without any type of dial mechanism. Each sailor clicked the receiver once or twice and was connected with an operator at the base.

"Pasadena 5-1226," he said into the surprisingly heavy handset. "One minute," said the anonymous female voice on the other end of the line.

Jimmy surveyed those around him as he waited for his connection, and saw five or six of the sailors from his ship. Most of them were in the middle of some type of animated conversation. Tom Griffin, the lookout from his gun crew, was two tables to his left and he thought he heard him crying as he tried to explain to someone where the ship was docked and when he'd be home. Jimmy lowered his head and tried to focus his gaze on the center of the phone as if he too was connected to home, but he kept listening to the others.

"I'm fine. Really. I think I'll be leaving the yard in 10 days and then take the train home. I'm not sure exactly, but I'll call as soon as I get the tickets," Griffin said and wiped his eyes with the end of his uniform sleeve. Jimmy thought about getting up and leaving, but it was too late, a sound so familiar and so far away came through the earpiece.

"Jimmy? Is that you?"

It was his mother's voice, a sound he hadn't heard for more than three years, and almost magically, the simple tone from his childhood silenced the world around him. He was speechless. Without a conscious thought, he pulled on the spiral cord and sat a little closer toward the phone.

"Jimmy?" she asked one more time. This time her question was laced with the smallest amount of panic.

"Hi ... Mom, yes it's me," he finally said and settled into his seat. Within minutes, he explained where he was and that he was not hurt or in the hospital and that he would be getting out of the Navy soon.

"You'll be coming home? For good?"

Jimmy paused for a few seconds and then told her the story he'd been practicing for the last two days. "Just for a day or two, but I've got a line on a job in San Diego with the shipyard and if I get it, I'll need to start soon. There aren't going to be many yards left now that the war's over and I'll be lucky to find the work."

His mother was silent, but after taking another loud breath, she said it was so good to hear from him and she couldn't wait to see her son, even if it was only for a few days.

"I'll call you when I get on the train in Seattle," he said. "But I've got to get back to the ship."

"Jimmy ... I'm so happy you're home," his mother said.

"Me too," he said. Once the two simple words left his throat, it became increasingly difficult to breathe and his eyes filled with the tears of more than a thousand sleepless nights. He put the handset back on the phone without making a sound. Neither one of them said goodbye or mentioned Jimmy's father. That could wait.

Jimmy wasn't surprised when he received his discharge papers within 10 days. He and most of the other men on the ship packed what few belongings they had, said their goodbyes, promised to keep in touch with one another and left for the place they each called home. Jimmy, with a sea bag full of memories and sweat-stained uniforms, headed for the front gate and a shuttle bus to the train station in Seattle. He saw the skipper one last time as he stood on the fantail and saluted the ensign flying on the stern of the ship. Captain Fowler was standing on the bridge wing watching the men as they made their way from the ship, and he turned toward the stern as Jimmy stepped on the gangway. He didn't say anything, he didn't move, but every time Jimmy thought about his last minutes in the Navy, and he felt sure the old man had nodded to him as if to say goodbye.

Every seat on the shuttle bus was filled and the makeshift rack that was welded to the roof strained to hold each of the seabags tossed happily into the morning sky. The converted school bus was top-heavy and with every bench seat containing two or more sailors, it took more than a half-mile to pick up any real speed. The base mechanics knew what the old vehicle was in for and before it left the shop, the early morning shift had pumped the tires with an extra five or ten pounds of air pressure. The gray ghost of a bus dropped nearly to the pavement every time it went over a bump or found a hole in the road, but the men inside her hull didn't care one bit. A few passed around a bottle that had been stashed in their locker, and within minutes, the sound of happy, hearty, and homeward bound sailors pushed the tired transport forward with a purpose and a longing.

During the war years, both of the passenger train stations in Seattle saw their share of soldiers and sailors come and go, but after September 2, 1945, when the formal surrender documents between the United States and Japan were signed in Tokyo Bay, many servicemen and women used the stations as the first segment of their journey home. Jimmy asked a few people at the base about the trains to Los Angeles and was told there was no direct service, and he'd have to make a change in San Francisco. He couldn't buy the tickets until he got to the King Street Station, but the Northern Pacific Railroad recently added extra cars in order to accommodate the immediate influx of passengers and even if he didn't get on the first train to California, the next one would leave six hours later. Either way, he'd have a seat for sure. The old gray bus settled to a stop next to the granite curb and Jimmy and his now all-too-jolly friends rolled through the front door, and in a fit of excitement, lurched uneasily toward the station. "Home, home, home," he muttered more to himself than anyone else. The air was cold and wet, but to Jimmy it had a different feel to it, almost thick and palpable. The large, white-faced clock with ornate gold hands on the outside of the station showed that it was three minutes before 9 a.m. and he knew the first train to San Francisco left at 9:45. He didn't say too much to the rest of the group, but he hoisted his seabag over his shoulder and headed for the front door and the ticket counter beyond. "Gotta go, gotta go," he muttered as he slalomed between several standing passengers.

Once he was through the main doors, he panicked for a minute. "Ticket counter," he said in no more than a whisper and his head began to pivot from side to side, as it had often done when scanning the skies for an enemy plane, slow and steady, right to left. "There you are," he said and a small almost undetectable smile appeared. With a direction and a destination, he started moving again across the polished marble floor. There were two rows of bench seats in the middle of the station for the waiting passengers, but Jimmy gave them a quick glance and moved toward the closest ticket line. One person stood in front of him, a young woman with a plain blue suitcase that had an auburn symbol embroidered near the leather handle. She was neatly dressed and her ebony colored hair was cut close to her shoulders, in a fashion he hadn't seen for many years. Her hair was pinned neatly behind each ear and it was braided into a single, foot-long line that resembled the decorative ropes he'd seen in the Navy. Jimmy never saw her face but decided the line she was in would be the fastest. He glanced back toward the clock – 9:05.

"One for San Francisco," she said and Jimmy heard what he thought was a slight accent, maybe European. She opened the small pocketbook attached to her wrist and pulled out an even smaller change purse; it was the size of a ripe apple and it appeared to be filled with money. She peeled away a $10 bill and closed the purse before the clerk had a chance to look at her.

"That'll be $8.50 and you'll have to take one of the last two cars," the clerk said after he pulled her money through the caged window.

"Name?" he asked and pulled a thick ledger closer to the center of the window.

"Annie George," she replied, and with one continuous motion of his pen, the clerk entered her name into the train's manifest.

Jimmy heard coins slide across the wooden windowsill but not another word from the woman standing in front of him, and within seconds, she was gone. He was alone in front of the clerk.

"One for San Francisco, and do I have time for the 9:45?" Jimmy asked.

"I only have one or two seats left and they're in the last two cars, the colored car, but I have plenty of room on the 1:45," he said.

"That's fine – 9:45. I just want to head out," Jimmy said and pushed a crumpled $20 bill through the window.

"Tell them to put you in the front of the car. Name?"

"Connelly, James C.," he said in an automatic fashion that he'd learned during the last three years.

The clerk entered his name into the ledger and to Jimmy, it seemed funny to see the neat block lettering printed next to the girl's name - probably it was the fact that she had two first names. He shoved his change back into his uniform pants, grabbed his seabag and ticket, and he headed toward the doors marked for departures and the seats nearest to them.

He wasn't seated for long, probably no more than 10 minutes, when a whistle sounded throughout the station and an announcement was made that Great Northern 410 – departing at 9:45 - was ready for boarding. With a deep exhale, he stood up, grabbed his hat and seabag, and headed for the train. At the doorway leading to the platform, he saw the woman who stood in the ticket line in front of him. She turned her head to the left, looking for the end of the train and when she did, she raised a gloved hand to shield her eyes from the morning sun. After seeing a brief flash, Jimmy realized she was wearing a narrow silver bracelet. When she raised her hand, the intricately designed bits of silver and black formed a perfect angle with the sun and the morning light danced and sparkled from her wrist. But as quick as it happened, it was over. The now stationary sailor saw the bracelet she wore was a combination of intricate artwork carved into the precious metal.

From where he stood, the metalwork resembled the knots they used to tie on the ship, but it was more than that. Without noticing the movement, he followed her toward the last cars on the train and with a ticket in his right hand and his seabag over his left shoulder, he hopped up to the wooden platform. A small bead of sweat fell from his forehead as he entered the car and tried to find the conductor and a seat.

The car was nearly full; the windows on both sides of the steel carriage were lowered and a soft breeze blew over Jimmy's uncovered head. His rarely exposed head felt cool as the sweat of his brow evaporated. Because of the musky, humid smell, the low lighting, and constant murmur of conversation, his mind instantly made a connection back to the forward end the destroyer that he had abandoned in the shipyard. During his first year on the Thatcher, the bunks he shared with the other men were stacked four deep along the hull of the ship and in the center of the space were cast-iron pipes that ran from the deck plates to the overhead, The bunks, their racks, were stacked four-high in between. Once he was settled into his rack, there was less than a foot from his nose to the backside of the sailor above him, not necessarily a comforting memory. Eventually, he was promoted to E-6 and his rack was moved to the back section of the forward berthing area. There, along with six other first class petty officers, he was given a small vertical locker and the bunks were constructed in such a way that only two sailors shared the same space. To Jimmy, that section of steel and gray paint was home, a place where he often dreamed of a future – a place where he once made a deal with the man upstairs.

Jimmy dropped his seabag and nodded in the direction of the conductor. He appeared to be in his mid-50s and was about a third of the way down the car, talking to two mess cooks from Jimmy's ship. The cooks hadn't been on the bus with him, but he knew them both on sight, they'd served him countless meals. The conductor abruptly ended his conversation with the men and made his way toward Jimmy.

"You must be in the wrong car," he said as he approached the sailor. "This is for coloreds."

Jimmy dropped his bag to the floor with a loud, dull,

thud, and glared at the man.

"The other cars are full and I just want to get home," he said and pushed his ticket toward him. The conductor pulled the ticket with enough force to nearly tear it in half.

"It won't be a problem," Jimmy said. "I plan to sleep most of the way to San Francisco."

"Well ... sit in this first row," the conductor said and returned the ticket with a hole punched through the top half.

Jimmy hoisted his seabag one more time and pushed it across the wooden floor until it sat half under the bench on the left side of the cabin. He rolled his dark blue peacoat into a makeshift pillow and straddling his bag, he took a seat nearest the train windows. During the last three years, he'd learned to sleep whenever possible, or as needed. Now was one of those times, and he propped his coat between his shoulder and the window, tilted his head slightly, and lowered his cap over his eyes. The smell of sweat and diesel fuel from the worn, wool jacket filled his nose and it was almost as if he was on the ship again. His body instinctively relaxed and he knew that in minutes he'd be asleep. He heard someone settle into the seat next to him, but he didn't bother to open his eyes, and as the train rolled slowly from the station, he thought, "I made it. I'm going home."

2 – Birds of a Feather

October 1945

The magical effect of the movement of the train and the comfortable smell of the ship in his old coat worked their wonders on the sailor. In less than 10 minutes, Jimmy Connelly was motionless and his eyelids settled into a comfortable resting place for the next few hours. The slow and steady rattle of practiced sleep could be heard throughout the front portion of the train. Without many other options, Annie George had taken the seat next to the sleeping sailor. By the time she boarded the train, the window seats were all taken and the only empty seat that seemed safe was right in the front row of the cabin. The open seat was next to the aisle and the door to one washroom on this end of the train. The smell of antiseptic and stale urine drifted toward her as each passenger in the car walked by and caused the air to move in her direction.

She placed most of her simple belongings under her seat and took out a small leather-bound journal from her traveling bag. With one last look in the direction of the sleeping serviceman sitting next to her, she placed the journal on her lap and watched the city slip away. It was the first time she'd ever been to Seattle, a city her father often told her was named after one of the great men of her nation. Now, after less than an hour inside the city limits, she was leaving her family behind and heading south, convinced a better life lay ahead.

Annie had been awake for nearly 20 hours before boarding the train and the warmth of the cabin, the gentle rolling motion, and rhythmic sound of the steel wheels traveling over the tracks worked their magic on her as well. Within minutes, her eyelids felt as if they needed to close for a second or two. Her eyes themselves were sore, she felt like they were covered with bits of sand or dust, and she knew the rest would take away some of the pain.

"It will be all right for a second or two," she thought. "I'll be fine." She convinced herself that while she rested, the conversations swirling around her would keep her awake. She tipped her head back slightly and rested her head on the upper edge of the seat.

Annie didn't move for nearly two hours and only woke up when a slightly drunken sailor bumped into her as he lurched for the open bathroom door. With a bit of panic, she woke up and for a second she forgot where she was.

"Hey," she said and put her right hand up near her face as if to cover the vulnerable section of her head.

"Well, well, looky, looky," said the sailor, in a voice thickened by drink and time. He hadn't seen her as he made his way to the forward end of the train. Some primitive piece of his mind had propelled him with a sense of urgency toward the bathroom and her presence stunned him. He tried to turn in her direction, but the alcohol in his system slowed his reflexes. He managed to twist at the waist and face her, but he wasn't in full control and the weight of his body kept moving forward toward the open bathroom door. It was more than his reflexes could handle and he ended up in a painful pile on the floor of the cabin.

"Sheet," he said and burped loudly as the gas in his chest and gut found the most direct way to escape. "Sheet, sheet," he drawled again and the gas trapped inside his torso discovered a more southern route to leave the sailor's body. Annie pretended not to notice and slid almost imperceptibly closer to the sleeping sailor on her left.

She smelled the sour, all-too-familiar, scent of half-digested whiskey and knew there was a better-than-even chance the liquid that shared the same space as the gas would soon seek its own way out. She turned away from the aisle, picked up her pen and focused on the journal in front of her. Annie started to systematically fill the page with copies of her signature.

Jimmy, oblivious to her task, had been dreaming of the ship's last mission, and he thought he was trapped below decks. In his dream, he and the other men on watch were crowded near the engine room hatch. He didn't know why, but they desperately needed to get to the main deck. They couldn't open the heavy steel hatch and he knew that if they didn't get out soon, they'd either drown or burn to death as the ship struggled to stay afloat. There were men on the other side and Jimmy heard them scraping on the gray, metal door, scratching as if they were trying to communicate.

"Hey, hey, ... Here!" he said and lunged toward the door in his dreams. Startled and trying to make sense of the landscape moving past his window, Jimmy awoke with a start and lunged forward. His head came to rest with a loud thud when he hit the metal bar that separated the top half of the train window.

"Damn it," he said more to himself than anyone else in his dream or anyone who happened to share the railroad car with him. He instinctively put his hand to the sore area of his forehead and turned his head slightly to the right. The woman next to him had stopped writing in the little leather book on her lap, but he could see the page and there was one name written over and over again in three neat columns on the page, Anna Martinez. The final Z in the name was written in a flourish of cursive script, and Jimmy thought of the images of the declaration of independence he'd seen as a boy in school.

"Sorry if I woke you," she said to the groggy sailor and shut her book.

"That's all right. I don't want to sleep too long," he said, straightening his uniform shirt as best he could. "I'm James Connelly," he said.

At first, Annie George didn't know if she should respond. For the last few years, she'd heard stories about sailors and what happened when they came ashore. Her teacher at the reservation school always told the girls that whenever they left their homes to see a movie or visit the stores in the city, they should travel with a friend, preferably two or three. But this sailor was different, he was subdued. He seemed consumed by his own thoughts and not the least bit interested in her.

"Anna Martinez," she said and turned once more toward the small aisle between the seats. She hoped this would be the end of the conversation.

"Are you heading to Los Angeles?" Jimmy asked, thinking about the name he'd seen the clerk enter into the manifest. It didn't match the name she'd given him, but right about now, that didn't matter.

"Yes. I mean no. I'm going to San Diego," she said. "I have a job there."

As she spoke with the sailor, she had the habit of raising her hands to her face, as if she wanted to cover her mouth and hide the words from anyone else who might be looking in her direction.

Jimmy glanced at his watch and saw that he'd been sleeping for nearly three hours. He was sore and hungry and he needed to find the head.

"I'm going to stretch my legs and see if I can't find a sandwich," he said and started to rise from his seat. "Would you mind watching my bag and do you want something?"

Annie didn't know which question to answer first, and she smiled at the sailor. It felt as if it had been a week or more since she last smiled for the world.

"No, I don't need anything and I'll watch your bag," she said.

Stepping around her and moving toward the front end of the train, Jimmy nodded and returned the smile.

The trip from Seattle to San Francisco was scheduled to take a little more than 24 hours and Jimmy knew he probably would be able to sleep most of the way, but he was also thinking about home and he wanted to make sure he had his story straight. After returning from the dining car, he settled into his seat again and tried to act naturally as he turned toward the young woman sitting next to him.

"Do you have family in San Diego?" Jimmy asked, hoping to think of a way to extend the conversation with Anna. She was beautiful and young, two things he hadn't seen much of during the last four years, and he wasn't sure exactly what to say.

"What kind of job do you have?" he asked, hoping this was a better question. Anna turned the silver bracelet on her wrist so the ornate eagle near the clasp was facing toward her chest, and she drew in a long breath. "My family is from Mexico and I have a job at a resort a few miles outside of the city. There's a small lake there and they need help with the cabins and the laundry," she said. "I am not exactly sure, I saw the ad in the newspaper and called them from school."

"Were you working there?" Jimmy asked and noticed that Anna had started tapping the cover of the book on her lap.

"I was helping the teacher, but I wasn't paid. I could live there and they gave me room and board, but there wasn't any real money. Sometimes at the end of the month, I'd get $5 or $10 if the farm stand had done well, but I couldn't count on it."

Jimmy gave her a look that was supposed to mean he knew exactly what it must have been like, but the whole time he was focused on the shape and color of her eyes and her profile. Her skin was dark, the color of lightly stained oak, but unlike his pale Irish complexion, she didn't have a single blemish, freckle, or any other mark on her face. He thought her face was perfect. Her hair was dark and the richness of the color only complimented the tone of her skin. She pulled her hair back into a single black braid and near the nape of her neck she wore a small silver barrette. It was similar to the bracelet she wore, but it appeared as if the piece of jewelry were created from a curved knot of metal rope. There was a short, wooden stick looped under her hair and through the barrette. He kept looking at the young woman and completely missed her conversation.

"Yeah, we got paid regular too," he said, not sure if that mattered to the woman. "Sometimes, though, we wouldn't get paid until the ship came back into port."

For the next two hours Jimmy told her about his hitch in the Navy, where he'd been, and the names of some of the battles he'd fought in. He tried to describe what it was like on the ship - what it felt like to be alone in the middle of the Pacific. He told her about the solitary moments when he found himself late in the day on the fantail of the ship, staring at the sea and sky. Even during war he noticed that the bottom of the clouds that hung from the oncoming night sky were the color of almost ripe plums and the sun was sitting large and low on the horizon. It comforted him – it made him feel as if things might be normal again.

He wasn't a storyteller by nature, but there was something soothing about the way she looked at him and listened. It was easy to talk to Anna.

The afternoon passed quickly, and Jimmy noticed that as time elapsed her eyelids were half closed. If she sat still for more than a minute, her head would start to bob toward her chest. It reminded him of the watches he used to stand on the ship, trying to stay awake at the end before his relief showed up. He'd been there all-too-often himself.

"Do you want to switch seats and rest your head against the window?" he asked. "You don't have to, but it'll be a long night if you don't get some sleep."

Anna paused for a moment and said, "No, I'm fine. Really."

"I'll watch your stuff and nobody will bother us," he added and gazed at her for 10 seconds or more. He didn't smile. He didn't frown. He tried to show her that it would be safe with him there by her side. "Really," he said and stated to get up.

Anna put the leather binder into her bag and stood up. Without a word, she and Jimmy exchanged seats. The train was rolling along a curved section somewhere near the Oregon coast and for the last mile or so, every time it went over one of the older railroad ties, it lurched – first to the left and then to the right. The track was repaired each year after the heavy spring rains, and with each washout, the maintenance crews tried to shore up this section using the volcanic remains of the local islands that had long ago washed ashore.

As they passed in front of their seats, the train rolled past one of these sections of the track and Anna stumbled as if she were going to fall. Without thinking, and before any words left her lips, Jimmy reached for her forearm and slid his other hand around her waist. After four years spent on heaving decks, he knew how to lean into the sudden movement and stay upright. He guided her to her seat.

Anna was grateful for the help, but in a practiced, nearly familial way, she kept her thoughts to herself. She was amazed by the sailor who sat next to her – she had heard so often at school about the men who were away fighting and how they would routinely turn aggressive and cruel in mere moments. They were not to be trusted. But this sailor was different. His stories, his voice, the gentle way he seemed to care for her was confusing and she wasn't sure where the truth about him could be found. She was grateful he was in the seat next to her. But even more confusing to her was the way she felt when he was physically close to her.

When he reached out and touched her arm and guided her to her seat, everything stopped for a second or two and she focused on his hand. It was not smooth, but not rough like the hands of the men who worked on the farm near her school. She was thankful he was there and astonished by her body's response to his touch. She was tired and she knew she needed to sleep soon, if only for a few hours.

Anna took the seat and rolled her scarf around her gloves to form a makeshift pillow. She placed it on her left shoulder as she had seen Jimmy place his coat on his own shoulder a few hours before. She shifted her body slightly so her head was not resting on the glass window but on the soft red, black, and brown scarf she'd had since she was a child. Her cheek was warm from the cloth and she closed her eyes, expecting to drift off any second, but her mind was now moving as fast as the wheels below her cabin. Her eyes were closed, but as tired as she was a few minutes ago, sleep would not come.

"Jimmy, James ... Connelly," she repeated to herself. "I wonder who you are."

Jimmy watched her lower her head toward the window and started to think once more about visiting home and seeing his parents after so many years away. He'd pulled a newspaper out of the trash bin in the dining car and brought it back to his seat. Every few seconds he would flip through the pages as if he were reading, but he wasn't even looking at the photos that were splashed across the pages. He got to the last page and folded the paper back to the beginning and started all over again.

Jimmy loved his parents. He thought of his mother, Grace, as affectionate, but only to a point. For her, life was a series of difficult tasks and there wasn't any reason not to work hard.

As a child, she'd said to him more than once "Everyone's got responsibilities. You need to meet yours head on. They won't manage themselves." This was her advice for everything he did in his life. "Your rest and reward will come in time."

The train rolled along the coast and eventually moved inland for the southern run toward the California border and its final destination. Jimmy couldn't sleep anymore. His thoughts were occupied with the young girl next to him and what he was going to do now that the war was over. He knew going back to school was an option but he couldn't imagine spending the next three years inside a classroom. What was he going to learn in school that he didn't already know? The war and his time in the Navy left a permanent mark on his personality and after facing death on more than one occasion, he couldn't imagine listening to teachers or professors drone on about subjects and lessons that didn't matter one bit to him. He had survived and been given the gift of time, and he didn't want to waste one second of that precious commodity.

The sun dipped below the tree line to his left and for close to an hour, as the light was pulled from the evening sky, Jimmy listened to the sounds of Anna breathing. As he watched her sleep, he saw her eyes twitch and he wondered if she was dreaming. Her breathing was regular and even, but every so often, she took a double breath and then she wouldn't exhale. To the sailor, it looked as if she stopped breathing for 30 seconds or more. The third time it happened, he thought he would have to touch her and wake her up, but then it came, inevitable as the miles ahead, she drew another breath and continued sleeping. The cabin was becoming colder - there wasn't any heat in this end of the train and Jimmy didn't want her to feel the chill of the winter night. He unrolled his wool jacket and gently laid it on her shoulders. Without touching her directly, he tucked it under one of her elbows and made sure the lower half of the coat covered her legs. He again noticed the silver bracelet on her wrist. This time, the silver and black eagle was turned in his direction and the ornate, regal bird watched as he comforted her. He smiled when she didn't wake up and he settled himself a bit more in his seat.

The train skated along the rails as it made its way

through the northern hills of California, and shortly after midnight, he felt Anna stirring next to him. The two had become used to the feel of one another and the warm silence brought comfort to them both.

"Excuse me," she said and in the dim light of the cabin and pointed toward the bathroom door.

"Oh yeah," Jimmy said and stood for her.

"Why don't you take this seat for a while," Anna said as she moved toward the aisle. "I don't think I could sleep anymore – thank you."

She didn't wait for an answer and made her way to the bathroom.

When she returned, Jimmy slid himself nearer to the side of the rail car and she was now sitting close to the aisle. He smiled when she returned to her seat. What he didn't tell her was how warm the seat felt when he moved over and propped himself against the window. Jimmy sensed her presence and the fragrance that defined her lingered in the open space between the seat and the window. The essence of who she was hung in the air for him, and before it left, he deeply inhaled. He wanted to carry her with him, to join him.

"How much longer do you think it will be before we arrive?" she asked, looking at her watch. From her ticket, Anna knew it would be at least eight hours before they arrived in San Francisco, but that had become both a blessing and a curse. She felt comfortable talking to the sailor sitting near her, but Anna knew he'd be leaving soon, heading back to his world, a world that was completely foreign to her. Where she was heading was still mostly a mystery to her.

"We'll be there in the morning, sometime after eight," he said, turning for a moment toward the passing darkness.

For the next hour or so neither one said much. Anna occasionally added another signature or two to her long list, and for his part, Jimmy tried not to notice. He wanted to sleep, but whether his eyes were open or closed, his thoughts kept returning to the woman traveling with him. The rest of the rail car had settled into a deep slumber, and he thought they must be the only two still awake.

After more than an hour thinking to himself, trying to find the right words, he said, "That's an interesting bracelet. Is that an eagle? I've never seen one quite like that."

Anna unconsciously pulled her wrist up and toward her closed mouth. She exhaled as if a decision had been made and said, "It was my mother's. She said it has been in our family for a long time and when I told her I was leaving, she gave it to me as a reminder of who I was – where I'd been and where I was going."

Jimmy didn't respond right away, and unconsciously he rubbed his own wrist. "Is that an eagle?" he asked, pointing at the silver bird.

"Yes," Anna said and paused for a moment as if she were trying to decide whether or not she should say anything else. "For me, for my family, it represents the strongest spirit - life. When I was young, I learned that if you carry that spirit with you, it will always carry you home."

Jimmy looked at her but didn't say anything. He

thought of his own childhood, the men who he'd known during the last four years who didn't make it home, and his own future, but no matter where his thoughts started they ended with the girl whose leg was now pressed steadily against his own. All he could do was nod his head in her direction. He wanted to hear more.

"Are you getting off the train in San Francisco?" she asked.

"No, I'm heading all the way to Los Angeles. My parents live about 20 miles outside of the city, near Pasadena," he said.

"Is that where you grew up? Is that where your family is from?" she asked.

"Yeah. My great-grandparents settled there right after the civil war, most of the family's been there ever since," he said.

Anna's head moved again in his direction and then after hesitating for a few seconds, she added, "I'm going to Los Angeles too, for a job."

"Is your family in Seattle?" Jimmy asked. As soon as the words left his mouth, he noticed her shift in her seat and her leg moved away from his own. The distance created by her movement allowed him to feel the cold air in the cabin, and she waited for nearly a minute before she replied.

"My family is not from Seattle. I grew up near Spokane," she said and measured the response from the sailor.

"Actually, it was a reservation. I am a member of the Coeur D'Alene tribe," she said and crossed her arms as if she were now expecting a fight.

"But your name - the book," he said pointing to the journal resting on her legs.

"At home, I had a teacher, Miss Martinez, who was Spanish and she told me that I reminded her of her family. She said I even resembled them in some ways," Anna said.

"I loved the land, my family, but if I stayed, there would be nothing for me. I saw some of the newspapers from Los Angeles in the small school library. There were a few help wanted ads from resorts near San Diego and I convinced Miss Martinez to let me use her mailing address. If I sent a letter from the reservation, I didn't think I would get the job."

She took a deep breath and waited to see what his response would be. She half-expected him to ask her to move to another seat.

"You got the job?" he asked.

"After about a month, one of the resorts near Lake Wohlford wrote back and they said that if I could be there before the first of May, I'd have a job," she said.

"They are expecting someone who speaks Spanish and can cook and clean. I thought it would be better to be Anna Martinez than Annie George."

Jimmy watched her again, and rather than say anything, he just smiled. Finally, as if he'd waited long enough for her to respond he said, "That sounds like a great job and a great place, Anna. I'd like to see it."

Now, it was her turn to smile.

Within hours, the train pulled into the station in San Francisco and Jimmy and Anna gathered their belongings before moving to the main terminal. The station and passenger area in Seattle was tranquil and orderly, but the railway building in northern California the complete opposite. It was filled with commotion as soldiers and sailors tried to find their way home or to their next duty station.

"If you want, follow me," Jimmy said to Anna. "I think we are on the same train to L.A."

Jimmy saw the huge board at the end of the hall that listed all the departures and he noticed their train was leaving from the other side of the terminal, but they had to check in and get their tickets before they could board the southern bound express.

"Let's get in the line for the tickets – do you need help with those?" he asked and pointed to the large, fabric suitcases by Anna's side. Jimmy had his seabag, but he flipped it and was able to put his arms through the handles and rest the bag on his back. With his arms free, he picked up one of the suitcases and walked, or more precisely, waddled toward the windows. It took them almost 20 minutes to move to the front of the line and receive the papers that would let them board the train. The customer service agent assumed they were traveling together and gave them a boarding pass to the same car and seats that were next to one another. Jimmy didn't try to correct him when he saw what the agent was doing, he simply passed the paper to Anna and grinned.

"Here you go. Would you wait a second? I want to try to use the phone before we leave," he said, pointing at a line of telephone booths.

It took him less than a minute to connect with the phone in his parent's kitchen in Pasadena and as the metallic clicking sound of the ringing phone filled his ears, he remembered the rough-cut boards that made up the walls of the space. Anna watched as he turned away from her when he heard his mother's voice.

"Mom. It's me, Jimmy," he said. "Yes, I'm fine. I'm in San Francisco and there's been a slight change in plans. I got a job at the yard in San Diego." As soon as the last syllable left his lips he thought he heard his mother exhale. To Jimmy, it was as if she was trying to catch her breath and figure out what to say next. He helped her.

Jimmy explained that about a week before before he left the Navy Yard in Tacoma, he had signed up for a job in the San Diego shipyard. When the train stopped in San Francisco, he'd called ahead and found out he had the job.

It wasn't exactly true, but he had saved almost every penny he'd earned over the last two years, and he was sure if he headed toward San Diego, he'd find a job of one type or another. After nearly 1,000 days on the same ship, he wanted to stay near Anna. He didn't know why, but every part of him suggested it was the right course of action.

"I'll get settled and then come home as soon as I know my schedule," he said. "It's a good job, but I have to get there."

If there was one thing his mother and father appreciated, it was hard work. Jimmy often thought of them as pious, and serious people who felt their just reward would come in the next life.

"I'll see you soon," he said. "Tell dad I said hello and I'm fine. My train is here and I've got to run."

As he gently placed the handset into the receiver, he wondered if he had done the right thing. Deception was not something he practiced on a regular basis and he wasn't sure why he didn't go home and then travel to San Diego after spending some time with his parents. He turned as if he might pick up the phone again and he saw Anna gazing in his direction. She didn't smile, but her eyes met his and they both stood still. His hands dropped to his sides and as he exhaled, he pushed his way out of the booth and toward his bags and the train.

"All set?" he asked as he approached her. Not waiting for a response, he continued, "Let's get on the train and find our seats."

Jimmy and Anna boarded the train and again sat in the front of the car, closest to the door and the bathroom, their space. For most of the passengers, the run from San Francisco to Los Angeles was just another long day, but for Jimmy and Anna, it was a chance find out who they were and where they were headed.

For the first hour after the train left the station, Jimmy told her about growing up in the hills near Pasadena and what it was like to have parents who firmly believed that to spare the rod would spoil the child. It wasn't that he was always looking for trouble or trying to go against his parents' wishes, but to him most of the pranks and stunts his friends suggested sounded like a good idea.

"My mom and dad thought of life as almost a practice run. They were always talking about the rewards to come, the next life," he said. "I wasn't so sure. I kept thinking that this life might be good enough."

Anna turned away from her traveling companion and spent the next minute or more staring at the passing trees and rocks. When she first sat next to this sailor, she almost expected the worst. She assumed that he'd probably spend the trip drinking and try to talk her into one of the sleepers. Now, he was talking about his vision of life and she wanted nothing more than to continue the conversation.

By the time the train pulled into the Los Angeles terminal, Jimmy had convinced himself and Anna that they should head to San Diego together.

"It's a Navy town and I'm sure I can find work somewhere in the city," he said.

Anna nodded, not sure if she should reply and not sure why she felt so connected to this sailor, but she hoped it was true. As soon as their bags and belongings were on the platform, she told Jimmy she needed to find a pay phone and call the resort.

"In the letter I sent them, I told them I would call when I arrived in the city and let them know when I expected to be in San Diego," she said. Jimmy pointed at a long line of phone booths on the far wall of the terminal and told her he would watch the bags if she wanted to call them. Never questioning his motives, she nodded, pulled her small, intricately embroidered change purse from her bag and walked silently toward the phones.

"Mr. Jackson, the owner of the resort, is supposed to meet me at the station in San Diego," she said, as soon as she returned and put her purse back inside the large traveling bag.

"I'm not sure what he looks like, but he said he'll

have a sign."

A small almost guttural sound came from the former sailor and the half smile on his face indicated to her that he understood. He picked up most of the bags that were piled near his feet and led her toward the windows that were selling tickets for the local trains.

"Two for San Diego," he said and raised two fingers in front of the elderly man who was seated behind the turquoise-tinted half-window. Without looking up at the owner of the voice, or moving his left hand that held a half-smoked cigarette, he made two simple scratch marks in the ledger and pushed the tickets toward the voice.

Jimmy slid a $5 bill back in the direction of the man, and he watched in some amazement as the clerk, without a single wasted motion, put the paper money into his cash drawer and almost magically replaced it with two somewhat worn quarters.

"Track 12 – leaves in about 20 minutes," he said without lifting his head more than an inch. He still hadn't seen the sailor standing three feet in front of him.

Jimmy collected the tickets and was relieved that he hadn't bothered to ask his name or the name of the woman traveling with him. The last ticket clerk he'd seen in Seattle had entered 'Annie George' into his passenger manifest, but now he knew her only as Anna Martinez.

"All set," Jimmy said, and he showed Anna the two tickets to San Diego. Anna leaned forward and again started to pull her change purse from her luggage.

"Don't worry about that," Jimmy said. "I was heading in that direction anyway, and I've still got all of my Navy money."

Anna didn't want to accept anything from him, but the train was leaving in a few minutes. She didn't expect the sailor to follow her to San Diego and beyond, but it was nice to have him here.

"OK, but let me get you a coffee when we get on the train," she said.

"Deal," he said and smiled to himself.

After traveling together for more than 30 hours, Jimmy was used to her company and he couldn't remember a time when he felt so good about the world, but it was three hours to the next stop and he wasn't sure she wanted to see him after that. He only had a few more minutes to figure out a way to stay in touch.

"Where did you say that resort was?" he asked again.

"Lake Wohlford – it's near Escondido," Anna said as they settled into their new seats.

The final leg of their trip was nearly silent. No more than a dozen words passed between them as the train made its inexorable progress toward the southern border of the state. Each of them thought about the brief time they shared and wondered if it would end when the wheels rolled to a final stop.

"Almost there," Jimmy said, as the train eased under a makeshift awning and into the concrete and wooden station.

Anna stood as the train slowed and tried to find his eyes. She didn't say anything, but she locked her gaze onto his face and before either one could speak, she exhaled and gathered herself.

"I can't thank you enough for the help," she said. "I have to look for the owner, Mr. Jackson. He said he'd be waiting by the platform."

"Can I write to you sometime?" Jimmy asked, hoping to continue the conversation.

"I'll be at the Lake Wohlford Resort," Anna said. "I'm sure if you send a letter there, I'll get it."

As the last words reached him, she turned and spotted the small crowd waiting for the train. A trim man, nearly six feet tall, who appeared to be in his fifties and wearing stained, tan work pants stood near the closest bench on the platform. He was holding a small white sign with neat black, block lettering: "A. MARTINEZ."

"There he is," Anna said. "Thank you again."

"Lake Wohlford Resort," Jimmy replied. "I won't forget."

Jimmy watched her walk away and as she approached the older man, he held out his hand to take her bag. He didn't smile, or nod, instead, Mr. Jackson wiped his mouth once and briskly led the way toward the brass-framed doors that led passengers away from the station. As the large metal and wood door swung behind them, Anna looked as if she were skipping to catch up with him. His car was parked three spaces from the granite curb, and in less than five minutes from the time the two of them stepped from the train, she was gone.

Jimmy followed through the same door not two minutes later and tried to find a bus, taxi, or some way to travel to the small city of Escondido. He wasn't sure where he was going to stay, or where he wanted to go. All he knew was that he wanted to be near the woman who had spent the last three days with him on the train.

For the next two days, Jimmy walked the streets of Escondido trying to find work and a permanent place to stay. He found a clean, cheap hotel near the town hall and took most of his meals at the only diner in the center of town. After two days of walking and looking for work, a rather portly, friendly waitress with the name Myrtle written on her name tag asked him if he was looking for work and if he was new in town.

"I just got off the ship ... out of the Navy," he said. "I was hoping to settle nearby – I'm trying to find a job."

"Bob Murphy, who owns the filling station at the end of Main Street was in here this morning before we opened for coffee, and he said he's been looking for a mechanic for a couple of weeks," she said. "The last one ran off to L.A. thinking he'd make it in the movies."

Jimmy Connelly took two small sips of coffee from his porcelain mug and purposefully turned toward the waitress.

"He's usually back for lunch," she said and pointed her pencil toward the clock on the wall. It was 11:45 in the morning and already Jimmy could feel the heat of the day building inside the small dining area. There was a large open window leading to the ovens and the kitchen, and the front half of the room had an equally large glass window that faced toward the east and the rising sun. It didn't take long to heat the small space.

"Certainly warm here," he said and sat on one of the empty stools at the counter.

"What'll you have?" Myrtle asked as she filled a sturdy white mug with steaming black coffee. "No such thing as a free lunch here," she said pointing toward the nearly-filled diner.

"How about a BLT and fries?" Jimmy asked without looking at the menu. Myrtle turned as soon as she heard the order and scribbled something on a light-blue slip, pushing it across a clean stainless steel counter toward the two cooks standing in the kitchen.

"BLT regular – Navy style," she said.

With the last comment, she took one more glance back at the man at the counter and nodded. She didn't smile or exchange pleasantries with him, but still, there was a message in her eyes and promise in the her voice that meant only one thing. She liked him.

Jimmy paid little attention to his surroundings and hadn't taken more than two bites of his sandwich when he heard the door to the diner open and saw a heavyset, older man with thick workman-like hands walk toward the end of the counter. Myrtle spun again in Jimmy's direction and gave him the slightest nod, but she directed her conversation toward the man standing next to the register.

"Hi, Bob," she said. "I'll grab your lunch. I'm sure it's ready."

Bob Murphy had been coming to the diner for nearly 20 years and every day he picked up the same lunch at 12:15 sharp. "I'll give the crowd a chance to come in first," he once said to Myrtle with as much of a smile as ever had.

"Pickup for Murphy," Myrtle said in the direction of the kitchen and walked through the swinging door that led from the counter area to the kitchen.

As the door swung shut behind her and bumped into

her ample backside, Jimmy stood and turned toward the man. He noticed that he was flexing his hands, open and close. They were strong and stained from years of working in the garage and as Jimmy watched him, he remembered the time he'd been assigned temporarily to the deck crew. Twice a day he and the other sailors working with him had to haul in the lines that tethered the destroyer to the docks. After about the third or fourth day, his hands were red and sore from pulling and coiling the nearly 500 feet of thick line, and the chief boatswain mate laughed as he saw the young engineer stretching and flexing his hands and fingers.

"Hey shit-for-brains! You think that'll help?" he asked. "Maybe you need to spend the rest of your tour up here in the sunshine."

Jimmy smiled to himself at the thought of the chief and then he remembered that he'd been swept from the deck during a storm. Two of the ship's lifeboats had broken free from the davits that held them securely in their cradles. The chief was trying to grab the bow of the second lifeboat when the stern of the first swung free and hit him in the back. In less time than it took to scream, he was over the side. The two men who were with him had clipped their belt to the railing, but the chief was old school.

Jimmy's smile faded as his mind traveled back to the diner and the owner of the garage.

"Mr. Murphy. I'm James Connelly – just out of the Navy – Myrtle said you might be looking for a mechanic."

Bob turned toward the young sailor and sized him

up the way farmers sometimes look at livestock. He didn't respond immediately, but he noticed the seabag resting against the shiny metal post of the stool where he had been sitting.

"I was a machinist's mate, first-class," he said, hoping that meant something to the man.

The air between the two men heated up a degree or two more before Bob Murphy finally spoke.

"Kid, what do you know about vehicles that don't float?"

Waiting for a second or two, Jimmy replied, "I know how to tear down and fix almost anything that runs on gas, oil, or steam."

As soon as the last words of his proclamation left his lips, he extended his right hand toward the man.

Bob Murphy shook the sailor's hand, and it soon became obvious to the older man that the young sailor standing in front of him had worked with his hands for more than a day or two. His grip was surprisingly strong and there was a hidden heft to his hands.

"Why don't you throw your bag in the back of my truck and head back to the station with me. We'll see what you know."

Jimmy grabbed his gear and headed for the front door. As he reached for the handle, he turned one last time toward the counter and saw Myrtle coming through the door with a brown paper bag. She had heard the whole conversation and knew where he was going. She held the bag out toward Bob, but smiled and focused on Jimmy.

"Good luck," she said. "And see you around."

In less than an hour, Bob Murphy knew he found someone who understood the value of a day's work and didn't need a lot of talk or chatter to get his job done. Murphy suggested that he stay in the boarding house three doors down from the diner. He'd pay him a fair wage, $1.50 an hour, for a fair day's work. People were always bringing their cars to the station for repairs and when he wasn't busy with a car, Jimmy was expected to help out at the pumps. Murphy suggested that he could have breakfast at the boarding house and he would pick him up each morning on his way to the station. At noon, it would be just as easy for Bob to pick up a lunch for two as it would for one, and Bob knew the sailor could take his dinners in the boarding house.

Jimmy worked Monday through Saturday and one Sunday afternoon, after about a month of fixing flats and changing oil, he told Bob he wanted to go to Lake Wohlford for a day of hiking and fishing. Bob let him borrow the old Dodge pickup truck that was normally parked behind the station. There weren't any keys for the truck, and there was only a small starter button on the floor near the gas pedal but by now, he trusted the young man. It didn't take Jimmy long to figure out where Anna was working. There were only two resorts on the edge of the lake and one of them had 10 or 12 small cabins surrounding a large, white bunkhouse. The other had a single, faded sign that announced there were vacancies, but there weren't any cars parked on the property, and from what Jimmy could see, there wasn't any activity at all. The front door was shut and from the amount of dust he could see on the black sedan parked closest to the office, the resort appeared deserted.

Determined to see if he was right, he drove back to the first resort he saw along the western edge of the lake and pulled the old Dodge into the gravel parking lot. Taking more time than he normally would, he walked toward the front porch and tried to remember the speech he'd prepared for Anna.

"Can I help you?" A deep rich voice came at him from the porch.

Henry Jackson, the owner of the resort, had been working on the heating pipes that ran along the door near the front entrance of the resort that never seemed to shut the same way twice. He saw the truck from town roll across the gravel driveway and park. The land the resort stood on had been owned by Jackson's family for more than five decades. And for as long as Henry Jackson could remember, he worked six days each week to make sure the property was kept up and ready for the vacationers and fishermen who made their way to the lake.

He was lean, tan, and nearly every day wore the same work clothes as he painted, repaired, and tended to the surroundings near the 14 small, two-bedroom cabins that dotted hills near his side of the water. As he approached 60, his posture had started to fade a bit and only when he stood as straight as the soft pines that surrounded him, did his height approach the six-foot mark.

He and his wife, Gert, raised twin boys on the land and for most of their life, Henry expected them to take over the business and raise their own children on the property. That all changed on a sunny, Sunday morning in December when the Naval station in Hawaii was bombed. Like many of their male high school classmates,

Billy and Howard Jackson volunteered for the service and three weeks after they received their diplomas, they also received orders to the Navy's training center on the Great Lakes.

Billy, seemingly forever on a boat of one kind or another, was assigned to a destroyer escort group in the Atlantic, and Howard, a more methodical and quiet young man, volunteered for the submarine service.

For almost two years, letters would appear at random intervals from the two boys as their floating duty stations found a port to refuel, resupply, or simply rest for a few days.

Then, within six weeks of one another, they were gone. Billy first. His ship was escorting a convoy of merchant vessels across the Atlantic and somewhere near the southwestern coast of Ireland, they were attacked by a group of German U-boats. From the letter and the information, the Navy provided, Henry and Gert found out that the merchant vessels were attacked first, and as the ships disintegrated in the cold northern seas, surviving crew members scrambled to cling to the remaining lifeboats and wait for help.

The lookouts on Billy's destroyer saw the explosions and as the Naval vessel raced to pick up anyone alive in the water, the U-boats circled again and lined up to fire its torpedoes. The U.S.S. Leopold was hit amidships and as her boilers exploded, the munitions lockers, both fore and aft, detonated and the ship became a mass of flying flesh and steel. The U-boats, now without any remaining torpedoes, surfaced and mercilessly used their deck guns to clear the seas of any survivors. Each body they came across, alive or dead, received a short burst and as the sub silently passed by, the cold waters covered them, pushing them to their graves below the surface.

The Navy sent a telegram to the Lake Wohlford Resort to inform Henry and Gert Jackson that their son, Petty Officer William Jackson, was lost at sea.

Four weeks later, as a small white pennant with a red border and gold star in the center fluttered in the cool morning breeze, a messenger from Western Union arrived again. Howard's submarine, the U.S.S. Cisco was missing and presumed destroyed. The Jacksons were not told where or how it happened, but the message indicated there were no survivors. As each parent tried to imagine a life without their children, the messenger retreated back toward his car and as he had done so many other times in the past two years, he felt warm tears settle on his cheeks as he drove away from the lakeside home.

Day by day, the number of words shared between Henry and Gert became smaller and smaller, but they both realized that with their sons gone, they needed help around the property. Henry was the first to bring up the subject, but in the end, Gert wrote the text for the help-wanted ad they placed in the local newspaper, and she was the one who eventually wrote to Anna and offered her the job. Now, both of them considered her an important element of their business.

"Hello," Jimmy said. "I'm looking for a friend of mine – Anna Martinez."

Henry put the wrench he was holding down and stared at the man standing near him.

"Who?" Henry asked.

"Anna Martinez," Jimmy said with a bit more volume and conviction. "I thought she worked at this resort."

As he finished, Gert came through the back door and watched her husband and the young man standing in their driveway.

"She's down back. I'll tell her she has a visitor," she said. "I'm Gert Jackson and this is my husband, Henry."

She extended her hand toward Jimmy.

"Pleased to meet you. I'm James Connelly," he said.

Jimmy turned his attention toward Henry and the open pipes.

"Is that the heating system?" he asked. Henry took a deep breath. He had no intention of making small talk with this man, but there was something about the way he stood there.

"Yeah, I think there must be a couple hundred yards of pipe running from the boiler out back to the cabins and the house," he said. "The hot water just let go."

"Are you trying to bleed the system?" Jimmy asked. "Almost every other week we had the same problem on the ship – one boiler and miles of pipe."

Anna was walking toward the house when she saw Jimmy and Mr. Jackson walking away the truck in the driveway and toward the cabin furthest away from the house.

"They may be a few minutes," Gert said as Anna approached the porch. "You can wait here."

Anna and Gert sat on the porch watching the lake and the two men move from cabin to cabin. By the time they arrived at the house, almost two hours had passed.

"Hi," Jimmy said as he put his tool box down and wiped his hands. Anna smiled. She had often thought about the sailor who helped her travel, but she never expected him to actually show up here.

Henry put his tools down next to Jimmy's and watched as the mechanic who appeared from nowhere rolled down his shirt sleeves and wiped his hands again. Henry couldn't help it. He thought of his sons.

"Are you working at the station?" he asked, pointing to the truck. "If you ever want to a change, we could use someone who knows his way around a wrench."

Anna smiled, lifting her hand toward her mouth. Jimmy once again saw the bracelet that caught his attention on the train and she closed her mouth and nodded in his directions.

"I think I'd like that," Jimmy said.

Within two weeks, Jimmy had finished at the garage and was working at the resort, and Henry and Jimmy spent the next six months overhauling the mechanical and electrical systems that were connected to each of the cabins. Even Gert had come around and now each week or so, she'd make a fruit pie of one sort or another for the young man. In late August, Henry called the local minister and asked him if he would come to the resort and perform a wedding ceremony. He said it was unusual, but having known Gert and Henry his entire life, he'd make it out there.

There were only five people at the wedding: Henry, Gert, Anna, Jimmy, the reverend, and Bob Murphy. Anyone who was standing there watching the ceremony, and the couple getting married, were not surprised by two things. It was clear that Jimmy and Anna loved each other. They laughed, smiled, and even giggled a bit at one point and it was equally clear that Jimmy and Anna were going to be parents. Four months to the day after they exchanged their vows, Jimmy raced for the hospital with his wife in labor. Three hours after they rolled through the emergency doors, a nurse came to get him and told the nervous father-to-be that their son, Robert Francis Connelly was born.

Anna stayed in the hospital for four days and as she healed and rested, Jimmy got their cabin ready for his family. Holding the young boy in her arms, Anna left the hospital and smiled to herself as her husband guided the wheelchair she was riding in toward the waiting vehicle. After helping mother and child to the car, Jimmy slid into the front seat of the Chevy and pulled away, slowly, from the curb. As the couple and their son traveled home, the needle of the speedometer barely moved above 30 miles-per-hour. Jimmy couldn't remember a time in his life when he had felt such joy, such promise, such responsibility. He knew this was a good place to raise his son. A good place to settle down.

Anna gently walked across the small stones leading to their front door and cradled her young son. As she settled into a rocking chair, she held him close to her breast and started singing. To Jimmy, the melody was familiar and distant but the words were not English.

Jimmy silently crossed the room toward his wife and listened to the words again. He didn't understand the literal meaning behind the words, but after watching the way she touched the baby, he knew she was passing something important to their son. The lullaby was not in English, not in Spanish but the depth and beauty of the words and phrasing were clear to him. He saw Anna close her eyes as she continued to sing to their son. What he didn't realize was that his son had heard these words and the melody before. For nearly nine months they had been a source of comfort and peace, a source of images and life. There was one recurring vision, one ephemeral idea that kept entering his infant mind. The baby, Bobby, had no idea what it meant or if its intentions were good, and he didn't have the ability to attach a word to the image, but he had seen it before and he recognized the ancient image of a bird in flight. A bird that in his young mind is meant to be free and meant to soar.

3 – The Boy from the Berkshires

December 1966

My family wasn't flashy. We didn't have piles of cash hidden in the bank, or own the paper mill down by the river. We lived on the same 100 acres of land where my grandfather was born, and the fields I walked as a teenager were the same stretch of earth where my dad hunted turkeys every fall. The gentle, rolling hills and valleys of western Massachusetts were my home and I thought I'd never leave. I was wrong – now I know I might never get back.

For 17 years I worked hard and learned the value of a day spent in the fields, the barns, and the garage. The Grondan dairy farm was about a mile and a half down the road and they always needed someone to help with the chores. There were two or three full-time hands, but my dad knew Mr. Grondan and by the time I was 14, I worked there every Thursday and Friday afternoon after school and then again on Saturday and Sunday mornings. Mr. Grondan paid everyone on Friday afternoon, a few minutes before quitting for the day. With the crisp bills neatly folded in their pockets, the other workers, Joe and Charlie, were anxious to spend the night in town. By the time the sun snuck over the horizon and said hello to Saturday morning, there was no waking them. That was OK with me. I kind of liked walking through the barns alone and tending to the herd. Days, seasons, and years were spent working the land and by the time I decided to quit high school, my body was accustomed to steady physical activity - haying in the summer, planting in the spring, working with the animals and crops in the fall and then plowing snow and repairing equipment all winter. The thick, rich smell of the land, the animals, and the machinery settled me. Everything in combination with each other made me feel like I was where I belonged.

"Russ, what are you going to do?" Mr. Grondan said to me one Friday afternoon in December. "Unless I've missed my guess, you're gonna be 18 soon, and you've got to register."

I knew what he was talking about, but I tried not to think about it. All the boys in the country had to sign up with the draft board when they turned 18, and I kept telling my girlfriend, Sandy, I was going to be picked. I stopped walking toward the big gray sliding doors of the barn and looked at the old man, trying to find the right words. "I don't know," was all I said.

For the last few months, this single issue or problem dominated almost every conversation I had with Sandy. One way or another, the subject always came up. We'd spend hours looking at the draft list in the newspaper. The small, handmade wooden dinner table in my house was turned into a library desk of sorts and we would spread the Springfield Union over the length of faded, chestnut colored pine boards. It wasn't unusual for 20 minutes or more to pass without a single word from either of us. We'd spend the time looking at the line of birthdays printed in the paper and wonder how long it would be before my draft notice was unceremoniously dropped into the plain, aluminum mailbox at the end of the driveway.

Starting on the second page of the paper, the numbers associated with the draft were listed 1 through 365 and next to each number a simple date was printed. The dates represented birthdays and the order of the dates indicated where you stood in terms of the draft. If your birthday happened to be near the top, you were likely to go. It didn't take me long to find my birthday, December 11. It wasn't hard to find; it was in the first few inches of black ink on the page. My number, lucky number 46, was likely to be drawn within a month or so. I didn't have many choices.

I wasn't going to college. I hadn't finished high school, and a lot of the guys I knew had already been drafted. They told me it was better to enlist. They said at least you had a chance to pick something other than the infantry.

Mr. Grondan and I finished getting the barn ready for the night. The stalls had all been cleaned and filled with crisp hay the color of freshly bottled honey. The old droppings, or floppies, had all been raked into the big black wheelbarrow that stayed near the front end of the barn. All I needed to do was grab the heavy, dense handles and with one extended effort, wheel them over to the "shit pit," the deep hollow in the hill behind the barn, and dump them. In the spring, Mr. Grondan would use the tractor and load the flatbed trailer full of the half-frozen composted manure. With one of the farmhands, Charlie or Joe, standing on the rough oak planking, he'd drive to the cornfields that surrounded the white farmhouse and together they'd spend the morning spreading and turning the dark brown chunks of hay and waste into the rich New England soil - land that would only become richer because of the hard, steady work.

Most years, in late April, after this work was done and a week or two before the spring planting started in earnest, the Grondan farmhouse would seem to emerge from a long winter's sleep. It stood alone, a single structure on a small, half-acre plot with deep green spring grass forming a barrier of sorts between the living and the land. As the inevitable afternoon winds came from the west, the solitary house was almost adrift, an island of green in a sea of soil.

By the time I returned to the barn with the empty wheelbarrow, I knew I needed to enlist. My birthday was next week, three weeks until the first of the year and the new draft. After that, I was fair game for all. Coming into the house from the farm, I knew my mother heard me open the screen door and the back door. She was cutting some squash for dinner and as I sat on the old milk stool near the coatrack, I heard the knife in her hand click every time she hit the cutting board. My boots were muddy and they had the aroma of the farm, but they weren't in the kitchen. From the smell of the pipe tobacco, I thought dad was close by, probably in his chair in the living room. The radio was on and I heard the newspaper pages rustle as he read over the day's events. Stepping into the kitchen and onto the faded linoleum floor, I took a deep breath and let the words spill from my mouth.

"Mom, Dad? My birthday's next week. I think I should enlist."

Mom put the knife down and I heard her exhale as my dad got to his feet. For a minute they stared in my direction. The silence was unnerving, and rather than stare at my shoes any longer, I started talking, trying as best I could to convince my mother and father this was the best course of action. I showed them the list of dates and talked about training to become a heavy equipment mechanic.

"It'd be nice to get out and get a job with the railroad," I said. "It's better than waiting for the letter to come."

The discussion didn't last more than 30 minutes, and without any other fanfare, it was decided. My mother, Verna Warriner, would drive me, the youngest of her children, to the recruiting offices in Springfield, Massachusetts. We'd go in a few days, next week at the latest. My older brother, George, was already in the Army and stationed in Germany. He was safe and at this point, it didn't look like he'd be heading to Southeast Asia.

"Communications and electronics," mom said, more than once. "That's what your brother's working on and he's at a base. You should think about it."

My mom worked downtown at the Williamsburg Savings Bank and they were closed on Wednesday afternoons. I thought we could go to Springfield after she got out of work and talk to the recruiters. My dad was not thrilled with the idea of me going into the service. His silence on the subject was proof of that, but what choice did I have? Dad left for the VA hospital at 5 a.m.

every morning and spent most of his time working as a baker making bread, rolls, and pastries for the more than 250 patients and staff members who ate there each day. By the time he got home at night, there was little left of him for us. He was just too tired. By the time Walter Cronkite said, "… and that's the way it is," it wasn't unusual for my dad to be asleep in his chair with his head tilted back at a funny angle.

Wednesday came and mom was home a little early. We left the house by 11 a.m. and headed the old black Buick south in the direction of Springfield and my future. Mom started in again about George and working in electronics, but I'd heard it all before. I wasn't my brother and I didn't want to repeat everything he did, even if it made my parents happy. I didn't want to make them mad or disappoint them, but I didn't want to be a copy of my brother.

It's funny in a way, my mother and I were comfortable with each other in the way that required little speech. Any words that were said on the ride often remained in the air waiting for the other person to take them in and make them their own. Sooner or later, they'd come back out wrapped in a new thought or idea. The 45-minute ride was quiet and quick.

"The offices for all the branches are close together, but I think the Army is the best choice for me," I said, as my mother drove the sedan into the open-air parking lot. The snow from an early winter storm had been cleared and only small traces of ice covered the black asphalt. When she turned the key and shut the car off, I was the first to reach for the door handle and leave the warmth of our drive behind.

Without a word, my mom followed me toward the nondescript brick building that contained the offices for the armed services. Posters of young, handsome men in uniform filled the windows that faced the street. Almost each one, regardless of the color or style of their shirt, stood with their chest out and their chin pointed straight ahead. To me, and my mom, they were a mature version of who I might become. I hoped that someday soon, I might be one of them – brave and strong.

When I entered the office, I was greeted by a tall, young man who wasn't much older than I was. He had three yellow stripes on his shoulder and I'd seen enough movies to know he was a sergeant of some kind.

"Master Sergeant Watson's gone to lunch, ma'am," he said in the general direction of my mother. "But he'll be back shortly."

He didn't even glance at me, and I thought about going to see the Air Force – they were right next door, but I waited. At the time, I was little less than six feet tall and weighed no more than 155 pounds. There were stretches when I thought I could eat anything and everything and still not gain an ounce. I'd become lean and strong from years of getting up early and working, and my hands were thick and calloused and I thought they were almost too large for the rest of my body. Sometimes I'd catch a glimpse of them in a mirror or see my reflection in a window and there they were, hanging loosely at my sides. They appeared almost swollen and heavy like a couple of pieces of misshaped produce – maybe a squash or a cucumber. I didn't think they were my hands. They were too old.

The sergeant standing in front me gave me a quick glance and I could've sworn he was sizing me up in the way boys sometimes do before they start swinging. I remembered the one fight I had in high school. Frank Costello. I was 14 or 15, still a freshman, and maybe it was my age or maybe it was the way he used to snicker in my direction every time I walked by. I am still not sure if there was a reason, but I lashed out and called him a dumb bastard. My pronouncement was met with silence. He stood there, hands turned into small fleshy fists, and Frank looked at me as if he were trying to decide if he wanted to swing. Apparently, the answer was yes. For the next two minutes we wrestled and struggled with one another and finally, I managed to get my arm around his head. It was hot and slippery, and he almost pulled away from me, but I locked my hands together and I pulled him closer to my chest.

I didn't think. I followed my instincts and hit him. After years spent lifting tires, rocks, equipment and countless bales of hay it was an easy swing. As soon as the crunching sound of fist hitting bone filled the small hallway, he collapsed in a bloody heap. I'd crushed his nose and splotches of bright red snot and blood oozed from his face falling to the dull green floor in globs and drops. I stared at the carnage I created. I felt bad, but what was I supposed to do.

Now, three years later, it felt like the same thing. I didn't think the sergeant was going to hit me, but I was sure he was sizing me up, trying to figure out who I was. I waited for him to tell me what to do next. I'd already been waiting for a while; a few more minutes wouldn't matter.

For last two weeks or more, I'd spent hours each night thinking about what was next, what was in my future. At first, I wasn't even sure what branch of the service I'd like, but as the nights wore on, and the panic and the reality of the situation set in, an idea started to form. I'd always liked working at the farm and working on the equipment there. The shops, barns, and fields were like my home. I could spend hours in the shop working on an old piece of equipment, and liked nothing better than listening to the music from the old AM radio and learning about the different parts of the tractor. Maybe I could become some type of heavy equipment mechanic, maybe even work on tanks.

"You know … like working in a garage," I thought.

I almost forgot I was standing in the front of the young recruiter.

"You can see Sergeant Watson now," he said and pointed in the direction of the older soldier who had walked through the back door of the office. He was standing near the front desk but turned away from everyone in the room. The broad expanse of his stiff, wrinkle-free uniform shirt turned steadily in my direction and it appeared as if he was placing a small brown bag into one of the lower desk drawers. Sergeant Watson didn't even look in my direction or make a noise; with hands that were even larger than my own, he waved me over. I tried to stand taller for a moment and then moved toward the single metal folding chair placed in front of the desk. All I could do was sling a few garbled words in his general direction.

"Sergeant Watson? I think I'd like to enlist. I'd like to be a mechanic. I was thinking about working on heavy equipment, maybe tanks."

I could see he was focused on what I had just said. There were rows and rows of important looking colored ribbons on the left side of his shirt and above the ribbons there was a small silver rifle pinned to a blue rectangle. It didn't look like a modern rifle or even the type I hunted with at home. I would have sworn it was something out of the history books. The sergeant put his pen down on the desk, on top of a small pile of green folders, and laughed. When he finally spoke, his words were measured.

"That's the last thing you want to do," he said. "It's not safe, you'll be right in the middle of it," he said, picking a folder from the middle of the pile.

"Right now, the Army needs lots of soldiers, and most of them will head to an infantry unit, but some will go in a supporting role. You should see if you qualify for one of those."

The sergeant became more animated and the volume of his voice rose as spoke for more than five minutes about the hazards associated with working on tanks and becoming a member of a tank crew. I didn't say a word. I watched and with each syllable or sound, in a strangely synchronized fashion, the medals on his chest bobbed and bounced with the rhythm of his voice. By the time he was finished, he convinced me that joining a tank crew, or working on tanks in general, was a pretty dangerous job and the chances of getting killed or wounded were more than I cared to think about. With each sentence and comment, I couldn't help but think about my chances of coming out of this in one piece. I don't think it helped that after uttering each fact or idea, he almost unintentionally started staring in the direction of my mother. The speech didn't seem practiced or an attempt to persuade me to do something that wasn't in my best interest. The sergeant suggested that instead of tanks, I should think about becoming an aviation mechanic.

"You'll work on planes and helicopters at a base – away from the action," he said, looking at some sort of calendar and list that was placed under the glass that covered the top of his dull green metal desk.

"There's a shortage now, so you probably should sign up today. I could probably guarantee you'll get into one of these companies."

I noticed he glanced quickly at the clock on the wall, and even though it appeared as if his mind had already thought of something else, he continued on.

"Besides, after you get out you'll probably go right to work for one of the airlines or airports, and their pay is pretty good. Let Uncle Sam train you and then get paid for the rest of your life."

I'd never been on a plane or a helicopter, but that did sound better. Near home, there were always plenty of planes flying over the hills toward Bradley Field or Westover Air Base. Sometimes they were low enough that I could read the lettering on the fuselage, near where the engines were attached. And I often wondered what it felt like to float across the sky, but I never had the chance to go for a ride. The sergeant said something about the needs of the service, but I wasn't paying attention and I didn't hear him. Thoughts of my family and my brother were running through my head and this time I was the one who turned in the direction of my mother.

"George was studying electronics and stationed in Germany, that might be good for me too," I thought.

"What do I have to do? Do I have to go to Vietnam?" I asked.

Sergeant Watson explained that in the next few days, I'd need to take a physical and pass a written exam, but if everything went well, I'd go to basic training and then to aviation school at Fort Rucker in Alabama. He pulled some forms from a manila folder and put a calendar on the side of the desk closest to where I was sitting.

"See – there's a class A school in July. I can get you to basic and then right into the school," he said. "Your training'll last at least six months before you head to a base. You'll probably even move up in rank. Who knows what'll be going on in Vietnam by then."

My head was swimming with all the details, but it sounded good. There was so much information on the papers, it made things confusing. He pointed toward the pay scale and the training schedule, and I thought of Sandy. We'd been together for more than a year and she knew I was here, but she wasn't happy. In the end, this would be better for us. I'd be able to get married when I got home and out of the Army. The sergeant didn't say a word. He let me look at all the material and watched as I tried to make sense of the new words, phrases, and abbreviations. I knew I wanted to go, but I did wonder how many others sat in this same chair and heard the same message. The dark brown folding chair next to his desk had a way of attracting warm bodies. I was one of them.

Sergeant Watson showed me the preliminary forms one more time and the commitment letter. He explained again about the shortage of aviation mechanics and said each recruiter would be trying to fill the schools. When they were full, that'd be a different story. With my signature at the bottom of the page, the enlistment process would start. They'd hold a spot for me.

"Is it Russ or Russell?" the sergeant asked as he copied some information from my driver's license. He was already filling out some form with the big initials DD on the top.

"My full name is Russell Stanley Warriner," I said, knowing that my connection to the Army was now becoming official. I exhaled once more, scratched the back of my head and formally signed the bottom of the page. I was in.

Sitting there next to the sergeant, I listened to his stories about flying as he built me a permanent folder. A little more than 90 minutes had passed from the time my mother and I left the icy parking lot and entered the office, to the point where I stood and shook hands with the sergeant and signed my enlistment contract.

I agreed to come back the next day and take the necessary academic exams and have a physical. The test took almost two hours and both sergeants had commitments later in the afternoon. The physical and medical portion of the processing might take as much as four hours. It was going to be an all-day affair, but at the end of it all, I'd stand with my right hand raised and swear an oath. Sergeant Watson dismissed me and gave me an official business card with his name and the phone number on it.

"If you have any issues, or questions, or need anything," he said. "Don't do anything stupid either. As of today, you're in the system, and after tomorrow, you're in the Army."

I wasn't exactly sure what that meant, but I felt kind of proud. I slid my coat on and took the card and a few papers with me. I was in. Mom and I walked back to the car deep in our own thoughts. I wondered what Sandy would say. She'd asked me not to sign anything until we talked, but this made the most sense. She'd see that. On the ride back, I couldn't help but notice that during the last few days winter had settled into the hills, and over and over again, I kept telling myself that this soon-to-be 18-year-old boy from the Berkshires was now Private Russell Warriner, US Army. I'd leave the only home I'd ever known in March, but I'd be back.

For most of the ride home, I didn't say much. My mother drove, and I even dozed off for a few minutes. I hadn't slept much the night before and in some way, I felt relieved. It was over. There was no turning back now.

After we got home, I wanted to sit down with my parents and convince them I'd picked a safe occupation and I'd be coming home before they knew it, but the truth of it was, I couldn't stop thinking about the next six months. I wasn't sure what would happen, and with each minute that passed, a deeper sense of dread began to seep into my thoughts. I'd never been out of Massachusetts and now they were talking about possibly shipping me to a base in Vietnam. I decided that conversation with my parents could wait. I wanted to see Sandy.

4 – Changing Habits

December 1966

My old Ford pickup didn't always start every time I turned the key - there was probably a flat spot on the starter gear - but sooner or later the engine would catch and the front end of "old blue" would shake and rattle like a dog trying to dry off after a swim in the river. All six of the cylinders would come to life as the old engine figured out a way to combine their power and work as one machine. I waited a minute or two as sound and rhythm of the truck became steadier and steadier, and then pulled out the light switch and eased off on the clutch.

The truck acted as if it knew instinctively where we were headed, and despite the dark and cold winter weather, we both bounced along at just the right speed for the four-mile trip across town. My hands floated above the worn steel steering wheel and I knew, if I kept my contact with the truck to a minimum, the cold of the day wouldn't work its way into me. My thoughts alone seemed to nudge the truck to the left or the right, and I was humming, but the radio was off. The sound resonated against the metal cab roof and that too felt normal. It felt like my life.

Sandy's mom and dad owned the only drug store in town. In the center of Williamsburg, there was a Civil War memorial on a small, square spot of land; it was an ordinary war statue of some guy on a horse with no expression at all on his face. His right arm was raised and his sword extended from his hand, pointing toward the snow covered hills that rose beyond the town limits. There were four streets that bordered the square and on each one there was only one business or store. On the north side there was Jack's, a clothing store and tailor shop, and at almost any time of day you could go into the store and smell the cleaning products that were used in the back room to press and steam the suits and dresses that were being altered. The store itself hissed and breathed like an old horse as the steam from the machinery found its way into the fabric.

As a kid, I'd go there once a year to get a new pair of pants and a coat for school. Jack would come out of the back with a cloth tape measure wrapped around his neck the way a doctor wears a stethoscope. With a thick Eastern European accent and a hint of a smile, he'd ask my mother, "Who is dis? It can't be Russell."

Before I knew it, I was standing on an overturned milk crate, trying on a new pair of pants and a navy blue blazer. Jack whirled about me as I tried to stand still and not scratch my legs or arms. The new material was stiff and abrasive as it moved over my body. The more I tried to stand still, the more it irritated me, and the more fidgety I became, but there I was in front of the three mirrors rimmed with polished brass. Jack used a small piece of soap the way a skilled surgeon uses a scalpel and marked the clothes for alteration. He'd pull, he'd poke, and sometimes, in an accent that came straight from the movies, he'd tell me to stop wiggling. It was always serious work.

"They'll be ready next week," he said to Verna, whose attention was focused on the single clothing rack that contained ladies' dresses. Within minutes, I was back in my old clothes and in the short time since I had left them in a pile on the floor, I had this almost overwhelming sense they were shabby and too small. With one last, long scratch, I headed for the front door.

"Don't forget," was all Jack said, but I knew what he meant. I turned to wave goodbye to the man holding my new clothes. They looked funny in his arms - the white lines from the soap making a roadmap of sorts on the fabric. I reached up toward the glass counter and stuck my hand into a small glass bowl filled with wrapped mints. I wanted two, but I took one. I still think this was the best part of getting ready for another school year.

Directly across the square from Jack's was Miller Drug. The boxlike, brick store was owned by Sandy's parents, Douglas and Elizabeth Miller. For most of the people in town, the store was part post office, part emergency room, and part soda fountain and restaurant. I'd heard bits and pieces of the family history many times from Sandy. She liked to tell it, and truth be told, I liked to listen. Her grandfather, Henry, started the store after he returned from the first war in France, a period of time he rarely spoke about, least of all to his wife and children. Henry was a medic in the Army and knew about drugs, medicine, and making sure patients knew what to take and when.

"His job was to keep them alive," Sandy said with a hint of pride.

Most of the men in Henry's family were farmers, but from the time he was a child, Henry wanted nothing to do with the open fields and steady work that filled his own father's days. With the money he saved from the Army, he came home and settled into a single brick building that was empty on the edge of the square, and he petitioned the town council to allow him to set up a pharmacy. At the time, the nearest doctor was a good 20 miles away, almost all the way to Northampton, and Henry promised to "do things the right way," but perhaps most important of all, he promised the town officials that he would "stay put." Along with his new bride, Henry and Miller Drug soon became the heart of the small New England town.

Not one to remain idle or pass up the opportunity to improve things, Henry saw the chance to expand his newly established enterprise. Within two years he was back before the town council and asked them if he could build postal boxes at the far end of the pharmacy. He'd written to the postmaster in Springfield and mentioned his service in the Army and his willingness to protect the mail and ensure it was delivered and handled according to the postal code. Henry received a simple response suggesting he apply to become a postmaster for the town. That was all he needed to hear.

The following summer he spent nearly every evening pouring through the Postal Operations Manual, trying to learn the rules and regulations surrounding the delivery and handling of the mail. Many nights, Elizabeth entered the kitchen and there, slumped over his thick book, was her sleeping, sweaty husband. There were more than a few pages in the manual that literally contained the sweat and hopes of the young couple. By the time the temperatures started to drop, Henry knew every rule and every code. Each page of the thick manual had been turned and read time and time again. The regional postmaster in Springfield was only too happy to meet with him, and schedule a time for him to sit and take the postmaster's exam. The regional administrator knew all too well how the government worked and having another town office under his jurisdiction would only improve his standing in the eyes of his superiors. Besides, it was clear to him that this industrious veteran and his wife were the type of people the post office needed most.

"Now, we have a future," Henry said when he put the framed postal certificate on the front wall next to the door and the 1923 calendar from The Travelers insurance company. At the bottom, in large, ornate, official script it said, "Henry Miller, Postmaster, Williamsburg, Massachusetts." A gold seal and the signature of the Postmaster General of the United States completed the page. To Henry it meant everything; it was going to be a good year. To Elizabeth, it meant they could now have a family. Sandy would always smile when she finished this part of the story, talking about her grandparents. It was like there was some sort of female secret there, something only she knew. With any kind of luck, she'd share it with me.

Henry and Elizabeth were soon expecting a child,

and within a year, the sound of a baby crying was heard throughout the store. They had a son, Douglas. But for most of his young life, his mother referred to him simply as Dougie. It wasn't until he was a 13 or 14-year-old boy who more resembled a man, that she forced herself to call him by his given name. For Elizabeth, from that point forward, it was always Douglas. Her only son, and their only child.

It seemed as if Elizabeth didn't have a problem getting pregnant, she just couldn't seem to carry a baby to term. During his childhood, there were at least four times when Dougie remembered being told to walk quietly and not to disturb his mother. He wasn't sure why, but she would sometimes grab him as he walked by and squeeze him as if it were the last thing in the world she would do.

She'd spend weeks, it seemed, locked in her room as she hoped for another mouth to feed. It never happened. The doctor came and went each time her pregnancy ended abruptly and made sure Mrs. Miller stopped bleeding. "With the right amount of rest," he'd tell her in a tired and matter-of-fact fashion, "It's just not your time, but you'll be fine."

Douglas grew up without a brother or a sister and for him, that was normal. He spent most of his spare time following his father around the store, and by the time he was in high school, he was often left in charge as his father made deliveries or traveled to Springfield to get something he needed for their business. Henry knew the store was the focal point of the small community and he was of a mind that he should be able to fix or install anything; a new soda dispenser, freezer parts, electrical equipment, or almost anything else.

"If you can take care of it yourself, you'll be better off in the long run," he often told his young son.

When his dad was gone and the other men in town came in for their mail, Dougie heard bits and pieces about the trouble in Europe, the problems in Washington, and sometimes the gossip from the farms. Practically every other week there was a headline in the Springfield paper about a bombing raid or a ship sinking thousands of miles away. He often asked his dad about it but was told, "it'll blow over. People can't be that dumb again." Sandy remembered every word from the conversations she had with her grandfather and often said that if he spoke 10 words in an hour, "it seemed like a waterfall of sound. He just wasn't that way." She was sure he had said exactly those words to his young son.

The storm didn't end, though, and sure enough, during December of Doug's senior year in high school, the Japanese attacked the naval station at Pearl Harbor with a fury that shocked the nation. Even on the eastern shores of the United States, mothers and fathers knew that many of their sons would soon be leaving. As a whole, the country was holding its breath; The United States was again at war.

"My dad turned 18 during his senior year and it was only a matter of time," Sandy said. "But by then, Grandma had already lost four babies and she wasn't about to lose her last. I think my grandpa Henry spoke to the local draft board. Dad was drafted into the Navy, and because of his training with drugs and medicines, and

Grandpa's connections with the board, after basic training, he entered the service as a pharmacist's mate. Luckily for him, and for us, he was assigned to a hospital in Melbourne, Australia with a group of students and doctors from Ohio. He spent 18 months there and late in 1943 he was transferred to a training base and hospital in Hawaii." Sandy always finished the story with a smile and a quick comment. "He did his part and then came home."

After his years in the service, Doug went off to the Massachusetts School of Pharmacy and planned to follow in his dad's footsteps. Four years later, when he came home for good, he proudly hung his diploma on the back wall of the store, next to the certificate from the Postmaster and the 1948 version of The Traveler's calendar.

"My son's a professional," he heard his father say one day to Jim Burke, the only lawyer in town. Sandy usually paused here when she described the younger version of her father. "He's a professional," she would repeat.

Doug did take over for his dad, and like his father, he married the only girl he ever loved. Together - they too had only one child, Sandra. Doug and his wife, Gloria, didn't live in the store or in the apartment next door; they built a new house on a small piece of land outside of town. There was a gently sloping stretch of old farm road, Thompson's Hill, and a short distance beyond the summit there was a five-acre patch of farmland that had remained empty for almost a century. The local rumor was that the field had once been an Indian burial ground and when the first settlers came to this part of

Massachusetts in the late 1600s, they drove off the people living nearby and used the fields for the first farming settlements. Now, the grasslands were used every summer as grazing land by the Grondan farm, and that helped keep the trees and wild bushes at bay, but the land was hardly settled. When the time was right, Doug approached his dad and asked him about the land.

"I'd like to help run the store, but we'd like to raise a family out there," he said one afternoon as they filled the daily order of prescriptions for the VA hospital.

Henry didn't say anything directly to his son about his wish, but within a few days, Frank Dolan, the mortgage loan officer for the bank, stopped in to see Doug at the store. He casually mentioned the land might be for sale, and if Doug were interested, he'd make a few inquiries. The bank would be happy to help him get the money needed to buy the land and build the house.

"That's the way it was done," Sandy said. "We've lived there ever since. Someday, I'd like to live near there with my own family."

Henry Miller had a way of making things happen. He'd received the contract for the VA hospital within days after he opened the new pharmacy, and in the beginning, a simple handshake renewed the arrangement every year. Almost every day since then, there were at least 30 drug orders to fill, sometimes pills, sometimes powders, and occasionally, liquid remedies for the former soldiers staying at the hospital. Henry made sure every order was complete and often became quiet as he read the instructions from the doctors. Once, as they were filling the orders, Doug asked him if he knew anyone there.

"Sometimes I think I know them all," he said. And then with a look that indicated to his son he was through talking, they completed the orders for the day.

Henry had an old Chevy station wagon that he used for deliveries, and late each afternoon, he loaded up the car and made the 8-mile trip to the hospital. When Doug was young, he often slid into the front seat next to his father on these trips and the two Miller men would ride in silence toward the hospital. Doug would look at the hills and forestland between the town and the hospital, and as the pair trekked from town to town, Henry would often stare as if he were in another place and time. When they arrived, Doug would wait in the parked car while his dad walked toward the back entrance and made his way to the office where the drugs and medicine for the patients were stored. Sometimes, he would be back in a few minutes, other times, it took him nearly an hour to return.

Doug never asked why it took so long to deliver the prescriptions, but now he made more and more of these trips by himself. Henry was nearly 73-years-old and Doug saw him almost every day at the store, even if only for a little while, but he didn't feel comfortable with him driving alone to the VA in the afternoon, especially with the sun low on the horizon.

"I'll take care of it, Dad," he'd say to his father. Often, without another word between the two men, Henry Miller would finish the cup of coffee he had poured for himself when he entered the store, he'd straighten his tie, and then leave through the front door to walk quietly around the small town square. In 30 minutes he'd be back at the store, but instead of entering again through the front door, he would continue past the sparkling glass windows and head for the staircase that led to his apartment attached to the backside of the brick structure. It too was the only home he'd known.

From the time I was old enough to go to school, I'd known the Millers. Sandy was one grade behind me in school and I always thought she was more interested in school and clothes than boys, and I certainly didn't think she'd ever be interested in me. By the time I entered high school, I wanted to be anywhere but inside a schoolroom and often skipped the last few classes of the day to head home or to the farm. The choice between math class and the barn wasn't much of a choice. The barn always won. It's funny, I do remember the first time I saw Sandy, the time when I couldn't shake her from my thoughts. One Saturday morning I'd gone to the drug store with my dad to mail a letter. He'd promised me a soda and at the time, that was something special. We didn't have them in the house and even though the fizzy, sugary drinks always made me burp for about an hour afterward, I never passed up the chance to get one.

The store wasn't busy and as Dad filled out some form he needed to mail to Sears, I saw Sandy standing next to her grandfather. She must have been a foot taller than the last time I noticed her, and she had filled out. All I saw now were curves. For a long time, she had reminded me of a young calf. As a kid, she had a big head and long limbs. She was all knobby knees and elbows and there wasn't even the hint of a female form. I didn't know where I was when it happened, but that all changed. She was round in all the places that mattered and her eyes sparkled every time she smiled. All at once my world changed - she smiled at me.

I sat on the stool at the end of the counter, took a nickel from my shirt pocket and waited. Mr. Miller came over to me and I slid the nickel toward his resting hand.

"Just a pop, please."

"That's it? Aren't you Ronnie Warriner's youngest?" he asked. "You've stretched some since the last time I saw you," Henry Miller said.

I didn't know what to say, nobody called my dad Ronnie; even my mother called him Ronald. But as he said it, he picked up the nickel from the counter and turned toward the shelf to get a glass for my soda. Sandy saw her grandfather talking to me and getting ready to pour a soda and she moved a little closer to my end of the counter. One shot of syrup and a long pull of fizzy water filled the curved glass in his hand, and within seconds it was in front of me. I stopped looking at the soda and noticed she had moved next to me. I mumbled an almost unintelligible hello and to my surprise, she said hello back. We have been together ever since.

Sandy often talked about our future together, our future in town, and our future as a family. I wanted to say more, to fill in the blank spots in the conversation, but as always, listening to her carry on was almost better than speaking. I was happy to have her talk to me. Her voice, her conversation, was like some sort of potion. It made me feel better and as the minutes ticked by, it also made me a little sleepy. Now, as Old Blue eased into her driveway, the lights on either side of the front door lit up and I knew she had heard the deep rumble of the truck engine as the vehicle crunched across the gravel. I smiled as I thought about the next few minutes.

We didn't stay long at her house.

"Hi, Mrs. Miller. I wanted to see Sandy and talk to her about today."

"I'm proud of you Russell, but I can't help but worry a little. Sandy said you might be working at a base or on equipment. Will they send you to school?"

Dressed in her evening housecoat and slippers, she stood in the doorway to the kitchen. The smell from dinner was still hanging in the air, a mixture of cooked meat, vegetables, and cinnamon.

"There must have been a pie," I thought, and without any conscious effort, I turned back to the counter.

"I will be going to school," I said, trying to focus on the question and find Sandy. "I'm not sure how it will work, but I am going after basic."

"I'm sure they'll help you finish your G.E.D. Who knows, you may even go to college when you get home," she said.

Having seen Sandy come down the stairs, I nodded.

"Ready?"

"We won't be long, mom," Sandy said.

Taking me by the hand, she headed for the door. The front hallway led from the street-side of the house to the back and on either side, there was an entrance to the dining room and the living room. On the way out, I saw Mr. Miller sitting in the living room with a newspaper in his lap. He wasn't reading, but he didn't get up either. Within seconds we were out the door and into the cold night air.

As we jumped into the truck, Sandy smiled toward me, and I wanted to say something. I wanted to tell her how much she meant to me and I wanted to promise to return in one piece, to come back home to her. But instead, without any grace or flare, I fumbled for my keys and got in.

As the truck rumbled to life, I turned on the heater and asked, "Do you want to go somewhere special?" I smiled as the words tripped out of my mouth, hoping she would get the hint. Sometimes, we would sit in the truck on Thompson's Hill and look down toward the river, watching the world and thinking about the future. If it was a good night, the windows would steam up and most of the looking would be inside the cab.

"I do want to hear about the Army, about what happened, what you signed up for. But would that be OK?" she asked.

The truck now felt at least 20 degrees warmer and we turned left out of her driveway and headed to the hill, our spot. There was an old cow gate at the end of the field that marked the entrance to the pasture, and even in the winter, Mr. Grondan made sure the gate swung free and the road remained plowed. I knew this, but not many others did. Sandy and I would often head there to spend time together. I didn't know much about girls, but I knew I liked her, and I knew she felt good. I'd had only one other girlfriend, Sarah Wilkins. But that was in the ninth grade and I don't think she really counted. We'd kissed a few times and once our tongues even touched, but that was about it. Sandy was different. She liked to kiss and didn't mind if I held her close while we did it. She moved when we kissed. I liked that.

I was thinking about that and almost drove past the entrance to the field.

"Whoops – here's the gate," I said.

"Go quick. It's cold"

"Well, I can warm you after," I said with a smile on my face.

"Maybe ...," she said and pushed me from the truck to open the gate.

We drove over the old farm road and parked on the northern end of the hillside. The field was a blanket of snow covering the dormant grass and plants. It resembled one of the lumpy quilts that often covered my bed and when I turned off the truck lights, the lumps turned a bluish black. Now it actually looked like my blanket. The engine was idling quietly and Sandy slid across the bench seat as the light faded in front of us.

"Tell me about the Army. Tell me what happened," she said and touched the side of my face. I turned to speak to her but instead, I found her lips.

"No," she said. "Tell me first."

I told her about the training, the school, and becoming an aviation mechanic. She listened, often playing with the hair that hung near the side of her face.

"South Carolina and then Alabama?" she asked. "How long?"

"Combined, it should be about nine months. Then I

get stationed at a base."

"You really like the mechanical stuff? Where will they send you?

"Probably Vietnam, but it will be a base job," I said and as soon as the words left my mouth, I wondered if I would go to Vietnam. George had ended up in Germany. I could go there too.

Sandy leaned over and I noticed that her coat was unbuttoned and the windows were steamed.

She kissed me again and as she did, she leaned into me. I forgot about everything else and wanted this moment to continue. She moved away from me, smiling, watching me, and we both slid out of our coats. I pulled her close and kissed her again. I wanted her to know how much she meant to me. As unsure and excited as I was, it worked. She came alive and her body started to move as we kissed. I was holding her and my hands seemed as if they were not connected to the rest of my body. I felt every curve, button, and strap, and with each inch of cloth, the intensity multiplied until I was uncomfortable. But I wasn't about to stop.

"Russ – promise me you'll be careful," she said and moved one of her hands along my leg, pulling me closer.

I couldn't say anything. "Maybe when you come home you can become an engineer, we can have a future," she said in no more than a whisper.

"Yeah – a future," I said and pushed one of my hands along her legs, and when I did, she moved her hands again and brushed against me, all of me. We had been here in the field for no more than 15 minutes and I didn't ever want to leave.

She must have known what happened and how I felt because she moved her hand harder and pushed against me in a way that only made it better. I couldn't help what happened next.

I pushed her away, hoping she hadn't felt it, and reached for the window handle.

"Sandy, hang on ... we should get back."

She smiled and said, "OK."

I stepped from the truck and adjusted myself, hoping she wouldn't see the mess I'd made. Within minutes, we were back on the road and headed home. Well, she was headed home, and I was headed somewhere else.

5 – Death has a Name

May 1967

As the landing skids of the Huey accepted the weight of the helicopter, Bobby Connelly began to grin. He was waiting to hear the words from his instructor pilot, CW2 Wilson, but he knew he'd passed his last check ride. For Bobby, flying had become second nature. While some of his classmates at Fort Rucker struggled with the advanced tactical training they received, for Connelly, each lesson, each training exercise reinforced his belief that this was what he was meant to do. Flying had become everything he thought of and everything he wanted to do. It had gotten to a point where he felt as comfortable in the cockpit as he was walking around the lake near his home. He and the machine he piloted through the sky were almost one entity, one being.

If he thought about rolling the Huey to the left, his hands, feet, and head instinctively caused the machine beneath him to follow his commands.

"I don't know why you've got that shit-eating grin, Connelly," Wilson said as he made some last minute notes on a clipboard he carried for each check ride. "You've passed, but that just means you've earned a ticket to one of the shittiest places on the planet."

Wilson was only four years older than Connelly, but he had already served more than 12 months in Vietnam, flying attack helicopters for the 101st Airborne. He was thin, weathered, and not infrequently, he spent the entire night in the officers' club nursing beer after beer and smoking Marlboros until the doors closed. He didn't talk a lot to the men he trained about his time in combat, and there were times when he and Bobby were flying together when Connelly noticed Wilson's eyes were closed. Wilson would open the small window to his right so the warm spring breeze would drift over him as they flew above the barren Alabama countryside.

"You've got one thing left," he said as he watched the young man sitting next to him go through the shutdown procedures they both knew so well. When the overhead blade was nearly stopped, he opened the door on his side of the Huey and slid out of his safety harness. In a matter of seconds, he was standing next to the cooling aircraft and searching through his flight suit for a cigarette.

"E & E tomorrow or the day after," he said, turning back toward the helicopter and flipping an unlit cigarette into his mouth.

"Pass that and you'll be one more leaf in the wind," Wilson said.

Bobby didn't respond immediately, but he knew what his instructor meant. He'd be gone.

Wilson watched as the young pilot secured the aircraft and as he approached him from the tail, he rubbed his forehead as if he were trying to make one last decision.

"The course is called Escape and Evade, but it's really survival training," Wilson said. "If you do end up on the ground, the object of the game is to stay hidden until the good guys find you," he said. "Then you get a ride home."

Bobby stared at the older pilot and thought about what he said. He was 19-years-old at the time and despite the protests from his father and mother, he'd left college after three semesters to enlist and become a pilot. After boot camp, primary flight school and now advanced flight school, that was about to happen. If he could get past this one course, he'd be given his wings.

"Did it ever happen to you?" Bobby Connelly asked and moved his head in his direction.

Wilson pulled the cigarette from his lips and turned his attention to the young flier.

"Once – it was a night mission and some VC shithead got a lucky shot into our transmission," he said and pointed toward the top of the Huey.

"We couldn't get back so I decided to set it down on what I thought was our side of a small hill, and the three of us laid low until the sun came up. By then we were four or five clicks away from our Huey and one of the jolly greens came screaming in and picked us up."

He put the cigarette back into his mouth and drew a deep breath. There was a large gap between his two front teeth and as the cool evening air entered his windpipe, a deep and unexpected whistling sound emerged.

"If you go down, find a hole and stay put. You won't be alone."

Bobby half-nodded to the older flier and without

another word, he started to walk toward the maintenance buildings that surrounded the field.

"They'll give you maps, lights, and all kinds of shit when they take you to the boonies," Wilson said, referring to the course. "Keep your head and keep low. Survive for 24 hours and get to the pickup."

Bobby fidgeted as he tried not to think about the next day alone in the woods.

"Over there it'll be different. Remember, you're not out there alone. Your job is to get yourself and your crew home. Don't be a fucking hero," he said, looking directly at the young warrant officer.

Bobby nodded again and as they crossed from the asphalt tarmac to the concrete apron of the hangar, Wilson headed toward the instructor's office, and Bobby made his way to the training locker room. "I'll make it," he thought.

Just as CW2 Wilson said, the truck taking the pilots to the E & E course arrived in front of the barracks at 05:30 and two sergeants hustled into the silent brick building looking for 14 pilots. Connelly and 13 others were pulled from their racks and told to get into their flight suits and dress as if they were heading for another training flight. For Bobby, that meant pulling a small ditty bag from his foot locker that contained a clipboard, extra pens, a spare magazine for the sidearm he was required to carry, and a t-shirt and socks. What he never told anyone was that it also held the silver bracelet his mother had worn most of her life.

She had given it to her son a week before he was due to leave for boot camp, and in many ways, he risked everything by hiding it in his locker and not shipping it back home with the rest of his civilian gear. It was no more than a quarter of an inch wide and appeared as if it had been hand-hammered from a single piece of silver. Where the two ends came together, one end had been fashioned into a hooked clasp that resembled the talons of a bird of prey. The other end had been flattened and sculpted into the shape of an eagle's head. The beak was curved in such a way that it connected with the talon.

Bobby couldn't remember a time when he hadn't seen the bracelet on his mother's right wrist. In fact, when he was no more than an infant and he was fussy from teething or a fever, she would let him play with the clasp and the bird for hours as she rocked and comforted her only child.

Two days before he was due to leave for the Army, she said, "Bobby, you should take this with you. My spirit, our spirit, will be with you wherever you go."

He didn't know why at the time, but he took the bracelet and made a promise to himself that he'd always carry it with him.

Bobby and the other pilots assembled in the day room of the barracks, and within 15 minutes, they were shuttled from the building to the back end of a transport truck. The sides were covered in thick green canvas and the sergeants hoisted half of the canvas covering the rear of the vehicle so they could sit on the bench seats that were bolted to the steel sides of the truck. The other sergeant, the duty sergeant, half-stood at the end of the truck closest to the cab and was holding what resembled strips of black ribbon, and he snapped orders at them.

"Not another word until we drop you off. Your eyes will be covered and we'll pull you from the truck when it's your turn to run. Now sit the fuck down and put your gear at your feet."

Bobby saw the other pilots drop their bags as they lowered themselves to the planks. The bags were pinned between their boots, and each pilot knew intuitively what to do next. As if they were one person, they lowered their heads and waited for the sergeants to tie the black cloths around their heads.

"Remember!" barked the duty sergeant, "If I see one of you fuckers looking in my direction or at each other, I'll throw your ass from the truck and you'll be set back."

That was more than each man needed to know. They waited without a word as two of the sergeants hopped from the truck and jumped back into the cab. The duty sergeant, a man who was rumored to have already served two tours in Vietnam, sat on a small jump seat that folded down from the back of the cab. The pilots didn't see it, but he was smiling and thinking to himself, "What a bunch of dumb fuckers."

As Bobby sensed the truck pull away from the barracks parking lot, he felt the two rubber bands he had placed on his forearm pull at the hair on his arm. The harsh and painful pinch reminded him that he was wearing his mother's bracelet. Every time he put on his flight suit, he managed to place the bracelet halfway up his forearm. As soon as the clasp was closed, he put two thick rubber bands below the eagle's head. This kept the loops of silver from sliding to his wrist and being seen by anyone else, but he always knew the bracelet was there.

Every once in a while, he scratched the thick sleeves of his flight suit trying to stop the itchin. Unconsciously, he wanted nothing more than to connect with the silver bird.

    The truck rolled and bumped along the road until there weren't any other road sounds, and as the silence settled over him, Bobby thought of the quiet he often found at home. The rhythm of the ride and the heat inside the canvas truck made him sleepy. Bobby's mother had often taken him for hikes into the hills that surrounded their lakeside home. When he was no more than 10 or 12, she and her only child walked together through the hills, valleys, and lakeside trails nearly every Sunday morning. It was the one day both of his parents didn't work and his dad like to sleep in a little later than usual. His mother, always the creature of habit, got up at her usual time, 5:30 a.m., and most of the time, Bobby would awaken to the smell of breakfast cooking.

    After quickly and quietly eating, they both would put on a pair of ankle-high work boots, jeans, and long-sleeved cotton shirts. Bobby usually added a baseball cap from his favorite team, the New York Yankees, and they would be out the door. Each had a small pack with extra water, Band-Aids and a small roll made up of old t-shirts that were cut into long strips. Anna taught her son that it was better to have these things in case they fell or were injured. Bobby carried a small pocket knife in his jeans and his mother didn't tell him, but she also carried a weapon, a .38 caliber pistol. Anna grew up in a section of the country where wildlife, especially predators, were an ordinary element of the landscape and even at this end of the state, there were still large cats roaming the hills looking for deer.

Anna and Jimmy Connelly lived on the same property for more than a decade before she started taking her son on the walks through the back country near the lake and by then, she had three favorite routes. Depending on the time of year, the temperature, and the weather forecast, the hike might last anywhere from two to six hours. As the truck filled with pilots continued to roll along the back streets that ran along the perimeter of the base, Bobby remembered the only time he felt scared while he was with his mother.

They had been walking for nearly two hours and as usual, the silence between them was comforting. Each was lost in their own thoughts and Bobby knew they were about to descend a small hill and enter a clearing near the northern end of the lake. There were large boulders marking the edge of the opening and when the sun was out and it was warm, they often stopped there to get a drink and have a bite or two of the food they carried in their packs. From the clearing, they would walk along the shore until they got to their home.

As they approached the open area, and Anna stopped abruptly and raised her hand, silently communicating that she wanted Bobby to stop as well. They were still surrounded by small brush and trees, but Bobby was crouched next to a small stand of bushes and he was focused on the clearing. He was about to ask his mother why they stopped when he saw her put her hand to her lips. With her other arm, she pointed toward a single, small deer, not much older than a yearling, that was grazing on the far side of the open glade. The bracelet on her wrist moved back and forth as she raised her arm.

As he had done so many times before, Bobby lowered himself toward the ground in hopes that he'd see what she was looking at, why they had stopped. Almost 30 yards ahead of them, Bobby saw the young deer lift his head from the sweet, spring grass and turn in their direction. The deer that lived in the hills surrounding Lake Wohlford expected to see humans, but in almost every instance, their instinct was to flee at the first sound or sight of their noisy neighbors. This young buck must have been hungry because, after a few seconds of listening, looking, and smelling the morning breeze, he lowered his head again and continued to feed. Bobby didn't realize at the time that he and his mother weren't the only creatures watching the scene in front of them.

A mountain lion, rare for these parts, but not unheard of, had been watching too from the northern edge of the clearing, no more than 10 yards from the young deer. As soon as the nervous animal lowered his head, the large cat attacked. To Bobby, it happened in a blur of fur, noise, and blood. Without thinking, he started to scream.

"Arrgh," he said, but before he could form a single word, his mother's hand sealed the space between his lips. He was silenced.

"Don't," she said in a voice that was no more than a whisper. Bobby saw that she had dropped her pack and was now holding the loaded pistol in her other hand.

"Shoot it," Bobby tried to say with his mother's hand still covering his mouth. She shook her head no, and

Bobby turned again toward the water. The large cat had surprised the young deer and as he took a second leap toward the animal, he sunk his teeth into the side of his prey's neck and tried to slam his jaws shut. At the same time, the muscles running from the cat's shoulders to his jawline helped him whip his head back and forth in a violent but efficient movement. The sound of the young deer's neck snapping signaled the end of the struggle. And in less time than it takes to cross a busy road, the cat was holding a dead carcass in his jaws.

Bobby slumped and he could feel the sting of his tears as his cheeks became wet. His mother, with the gun still in one hand, reached for her son and started to walk silently away from the area where moments ago they intended to rest. Ten minutes or more passed before he spoke to her.

"Why didn't you shoot? We could've saved the deer," he said to his mother and pulled his hand from hers.

She stopped walking and because of the look on her face, he stopped too.

"Bobby – I know this doesn't seem right, but death is as natural as life," she said. "That lion needs meat to survive and the deer provides that for him."

Bobby watched her as she pulled some water from her pack and passed it to her son.

"Both the deer and lion have their part to play," she said and put the water away. She reached again for her son's hand and they continued their silent walk home.

The truck Connelly was riding in lurched to a stop and the duty sergeant stood up.

"Not a word," he said and pulled the man closest to

the rear end of the truck to his feet. The tailgate of the truck was lowered and the prospective pilot was roughly helped to the ground. One of the sergeants from the front of the truck had come around to the back and put a small sack into the pilot's hands.

"You've got a map, a compass, and instructions," he said. "Meet us at the pickup point tomorrow at 18:00. Don't take your blindfold off for two minutes."

With only those simple instructions, the sergeants jumped back into the truck and it pulled away. That process repeated itself six more times until it was finally Connelly's turn. By then he'd memorized the commands and he was ready to go.

Standing alone and abandoned, he couldn't hear the truck anymore and as he pulled the blindfold from his head, he saw he was standing in some type of wooded area. There were no buildings, no roads, only trees and brush. The scrub pines were everywhere and he had no idea where he was in relation to the base or where he needed to go in order to meet the truck that would pick them up. He remembered nothing but the plan he'd made on the ride here.

"Food, fuel, and silence – that'll get me home."

Connelly opened the small, cotton sack that each candidate received as they were dropped off. It contained four pieces of equipment and nothing else. There was a small waterproof map. Not much of a map, really, it was a section removed from the large aviation charts that all the pilots had become accustomed to reading. The piece they were given was sealed in plastic and had two marks on it. One mark was a small black X indicating where they supposedly went down, where they crashed. The second mark, a red circle about one-quarter of an inch in diameter, was where the pickup would be in 24 hours. Connelly didn't recognize either mark on the map, but given the scale they normally used, he calculated that he must be about 10 kilometers, or 10 klicks as he had learned to say, from the pickup. He had to move to the northeast and up and over a hill that was marked as 1,460 feet above sea level.

There was also a small, empty aluminum canteen in the sack, a compass, and a handheld radio. The radio felt as if it weighed around five pounds and Connelly knew the range of the device was limited to about one mile. They were told it was to be used only in emergencies. A light infantry unit was moving through the area and if they came across any "downed" flyers, the pilot-candidates were to be captured and brought back. The infantry had radio receivers that could identify the position of any transmissions. Connelly knew that if he turned the radio on, they'd track his signal and he'd be sent back, and he had no intention of letting any grunt find him or act as some type of impediment to his graduation.

After looking at the position of the sun, the black X on the chart, and his compass, Connelly slid his equipment over his shoulder and headed northeast toward a small rise of land.

Every 100 yards or so, Connelly stopped and listened. He knew that as he walked, the sound of his movement obscured the other noises in the forest, and he didn't want to be surprised by anyone else.

After two hours, he crested what he assumed was the hill between his original position and the pickup point. Looking down from the hill, he saw the creek that was marked on his chart, and he also saw a small outcropping of rocks and dead trees. He decided that would be his home for the night. The opposite side of the creek was open terrain and there was little if any cover to hide under.

Connelly moved from tree to tree as if he was being watched every step of the way. He walked with short, deliberate steps until he came to the gray and black boulders that seemed to grow like some deadly disease from the side of the hill. The small pine trees that filled the surrounding land left a layer of loose, organic material on the forest floor. When Connelly finally made it to the front of the boulders, he saw that if he removed most of the loose leaves, pine needles, and topsoil, there was more than enough room for him to get out of the elements and hopefully remain undetected. Using one of the flat loose rocks as a makeshift shovel, he dug a trench for himself and lined it with the leaves and pine needles.

"If it rains, I won't get wet. The rain will roll right down the hill past me and it can't be more than 30 minutes from here to the pickup point," he thought. "I'll be fine."

As the day wore on, Connelly managed to make his new home even a little larger. He removed a few more loose rocks, and the depression where he was hidden, his temporary shelter from the elements and those searching for him, was now almost six feet long and more than two feet wide. It reminded him of the single-person canoes he sometimes used on Lake Wohlford. With the loose branches and leaves placed in front of him, he was completely concealed. Now, he had to make it through the afternoon and evening. He knew that if he remained still, he wouldn't expend much energy and after the sun finally set, using the darkness as an ally, he'd make his way to the creek and get some fresh water.

The warmth of the day and the moisture of the surrounding vegetation made his makeshift home muggy, humid, but not uncomfortable. Nestled in place and despite his best intentions, his eyes kept closing and he found himself dozing for minutes at a time. Once, late in the afternoon, he woke to the sound of voices that seemed as if they were coming from the space directly above his shoulder. After holding his breath for nearly a minute he remembered how far sound carried in the forest. "They might not be that close," he thought.

The infantry unit, at least that's what he assumed was the source of the conversations, sounded as if they were nearly on top of him. Without moving more than a finger or two, he pushed some of the leaves and branches aside and saw boots walking past him. He drew a deep breath and waited.

"I can't believe we have to hump through this shit," one of the soldiers said as a clump of tobacco juice landed inches from Connelly's face.

Connelly could smell the sweet organic fluid and it almost made him sneeze. He held his nose and closed his mouth.

"At least we won't be here all night," another voice said, now a little further away. "The 15th got the short end of the stick. Those fuckers will be here until dawn."

The voices started to fade even more as the boots made their way down the hill. Connelly tried to settle back even further into his burrow and within minutes his breathing and heart rate slowed once again. The forest was as still as his thoughts and he dozed.

Somewhere in his dream, he heard a loud snap and he woke once again. It was late but with the moon high in the sky there were shafts of light that made it to the forest floor. He turned to his right, the direction from the noise and pushed his watch toward his face. The digits glowed in an almost eerie shade of turquoise and he knew it was shortly after midnight. Then he heard the snap again.

At first, he thought it must be some creature rooting around through the trees, but the noise was more regular, more measured. Connelly thought it must be someone from the infantry unit on patrol. He convinced himself that his breathing had slowed and whatever breaths he took, he tried to push them back through pursed lips that were no wider than a pencil. He tried not to breathe too loudly.

A voice, not really words, but more like a grunt came to him through the crisp, still, night air.

"Shit," he whispered to himself, and Connelly moved his eyes in the direction of the voice. It was another one of the pilots who had been pulled from the barracks with him, Jon Frankel.

Frankel was from New Jersey and one of the brains of the unit. His family owned a small drug store in Morristown, and Frankel didn't want to go to pharmacy school and follow in his dad's footsteps. He dreamed of becoming an engineer or architect and working on the magnificent buildings that lined the streets of Manhattan. He had enlisted within weeks after he turned 18 and his test scores qualified him for almost any job the Army had to offer. Without consulting his family, he'd picked aviation and with a single signature he was ready to become an aviator.

Frankel was a whiz in the classroom, and he often helped the other men in the unit with their studies, but when it came to the physical side of the job, he fell far short of his peers. More than once, he flirted with being washed out of the program.

The drill sergeants were fond of barking in his direction. "If you slow down any more, you'll be humping it in the infantry by the end of the day!" Fear alone boosted the adrenaline that coursed through him and he finished whatever physical task was demanded of him a few seconds before the mandatory cutoff time.

Connelly, in his makeshift cave, watched as Frankel tried to make his way down the hill as fast his legs would take him, and when he was no more than 25 yards from Connelly, he veered to the left and it looked like the top half of his torso was weighing him down. One foot had found a small hole in the forest floor. He bent over at the waist and the physics of having the upper half of his body moving forward so quickly caused him to lose his balance. He tried to hop forward, to place his feet underneath his body but his other boot became stuck on one of the roots that rested under the leaves.

"Ughhhh," he said and rolled forward. He had the

sense to tuck his head and avoid contact with the ground, but because he was on a hill, all that did was turn him into a flying ball of arms and legs. He made two quick revolutions, picked up speed, and then came to an abrupt stop. A loud wet, smacking sound was all Connelly heard, as he moved from under his rock.

He cautiously jogged toward the still form in front of him. Frankel's head, arms, and body were all at odd angles to one another, and when he was within 10 yards of him, Connelly stopped, stood next to a sturdy pine and crouched to the ground to watch the fallen airman's chest. For almost 20 seconds it didn't move and then slowly, Connelly watched it rise and fall. For the next minute, he watched, waited, and counted. No more than eight shallow breaths passed from Frankel and Connelly thought the distance his chest traveled with each breath was becoming smaller and smaller.

He moved away from the side of the tree and approached his fallen comrade. Frankel's small satchel was tangled on one wrist and his eyes were half-open. There was a growing pool of thick, dark, crimson liquid forming around his head, and as he approached, Connelly called to him.

"Frankel, Frankel, do you hear me? Don't move."

Connelly settled into a crouched position near his head and looked toward his eyes for a response. They didn't move. He leaned down further and saw the side of Frankel's head had come to rest against a flat rock that was covered by a thin coating of pine needles. The force of the collision shattered his skull and the side now resting on the rock had been violently forced into the shape of the stone.

Connelly pulled Frankel's eyelids back and waved his hand in front of his face. There was no response and as he stopped, he tried to listen for his breathing. Even in the stillness of the forest, he couldn't hear anything. Connelly tried again and with Frankel's eyelids once again pulled open, he used his other hand to quickly cover Frankel's eyes and then pulled his hand away. Even in the moonlight, he was hoping he'd see the pupils respond. They didn't move. They pupils nearly covered the colored portions of his eyes and they didn't move one way or another as the changing amounts of light entered his vision.

"He's dead. He just doesn't know it," Connelly thought and slowly stood up.

Connelly wondered if he should carry him out, use his radio to call for help, or do nothing. He doubted that if by calling for help, he'd fail the course and be sent back, or worse yet, washed out, but this was the Army. He'd learned that what might make sense in the real world, didn't always translate to the way things were dealt with in the Army. He turned again toward Frankel. This time he couldn't detect any movement in his chest at all. He was gone.

Connelly looked again at the small sack tangled on Frankel's wrist and knew what he'd do. He opened it enough to pull Frankel's portable radio out and placed it near the fallen soldier. With a sense of urgency, he placed the radio under Frankel's lifeless hand in a small furrow he dug into the forest floor. Using the now dead weight of his arm, he positioned Frankel's arm and hand on top of the transmit button. He knew if he could leave the radio in transmit mode, the signal would get out and the command sergeant would pick up the signal. It might take them a while, but Connelly knew they could home in on the transmission. They'd find him.

With a tree branch that had fallen to the forest floor, Connelly smoothed out the area near Frankel's body, and with one last look, he made his way back to his temporary home on the hill. He collected his belongings, pushed leaves, dirt and other debris into the hollow under the rocks and with his small survival pack looped over his shoulders, he made his way toward the small creek.

"Sorry Frankel," he thought. "But if they're busy with you, they won't find me."

Despite the late hour, Connelly wasn't the least bit tired and he made his way to the running water in less than 15 minutes. Using his canteen as a cup, he took two long drinks from the cold stream and refilled his canteen one last time. He had a good idea where he was and as near as he could tell, it was about two klicks to the pickup zone. He covered that distance in a little more than an hour, and after confirming his location he headed to a small hill that overlooked the pickup area. He'd wait there until daylight. With his face, hands, and head covered in dirt and leaves, he was nearly indistinguishable from the rest of the forest as he sat with his back against a tree and waited. Three hours later, the trucks showed up that would carry him back to the base.

As he took a final step toward the truck, one of the sergeants who drove the vehicles stopped him and said, "Good to see you, Sir. Did you happen to see Frankel while you were wandering through the woods?"

It was the first time he'd been formally addressed based on the rank he would now carry with him to Vietnam.

"No," Connelly said. "I just hid and waited for you to get here." He lowered his head and jumped into the back of the vehicle. His training was over.

Book II — 365 and a Wakeup

6 – Meeting the Family

August 1967

Two days. I had two lousy days of training left and then we'd graduate, at least that's what the drill sergeants and warrant officers kept telling us. It didn't seem possible, but I'd been in the Army for six months and in two days, I'd be through with school. As they kept saying, "I might just be a useful weapon after all."

Our final, written exam wasn't that difficult, and I scored an 82 percent – not exactly the best in the class, but I passed. I'd earned my MOS designation and I'd be moving on. I had pictures of Sandy, and my Mom and Dad, taped to the inside of my foot locker, but in my mind, the only memory of my life that mattered began on a cold, starless night in March when I stepped from a drab, gray bus and walked into the processing center at Fort Jackson, South Carolina.

For nearly 180 days, I did things the Army way. From one waking moment to the next, my days and nights became one long training session. I learned to dress, to run, to walk, to eat, even to shit on command. Green, gray, brown and black – those were the colors of my rainbow and most of my world contained only objects that were painted or stained from that particular palette.

The last civilian colors I remembered came from the red and black plaid hunting jacket I wore on my way into the induction center. In less than 12 hours I had traveled from the safe confines of my home in the hills to an Army outpost, a factory for creating soldiers.

"All right, pukes!" the sergeant who greeted the bus screamed as the tired wheels lurched to a stop. "Get your sorry asses inside and line up on the faded yellow line facing the front of the room."

It wasn't that cold outside, certainly not as cold as when I left Massachusetts or Connecticut, but as we trotted toward the open doors of the building I started to shake as if I had been outside too long and the cold found its way into my bones. I tried the best I could to keep up with the person in front of me, and I struggled to remember where he came from. I thought he said Ohio, but now as I ran behind him, I wasn't sure.

"Drop your bags and face me," came a booming, deep voice from the front of the room. It sounded like God himself had decided to pay us a visit. Not one of us spoke and I tried to stretch and give myself another inch or so of height. I wanted to see the man who was barking instructions in our direction.

Staff Sergeant Wilson Ames wasn't standing at attention, and from where I was standing, his six-foot, two-inch frame filled the front half of the room. He wore a drill sergeant's campaign hat low on his head and angled toward the bridge of his broad, black nose. His uniform shirt fit in a way that I knew I would never be able to duplicate, and his forearms appeared to be made of ribbons of some smooth metal. His skin was simply a covering for the destructive power his body contained.

"Not – a – fucking – word," he said in a slow, low throaty growl.

"It's bad enough I have to be here babysitting," he said and turned away from the recruits.

For the next 20 minutes, Sergeant Ames proceeded to explain where we'd be spending the night and how we might survive to see the dawn tomorrow, but we had one job to do before we could retreat to our barracks for the few hours we'd have to ourselves.

"Time to say goodbye to your life," he said and laughed more to himself than any of the soldiers standing in front of him. "You're mine now."

There were 60 of us assigned to the barracks and I saw more than one of the men in the room appear to shrink in size as the sergeant continued to speak.

"You'll be given a uniform for tonight and tomorrow. Take the sorry-ass civilian shit you brought with you and put it into the boxes. Stick a label on the outside and send it back to your momma."

As the last instructions filtered into our heads, I wondered for the first time if this was some strange mistake. I had volunteered.

There were privates and corporals at the ends of each row of recruits and within minutes, they had distributed our first set of greens.

"Strip and get your asses in gear," came a final command from the front of the room.

Hat, coat, shirt, pants, and shoes - I couldn't get

them off fast enough. As I folded the clothes and stuffed them into the half-bushel sized cardboard box with the words "U.S. Army" stenciled on each side, the sergeant yelled again.

"Your shitty-ass drawers too. You're all Army now." I froze for a moment. I knew what he wanted us to do, but it didn't seem right. The harsh fluorescent lights above our heads only accented every dimple, every roll, and every imperfection we all carried. The sound of fabric sliding against skin told me the other recruits knew we had no choice.

We stood there, naked as the day we were born, more like cattle than men, and pulled on the Army boxers that were given to us. Shirts, pants, and shoes – we now stood as silent rows of raw, green recruits. No longer individuals, but not yet soldiers. That would come.

Not the best, but not the worst recruit - I survived and now as I waited for the training to end. The uniform I wore each day was more like a second layer of skin, a layer that defined who I was and who I would be for the next year in Vietnam. We wouldn't get our final orders until we reported in at MACV in Saigon, but I thought about my days ahead. I couldn't help it. It was finally going to happen. At least I'd be assigned to a base.

I had to get through the next two days and then head home for leave. Sandy would be there and that would make the difference. Each morning as I opened my locker and pulled out a clean pair of socks and boxers, I stopped to look at her picture and think about the time we spent together. I remembered the face, but I couldn't remember her voice or the way she felt as I held her. What I did think about, what I did remember, was the smell. She always wore the same perfume and before I left, she put several drops of the perfume on the back of her photograph. Now, as I knelt near the locker and pulled out my clothes, I'd pretend to look for something that I had misplaced near the bottom of the locker, but more than anything, I wanted to push my face a little closer to the picture. Even after six months and moving from Fort Jackson to Fort Gordon, and now here at Rucker, it still smelled like her. That fragrance, that memory, if nothing else, it strengthened me.

At first, I'd written to her almost every day, but I didn't mail the letters until we were allowed to double-time it to the base post office at Fort Gordon, my home for 10 weeks of basic training. By the time we were allowed to mail the letters, I wasn't sure I wanted to tell her about the Army or life in the barracks. I certainly didn't know what to tell her about our week in the mess hall.

I only spent a few days at Fort Jackson before we were all bussed down the road to Fort Gordon, Georgia. The ride was dusty and hot. And after two, four-hour stints cramped into a glorified school bus, I smelled like most of the animals I tended to at Grondan's farm. For the next five weeks, I trained with 47 other recruits as we tried to make it to the end of boot camp. I knew that I'd be going to advanced training once we got to the end. Our only job was to survive until then.

It seems that each recruit company has to spend a week of basic training in the mess hall. No job is too big or too small for a soldier, and about the time we all qualified on the rifle range, it was time to peel potatoes and sling hash. Tommy Sullivan, our recruit company commander, was responsible for getting us to the mess hall in the morning and making sure we all followed orders until the end of the day.

During basic training, the racks in the barracks were nothing more than steel-framed bunk beds, and Tommy Sullivan and I shared the end bunk closest to the front of the long open room. On either end of the bed we stored our footlockers, and during the few minutes we had to ourselves before lights out, when most of the guys in the company were writing home or bragging to each other about what they were going to do once we were given a pass off the base, Tommy would talk about Boston. He'd talk about his family. I didn't have anything to add to the conversation, but I liked to listen. It made it easier to sleep. But every morning started the same way.

"Up and at 'em boys," Sullivan said with an accent that was one generation removed from the fields of Northern Ireland. Tommy said he grew up on the tough streets of Dorchester, Massachusetts, but despite his temperament, he'd managed to impress the sisters who ran his parish elementary school. By the time he was ready for the eighth grade, Sister Alice-Marie convinced his worn and weary mom that he should go to high school and even college.

He laughed when he told me the story.

"'Mrs. Sullivan - God's given him a gift,', the nun said to my mother one Sunday morning at the end of mass. 'He'd make a fine teacher, doctor, or lawyer.'"

Tommy said his mother didn't respond right away,

but later that same week, she did give him a note, in a sealed envelope, to bring to school. She'd never made it much past the fifth-grade and the idea that her son might make it out of the streets was more than she'd hoped for. She wanted to know what to do.

Tommy said that Sister Alice-Marie must have seen something special in him. She took a liking to him. I imagined he was a rugged, bright, street-smart kid, and she convinced him to apply for a scholarship to nearby Malden-Catholic High School.

Tommy told me more than once about his high school. The school, built in 1932, was an academically tough, city school run by the Xaverian brothers. The brothers believed in the basics and demanded only excellence and obedience from their students. Laziness, rude behavior, and a dull work-ethic were not tolerated. Most of the students who marched at graduation were not only academically ready for the rigors of college, but they often had a stronger sense of place and purpose than their peers.

Tommy Sullivan said he graduated with honors in 1962 and immediately enrolled at Boston College. Working for his dad, who he described as a hardworking and hard drinking bricklayer, he was able to save enough for tuition, but not room and board.

From the beginning of September until the end of May, Tommy traveled every morning from his home, a third-floor walkup in Dorchester, to the plush and foreign looking neighborhoods surrounding the Chestnut Hill area of Boston. I was not all that religious; my mom would bring us to church on Easter and Christmas, but most Sunday mornings we'd spend the time working around the house or getting ready for family dinner. Tommy explained to me that at Boston College, religion classes were required of all students, but he spent most of his time studying history and philosophy.

He was older than most of us and had graduated from college, I still think that's why they made him the squad leader, but I couldn't figure out why he wasn't an officer. One afternoon as we were waiting to enter the mess I worked up the courage to ask him.

"Three days before my graduation at BC, the letter from the draft board arrived. I knew it wasn't good news," he said. "Both mom and dad were sitting at the table when I came home and Dad was holding the shiny white letter and looking at it as if he were trying to decipher some sort of message."

Sullivan told me he had 14 days to report for a physical or contact the draft board and apply for a deferment.

"I already had a deferment when I was in school," Sullivan said. "And I knew if became a teacher or got married, I might be able to apply for another one. But that didn't seem right."

Tommy Sullivan told his parents it was his turn to step up. "I just told them I was going to go," he said.

Sullivan had more choices than I did, but in the end, he figured that if he enlisted and signed up for the infantry or the artillery, he'd only have to spend a year, two at the most, in the Army. If he went to OCS and became a 90-day-wonder, he'd have to give them four years.

"That wasn't going to happen," he said. "But I had no idea it was going to be like this."

I didn't know what he meant at the time, and in some ways, I still don't, but as the days turned to weeks, Tommy spoke less and less about home and sometimes at night I would hear him toss and turn in the bunk below me. I was sure I'd fallen asleep before he did. The nights were painful for most of us, not that we'd ever admit it, but for Tommy, they were especially difficult. In less than a month, we were due to graduate from basic and I knew I was headed to Rucker and advanced training. Tommy was going directly to Vietnam and an infantry unit.

Our turn in the mess hall came during our sixth week of training and already some of the guys in the squad were making plans for graduation from boot camp. I was just excited we were allowed a five minute call home.

"Don't worry about my graduation," I said to my mother on the Saturday before we started working in the mess hall. "If you want to come to graduation, why don't you and Dad see if you can come to Fort Rucker. Do you think you could bring Sandy too?"

The number of letters I received from Sandy had mysteriously started to dwindle. I hadn't heard from her in the last two weeks, and most of the time, I could count on at least two or three letters each week.

"Have you seen her lately?" I asked, hoping there was some news.

"I stopped into the store the other day to mail you a package, and I thought I saw her by the counter," she said. "But when I turned around, she was gone."

My mother and Sandy never really saw eye-to-eye on things, and I wasn't surprised when she didn't speak to her in the store.

"Well, I'll send you and Sandy my graduation date and if you can come together, that'd be great," I said.

Normally, we'd roll out of the racks at 5 a.m. for morning P.T. before we'd double-time it from the exercise fields to the mess hall for breakfast, but during the week that we worked in the kitchens, we were invited to roll out of the racks at 4:30 a.m. There was no P.T. and sleep was a distant memory. Tommy was always the first one awake and he roamed up and down the aisles of the barracks as if he were getting us ready for a mission. Like the born leader he was, he managed to rattle our chains and got the platoon assembled and ready for the day.

Within minutes, we were dressed and slowly running in the dark down the gravel road – as soldiers do after living together for months on end, we traveled as if were one person. Our steps in sync with the cadence we all knew too well and our collective voices carried us toward our work.

Everyone had a designated job, some were cooks' helpers, some worked on the chow line and served the food, and others were members of the crew that constantly tried to keep the place clean and organized. I was assigned to one of the big commercial dishwashers. I'd seen a machine like it before at the V.A. where my dad worked but I had no idea how uncomfortable the steam and heat from the machine could be.

There was a long stainless steel table behind me,

and near the end of our breakfast shift, two or three of the recruits in our squad were assigned prep duties for lunch. This usually meant heading to one of the huge coolers at the back of the room and bringing back trays of beef and ham. It needed to be sliced. The large, dripping slabs of meat were placed on the steel table and after the trays were washed again, the sliced meat was piled back onto the trays, covered, and returned to the coolers for the noontime meal.

I was hardly watching the process when Tommy came back and yelled at the two recruits who were goofing off and not interested in finishing their work.

"Listen, you stupid shits," he said. "We don't need to do any extra PT because you can't get your ass in gear."

As the last comments settled on me, I saw him move toward the table and pick up what might have been a 25 or 30-pound piece of ham. He hoisted it up near his head and with a sickening, wet thud, he dropped it into the meat slicer. Juice from the meat splashed across the upper half of his uniform shirt and rolled from the table to the tile floor.

"This is not exactly tough," he said and flipped the switch that provided power to the slicer.

There was high-pitched hum as the 14-inch, stainless-steel blade came up to speed. He pushed the handle down and secured the food before he started moving the cutting mechanism back and forth, and as it was supposed to, slices started to appear from the bottom of the machine.

Tommy turned toward me and then swung his head back in the direction of the two recruits and the machine.

He stopped speaking and listened for a second to the whirling blade.

"I shouldn't be here," he said and as the last words left his lips, he started moving the ham again toward the blade. He must have forgotten about the mess he made on the floor because he tried to shift his weight in order to put more leverage behind his movements. His feet found the puddle of jellied juice from the meat and he slipped.

His arm lurched forward as he tried to catch his balance and his hand skidded off the handle and came to rest in the small open space before the meat met the blade. Instinctively, he pushed his hand forward and his fingers became wedged beneath the blade. It stopped moving.

Tommy saw what happened, saw that the blade was no longer moving, saw four of his fingers drop into the serving tray. I heard the machine start spinning again and saw the blood.

Tommy grabbed his hand, but the blood and the injury were too much for him and he fainted. I yelled for the mess sergeant.

Tommy Sullivan lost four fingers on his right hand that day, and within a week, he was back home in Dorchester. Each member of the squad had to talk to an officer who gave us the impressions that Tommy might have done it on purpose. I didn't know, but we continued in the mess hall the next day and within a few weeks, we were finished with basic. I was on my way to Fort Rucker and ready to learn something that might clear the way for my future.

Our company graduated from Fort Gordon on a Thursday and most of the squad cleared the barracks that Friday. Some were given 30 days leave and sent home to get everything in order before shipping to Vietnam, a few were assigned to a post somewhere else in the world, and about half of us had orders to report for advanced training. I spent the morning making sure my gear was packed and I had my travel vouchers. It was only 300 miles from the Fort in Georgia to Fort Rucker. I studied the map, and it was nearly a straight shot further to the south-southwest from where we were. With a few stops, I thought it would take the bus about eight hours to get there.

I tried calling home before I left the base, but nobody answered the phone and I didn't want to try Sandy's house. I knew her mom would be home, but what was I going to say to her? A few minutes after 9 a.m., I threw my bag into the cargo bin under the bus and settled into my seat. The one lesson I'd already learned in the Army was to sleep whenever you can.

I don't think the old, slow Greyhound bus was more than a mile down the road before I was dozing off. I didn't expect to see Georgia again.

Fort Rucker was everything Fort Gordon wasn't. There were still orders to follow and plenty of rules and regulations, but for the most part, I was almost treated like a normal soldier. I felt like I was in the regular Army and even though training didn't start for a week or so, I soon became comfortable with the routine.

After I reported in, I was temporarily assigned to a maintenance company and I was told to report in at the airfield on Monday morning at 0700. The temporary barracks for soldiers reporting into Rucker was on the main road and there were shuttles starting at 0530, every 30 minutes, between the barracks and the airfield. As the company clerk, a corporal whose last name was Gendron, accepted my paperwork and explained everything to me, it started to sound like this would be a great job for me.

"You'll have about a week before your training class begins," he said and pulled paper after paper from my records. "Make sure you check in with Sergeant Dixon on Monday. He probably will be one of your instructors."

As the last words left his lips he finally lifted his head and turned his gaze toward me. The sides of his head had been shaved and only the top portion of his head remained covered with a thin coating of brown hair.

"You might want to visit the barber before you meet the sergeant," he said and his hands moved to his temples. "High and tight – it's never a bad thing."

I found the shuttle that was heading toward the barracks and as I took my seat, I asked the driver if he knew the hours for the base barber.

"Most days, eight to two," he said as he closed the door and pulled away from the main building. "Saturdays too."

I took the corporal's advice, and the next morning I left the barracks and headed for the barber shop. I didn't want to start things off on the wrong foot. On Monday, I was nervous, but I made sure I was up early and I stood alone in front of the barracks at 0530 waiting for the bus. I didn't know what to expect and I didn't know what I'd be asked to do. The weather in Alabama at the end of May felt like Massachusetts in the middle of the summer. I couldn't help it, walking to the place where the shuttle would pick me up, I started to sweat.

The driver smiled when I told him I wanted a ride to the airfield, that I was checking in, and when I stepped out at the gate to the field, I knew why – the place was empty. I tried to focus on the guard by the entrance, but I couldn't create eye contact. In the end, he rolled his eyes at me.

"You'll have to wait here," he said. "No one's here yet – have a seat."

About an hour later, cars started approaching the gate, and slowly the field came to life. At nearly 0650, a blue Ford F-150, not too different from the one I left at home, pulled up and the guard announced to me that this was Sergeant Dixon.

"Get in," he said in my direction and moved his hand toward the empty bed of the truck.

I jumped over the side and about the time I sat down, he pulled forward. It wasn't more than 500 yards to one of the largest hangars standing next to the runway, but it took more than five minutes to get there.

"Get inside while I figure out what to do with you," he said and pulled a pack of cigarettes from his uniform shirt. "For the next 10 weeks, your sorry ass is mine."

Staff Sergeant James Dixon was a 30-year-old veteran

from Magnolia, Ohio, and I learned that he'd spent the last 14 months as a crew chief with the Army's 175th Assault Helicopter Company. What I knew on the first day I met him, and saw the patch on his shoulder of a bull's skull with blood red eyes, was that he had been there. He'd seen some serious shit, but he'd come back and I hoped he'd show me how to do the same.

For the next ten weeks, I walked in fear of the sergeant. He didn't say much and his job was to shepherd 20 of us through the practical side of our training. He'd been a crew chief for a gunship company and I assumed he'd spent a lifetime, or at least 10 years, in the service.

More than once, he'd told us, "your only job is to keep the birds flying - help the pilots, shoot the bad guys, and get back to the base." I wasn't always sure what he was talking about and I didn't want to tell him that my recruiter slotted me for a large base in the south. I should be safe there.

Once our official class started, I only saw Sergeant Dixon about half the time, each day. For the first five weeks, we spent every morning in one of the large hangars with him, and he taught us about aerodynamics, hydraulics, fuel systems, and electronics. He made it quite clear that he wasn't going to go into great detail about the inner workings of the engines that kept the helicopter in the air. For our designation, we were told how to keep them running, not how to tear them down and rebuild them. If we needed to, we could replace an engine, but we didn't want to take one apart in the field.

"Leave that for the techs with the lab coats," Dixon said. "Those fuckers have a deal and they know it."

During the second half of the training, we flipped our schedule and spent the mornings in the classroom and each afternoon out by the airfield. Dixon was different in the afternoon. As the temperature of the day built up and waves of heat could be seen over the asphalt and concrete runway, his mood worsened. More than once, I thought he smelled like the backroom of Sandy's pharmacy. His eyes were red and he always had to have a cigarette or a stained, half-filled coffee cup in his hands.

By the time we approached the end of our training, we'd gone over nearly every bolt and rivet on the UH-1C, and I felt like I knew the aircraft well. For me, the mechanical training was the best. When I had a greasy rag in my pocket and a wrench in my hand, I felt at home. At the end of the 9th week, I was alone with Dixon in the back of the hangar putting the tools away and trying to sweep up before we shut down for the day when I heard the sound of a zippo lighter click. By now, that sound was as distinguishable as my own voice. Within seconds it clicked again and Dixon pulled fresh smoke from the glowing cigarette perched in his mouth into his lungs.

"You really do know how to use these tools," he said. Watching him flip the lighter back and forth, I knew he was speaking to me as if I were another person and not one of his puke-ass students, as he often called us.

"I worked at a garage and around the farm at home," I said and glanced toward the older man.

His arms flailed at his upper body as if he were suffering from a constant itch. He was scratching at the place where his bulky arms connected to his shoulders, and any second now, I thought he was going to draw blood.

"Where was that?" he asked and sat in the open bay of the helicopter we were using for training.

"Massachusetts, in the hills near the New York border," I said. He didn't move or say anything to me for almost a minute. The hangar was quiet.

"I came from farm country too - Ohio," he said. "You have family there? A girl?"

Now it was my turn to stop and think.

"Family yes, but I am not so sure about the girl. I haven't heard from her since I got to Rucker," I said. It was the first time I'd said the words out loud about Sandy. I was sure something had changed. Every time I tried to call collect, her mother accepted the charges, but told me that Sandy wasn't home. She said she'd give her the message, but I hadn't received any mail.

In about a week I was going to graduate, and when I got my orders, I was heading home for almost a month before shipping out for Vietnam. Sandy was all I'd known and most nights, even here in the heat of Alabama, she was all I thought about. I forgot where I was for a second or two and Dixon's voice snapped brought me back to reality.

"We don't make good husbands or boyfriends," Dixon said. "At least I didn't."

I didn't know what to say, and I didn't want to argue with him, but I knew he was wrong about me.

"Let's get out of here," he said. "We've got a fucking test flight in the morning and then you're almost finished."

He jumped from the bay of the Huey and without much of a thought, he patted the fuselage twice and walked from the building. Not knowing what else to do, I patted the aircraft too and followed the sergeant.

~ ~ ~ ~ ~

The night passed as so many others had during the past five months. No matter what I did or how much I worked during the day, sleep came slowly, almost painfully. I couldn't shut my head off and most of my thoughts were filled with two subjects - Sandy and the war. After a while, I didn't recognize the difference between the two.

On the morning of our check rides, I woke up as I always did, 15 minutes before we were supposed to be out of the racks. My head had become a clock and without knowing why or how, even in my sleep, I was able to gauge the passage of time.

We all dressed in our fatigues, but there was far less chatter, less horsing around. We all knew this was the last step before graduation, and before we received our orders.

Within an hour, as a company, we had eaten and run to the airfield. Our movements were always the same and it felt like we ran everywhere. I had become accustomed to the warmth and easy way my body settled into a slow, loping run - one mile, two miles, or ten. It didn't seem to matter - the pace was the same and my body responded to the commands without a single conscious thought.

Sergeant Dixon was waiting for us at the airfield and

he had already moved one of our training Hueys to the pad beside the hangar. There were long yellow streamers plugged into the main wing over the cabin and the tail rotor. The Huey had been sitting as a classroom specimen for more than eight weeks, but on this morning, it more closely resembled the dangerous thoroughbred its designers dreamt of. It too was ready to take to the sky.

I wasn't sure what to expect; I had only been on one flight and that was from Bradley Field to boot camp, hardly a small plane or helicopter. But before any of us had a chance to ask questions, Dixon made it clear he was in charge and this was his area of expertise.

"Get your sorry asses in the hangar and find a helmet and a flight suit," he said.

As we jogged toward the open hangar door his booming, smoke-deepened voice rolled over us again.

"If one of you fuckers blows chunks in my bird, you'll be playing with the dirt dogs by the end of the day."

We found two rows of flights suits, harnesses, and helmets. The cargo bay of the Huey had been cleared of gear and three of us would be assigned to a bench seat facing forward. Two others would have jump seats facing the rear end of the Huey and our backs would press against the steel and canvas of the pilot's seat. I hoped for the bench seat.

"We're only taking five of you at a time," Dixon said. "If it's not your flight, you'll wait here and stay the fuck out of trouble."

We exchanged glances and few of us tried to sort out our positions in line.

"Now listen up," he said, and without any more discussion, he called out the first five names and assigned seats. Mine wasn't among the names called and because of the omission, I could breathe again.

"Wait here until the pilots run through their checklists, and when you see me wave you over – run."

The first five men nodded as if they knew exactly what to do, and collectively they bent over at the waist as the pilots removed the warning streamers and settled into their seats. In seconds there was a loud pop as the fuel in the turbine engine ignited. The main blade started to slowly increase in speed, and Dixon left the hangar.

We could see him hop into the Huey and lean forward as he spoke to the pilots. The conversation couldn't have been more than a few words, but he smiled at something they said to him.

His looked familiar and comfortable inside the helicopter but that all seemed to fade from his face as he turned back toward the hangar and waved the first section over.

They scurried toward the Huey and one-by-one, Dixon pulled them aboard. We couldn't hear the conversation, but we did see them connect their harnesses to the aircraft.

"Locked and loaded," Frankie Rodriguez said to me in a low whisper as we both waited for them to leave the safety of the field.

The noise from the engine deepened and like a dog looking for its supper, they were off. In seconds they were 50-100 feet off the ground and moving away from us. I couldn't imagine what it must have felt like, but despite the cool morning breeze, I started to feel water pooling at the base of my back.

"How long will they be gone?" I asked Frankie.

"Beats the shit out of me," he said and turned away from me. "But we're next."

They were gone no more than 10 minutes, but the time dragged on, and I wondered what the ride would be like. All I kept thinking was I probably wouldn't have to go on too many check rides once I arrived at my base. But who knew?

The Huey arrived over the hangar without a lot of warning or noise and I thought they were moving far too fast to safely land, but at the last minute, the aircraft pitched up and settled as if it found a large pillow of air.

They were back, and Dixon's job had changed. Before the flight, he'd helped each one into the aircraft, and now he was intent on pulling them from the cargo bay and pushing the returning soldiers toward the hangar. Some of the faces were pale, some were smiling, some looked as if they might be sick, but they all appeared to have changed.

"Go, go, go!" Rodriguez said to me and hit my shoulder. "Dixon wants us," he said. Without thinking, five of us hunched over and ran for the Huey. The main rotor slowed, but it never stopped spinning.

The tarmac was hot and the air rolling off the blade hit us when we were about 50 feet from the Huey. It was as if someone opened the door to a furnace and turned on the fan. I put my hand up to shield my eyes and as I lifted my head to judge my distance to the Huey, I felt Dixon's grip. Vice-like, his fingers closed around my harness and as he pulled, I jumped aboard the bird.

"Here," he yelled in my direction and pushed me into one of the jump seats and clipped my harness to the safety hook welded to the frame and fuselage. The open doorway was no more than six inches from the front of my helmet and the early morning sun filled my vision. I thought about lowering the glare shield on my helmet, but I didn't want to move.

In seconds, Dixon had everyone aboard and clipped in and before we could say anything else, he tapped one of the pilots on the shoulder and swung his index finger in a circular motion. We were off.

Dixon himself clipped into a safety hook between the two jump seats and sat on a couple of ammo boxes that fit in the space between the pilots. One by one, he gazed at each of us and tapped his headset, a wordless reminder for us to plug in our flight helmets. Despite the rush of air coming from every direction, I heard him again.

"Stay in your seats and hang on. We're going to roll through a few basic attack maneuvers. Watch and learn."

We all had microphones embedded into our helmets, and even though we were connected electronically, most of us didn't speak. We didn't need to - a simple nod told him we were ready.

The morning air was still and we lifted off without nearly a bump or any type of noticeable movement. The ground fell away without warning. It was scary how smooth the transition was.

"We'll make a few runs as if we were on our way to hot LZ," Dixon said. "First left then right."

With nothing more said, the helicopter changed its

position in the air. It was no longer flying straight and level. The nose dipped forward and the main rotor pulled the bird through the air with increasing speed. I felt my back pushed against the steel cage of the jump seat. The run lasted about a minute and then with unexpected, brutal force we were lifted face first toward the sky, and the helicopter rolled to the left.

I wasn't ready for the flight maneuver and instinctively let out a small grunt and slid an inch or two closer to the open doorway. Dixon smiled.

As soon as I got used to the force of the left-hand turn, the Huey rose another 50 feet toward the sun. The nose of the ship crossed from left to right and then dipped back toward the deep red Alabama clay. I felt my stomach rise too.

We raced back toward the airfield following the same track we'd taken on the ride from the base and as we approached an imaginary point of land, we swung up and to the right. Sunshine, blasts of cool air, and noises from the other recruits all came rushing into my head. At the top of the arc, I swore we were weightless for a second or two, and I wished I'd gone easy on the breakfast.

"Now for a few simulated landings," Dixon said and the Huey launched itself toward a small, bare strip of land surrounded by scraggly looking pines. I swore we were going too fast to possibly land or even slow down.

My hands found the railing of my seat and I tried to push against the weight of my body. Looking at the others flying with me, I noticed two others were doing the same thing. Only Rodriguez was smiling, but he smiled at everything.

We didn't exactly land in the center of the simulated landing zone. It was still a mystery to me, but the pilots figured out how to stop us about three feet from the ground. We hovered for about 10-15 seconds and then we were off again. They repeated the process three more times and as they finished for the final time, I felt my stomach roll.

"Crap," I thought. "I can't blow it here." I took a deep breath and focused on the far horizon, the place where the trees met the sky. I tried to think of graduation.

My mom and dad were definitely coming but I still didn't know about Sandy. The last time I called home, my mother said they were all flying down. Dixon's no-nonsense voice suddenly filled my headset and all thoughts of home vanished.

"Hang on – We're going to show you what it feels like to auto-rotate one of these bastards," he said.

Smiling more to himself than any of us, he patted the backside of the pilot's seat and gave them one last thumbs-up.

"If the engine gives up the ghost, this'll be the last maneuver you have before you hit the ground."

The Huey pitched up and we were gaining altitude at an alarming rate. The lower half of my body and my stomach felt as if some large presence was pushing me further into the webbing of my seat. The gas and bile that had once been calmly sitting in my gut now rose in the pipe between my mouth and my abdomen.

"Deep breaths," I thought again. And then as we nearly reached the top of our climb, the engine suddenly became silent. At the same time that the aircraft pitched forward, I saw Dixon smile and close his eyes, and we started to fall.

"The pilots will change the pitch of the blades to keep them spinning and let us build up some speed," he said with his eyes still closed and to no one in particular.

I thought we were going to hit any second, and I was doubly certain they'd made a mistake and we were going to end up in a bloody pile of steel. The whole helicopter pitched up again and slowed to a point where we nearly stopped any forward movement. We were no more than a few feet off the ground and for a split second, the Huey hung in the air – no engine, no sounds, only a smiling sergeant who knew what was about to happen. Then we dropped, we hit.

"Get your asses back to the hangar," Dixon said and pulled us, one by one, from our perches.

My stomach settled somewhere in the back of my throat and about the time I decided there must be some strange bag of greasy liquid hanging in my windpipe, I felt Dixon's death grip on my shirt. With a lurch, I was launched toward the ground and my feet managed to find their place underneath me. I wobbled and duck-walked my way toward the open hangar door. When I was within three feet of the doorway, I knew I wouldn't make it much further without splashing somebody's feet.

I lifted my hand to my mouth and sprinted for the locker rooms and bathroom. Rodriguez saw me coming and moved to the side of the narrow hallway that separated the hangar space from the locker rooms. The look on my face must have made it clear that standing in front of me would not end well for either of us. About the time I finished retching and heaving, I heard the door to the bathroom swing open again and from one knee I saw Dixon's shiny boot as he crossed the floor toward the urinals.

"Warriner," I heard him say as he emptied the coffee he'd been drinking all morning into the base's septic system.

"You might just make it. That happened to me on my first ride too," he said as he finished his business. "Get your ass in gear and join the rest of your unit. The Army's not done with you yet," he said and turned away from me. He had another group waiting for a check ride.

7 – Looking Back at the World

November 1967

The base was quiet for most of the day and as Bobby Connelly walked with a sense of purpose from the ops shack to the airfield, he scanned the horizon. Without thinking about it, he lifted both hands to shade the corners of his eyes and tried to see through the thin layer of clouds that were tethered to the lumpy hills and trees surrounding the base. He hoped that in minutes he'd see the Huey that carried his friends and fellow warrant officers - Tom Hooper and Billy Braxton. Sitting in the comm shack, he learned the pair were due back any minute and from listening to only one-half of the conversation he knew their Huey had been hit at least three times by ground fire. Connelly wondered where they'd been hit and what type of damage their aircraft had sustained. They were flying one of the oldest Hueys in the unit, and this wasn't the first time it had been knocked around in battle. The patchwork fuselage was almost legendary amongst the pilots - some even started to refer to the Huey as "old-thru-and-thru" for the way enemy rounds almost eerily entered and exited without hitting any vital wires, hydraulic lines, or machinery.

Better yet, the pilots and crewmen riding in the B model bird had always come back, most of the time without a scratch.

Connelly moved his head toward the northern and eastern section of the sky and remembered what he thought he'd heard Hooper say. "The engine's trailing smoke. I'm not sure if one of the oil or hydraulic lines has been hit, but Leonard's taken a round. He's not moving."

The comm shack became still as each man waited for another transmission and collectively they each sensed the gravity of the situation. All other conversation stopped as the radio operator continued speaking with Hooper. The operator turned toward the officer of the day and the two men nodded as an unspoken message passed between them.

"You'd better find a place for us to set down," Hooper said over the radio. "I've got her almost red-lined and we're coming in hot."

Connelly had flown with these men before and he knew that Staff Sergeant Leonard, the crew chief on the Huey, was a short-timer with about a month left before he was due to make his way back to the states. He'd arrived in Vietnam in a similar way as all the other Americans: somewhat unsure of his surroundings, with an almost mythical sense of who the U.S. soldiers were, and with a deep-seated fear that he might not make it home.

The young pilot scanning the skies heard the stricken Huey long before he saw it. True to his word, Hooper was flying with the engine turning at or above its normal operating range. The deep resonating sound of its engine and the almost comforting "whoop-whoop" of the main rotor as it sliced through the tropical air had been replaced with a high pitched mechanical scream as the gearing in the turbine engine fought to continue spinning. Connelly thought the noises coming from the stricken Huey sounded more and more like the shrill shrieks the birds surrounding his California home made when he shot at them with his dad's 12-gauge Remington. The Huey had been attacked and was hurt. Now, as if by instinct alone, all it wanted to do was get home.

"There it is," he said to no one in particular and pointed toward a dark spot, low in the evening sky. "Two more minutes and they'll be here," he thought.

The Huey crossed the ring of trees that marked the boundary of the compound and Connelly watched as the aircraft slid to a stop three feet above the greenish-brown dirt and dust that acted as the tarmac for the airbase. With all the heat, sun, and humidity, it felt like something was alive and growing, even in the strange and foreign looking soil of this country. The Huey settled onto its landing gear and the dust and air surrounding the aircraft spooled away in an audible burst as if the machine were alive and finally exhaling after a long sprint home. Immediately the turbine engine began to spool down. They'd made it back.

Without any warning or notice, Connelly saw the two medics rush toward the helicopter, but the chief hadn't jumped from the cargo bay to meet them. He was slumped forward in his seat and still clipped into the safety harness that was designed to keep him onboard during flight. His flight helmet was still on and even as the daylight started to fade, his shaded visor remained pulled down to cover the top third of his face. Despite the noise and commotion, he wasn't moving.

Hooper opened the door next to his seat and jumped from the cockpit. To Connelly, it looked like his boots were moving furiously toward the back half of the aircraft before they even hit the ground. At the same time, Braxton made his way between the front seats and pulled the stricken crew chief toward him. He raised the sun visor on Sergeant Leonard's helmet and yelled for the medics. There was a dark stain on the top half of the crew chief's flight suit and it still shimmered, glistening as if it were wet. A dark circle highlighted the spot where his chest and neck came together. All Connelly could imagine was that the stain now resembled a bullseye of sorts. Somehow, someone or something had put one in the center ring.

As soon as the medics arrived at the Huey, they removed Leonard's helmet and laid the stricken man on the shiny, aluminum deck of the cargo bay. They pulled the helmet from his head and without changing their focus, they tossed it to the ground. When Leonard wore the helmet, the gold wings painted about an inch above his visor were usually pointed straight toward the sky. Now, in a bizarre way, they were tilted down toward the unmoving earth underneath the helmet. Connelly slowed his approach to the aircraft and let Braxton and Hooper have their time with their injured crewmate.

"I wonder who'll be the new chief," Connelly

thought, already accepting the fact that Leonard's days flying with them were over.

The medics jumped from the cargo bay and opened the temporary stretcher they'd brought to the side of the Huey. Leonard's body was lowered toward the ground and the two men started moving in the direction of a jeep that was parked at the outer edge of the landing zone.

"Well wasn't that a pisser," Braxton said as he jumped from the cockpit and walked toward Connelly. "Those little bastards didn't waste any time shooting us up." Hooper joined him from the front of the aircraft and the two men started to see the damage on the fuselage for the first time.

There were three holes in the tail section, each about the size of a 50-cent piece, and one angry gash on the housing of the turbine. On one side of the tail, the metal was bent inward where the round first attacked the ship. On the other side, there was a vicious, elongated tear where the round fought to escape from the Huey. The three punctures on the tail section formed a straight line nearly two feet long, where the back end of the aircraft expanded into the rotor housing. The dark green paint of the fuselage was a stark contrast to the last light of the day that poked its way through the damaged section.

"Hey, Hooper. Do you think you think they can patch her up?" Connelly asked as he instinctively ran one hand over the damaged section but pointed toward the engine with his free index finger.

"These went through and through, but you were

smoking when you landed."

Hooper saw him but didn't respond. He thought of the last few months and the number of missions he'd flown with Sergeant Leonard. He'd heard about his family, his four kids, and more than his share of what it was like to grow up in the flatlands of Oklahoma listening to country music. Finally, as if he realized there was nothing more to do there, Hooper turned toward Connelly.

"I don't know what they'll do with this," he said and patted the tail of the Huey. "But if it's like anything else around here, they'll use it until there's nothing left."

Connelly and Hooper didn't have long to wait for an answer. About four hours after they landed, as they were nearly asleep, the door to their tent swung open and Captain Walsh stepped inside holding a clipboard with about 10 forms pinched between the spring clip and the aluminum base.

"It's pretty bad," he said pointing in the general direction of the airfield. "The linkage and hydraulics coming off the engine were hit, but they want us to fly it back to Tam Ky for repairs and they'll give us a replacement. I want you and Connelly to go. Take Lopez with you as your chief."

Hooper nodded and Connelly wondered what the change would mean. He didn't usually fly with Hooper. Most of the time, Braxton flew in the right-hand seat.

"I want to make sure Braxton's ready to move up. For the next few weeks he'll fly with me," Walsh said and his finger followed the notes on his clipboard. "For the time being, you and Connelly will be together."

Hooper nodded but neither he nor Connelly said anything.

"Pick up your orders in the morning, but I want you to fly it back tomorrow and then head back here once they give you the replacement bird."

"Two days away – yes, sir," Hooper said and nodded toward Captain Walsh before returning his attention to Connelly. "Pack up, kid – enough clothes for an overnight. We'll leave after breakfast."

Connelly had only known one duty station, and he couldn't sense what it would be like to be away from the shooting for a few days, but he was willing to find out. He understood that taking the damaged Huey back for repairs would be dangerous. The maintenance work here was temporary, at best, but after nearly six-months at the forward base, he thought the time away might be a chance to draw a stress-free breath again.

Depending on the way the fuel was used, the Huey had a range of close to 300 miles and Connelly remembered the base at Tam Ky was a little more than 120 miles south of Camp Evans. After more than 60 missions, he knew it was safer to follow the coastline and he expected Hooper would want to follow that route. It would extend their time in the air, but there would be little chance of taking ground fire again as they made their way south. Thinking about the trip to Tam Ky, the day away from the steady stream of missions, and Leonard's last flight made sleeping nearly impossible - but at some point, darkness filled the tent.

The next morning, with the sun creeping relentlessly higher in the sky, Hooper and Connelly walked without a word from their tent to the damaged Huey. Finally, Hooper saw the chief getting the stricken bird ready and rather than say something, Hooper smiled. "Just us and a load of fuel," he said after a few minutes.

Lopez nodded and both pilots tossed their bags into the empty cargo bay behind their seats. Connelly untied the Huey and moved toward the right-hand seat. Within minutes, they were up and away. Hooper leveled them off at 3,000 feet, high enough to be out of the range of rifle fire, but not high enough to attract attention from the Russian fighters that randomly crossed the sky to the north. They were heading south toward the coast and for now, everything appeared to be normal, as normal as a mission in Vietnam could be.

Nearly two hours later the Huey settled on the landing pad at Tam Ky and as Hooper and Connelly gathered their things, the maintenance crew was began talking to Lopez and looking at the stricken aircraft, taking notes, and talking about the repair process. They connected the landing skids to a trailer and tug and a tractor started pulling the Huey toward one of the two large buildings used for repairs.

"We should check-in, get a shower," Hooper said and started walking toward the largest semi-permanent building there, a Quonset hut that appeared to be rusting from the bottom up.

The corporal sitting inside took their maintenance orders and told them where the temporary quarters were located, where to get a shower, and suggested they check back in with him in a couple of hours.

"Are we done for the day?" Connelly asked Hooper when they left the building.

"Not yet, but let's not waste this," Hooper said and grinned for the first time in three days.

"I know I could use a shower and a beer," Hooper continued. "They have a club here somewhere."

Hooper and Connelly made their way to the structure that acted as temporary quarters for officers and pilots. There was a makeshift shower built behind the tent. It was actually more like a tall, wooden box standing on a platform with a hose attached to the top end. There were holes drilled into the floor, a door that swung shut to provide a bit of privacy, and when you wanted water, you pulled on the rope handle connected to the end of the hose. There was no cold or hot, it was lukewarm, mostly clear running water, but to Connelly, it was a gift. They didn't have anything like this at Evans and grinning as if he'd received the best present ever, he planned to stand under the streaming water for as long as he could.

Hooper stood in the stall next to him and for nearly 20 minutes, the two airmen took turns pulling their respective handles and letting the stress of their life at Camp Evans wash away. If Connelly closed his eyes and forgot for a second where he was, it almost felt like he was standing in one of the outdoor showers at Lake Wohlford. Almost like home.

After their shower, both men repacked their duffle bags and then with nothing else to do, they wandered back to the admin building in hopes they'd know more about their replacement bird and when they might be released back to Evans. When they entered the building, the corporal wasn't at his desk, but they heard him in the back of the room talking to a sergeant who was holding some part wrapped in one of the red maintenance rags that littered the back end of the hangar. The conversation was short and as the corporal turned back toward his desk he saw the two warrant officers.

"Sir?" he said in Hooper's direction. "Is everything all right? Did you find your quarters?"

Hooper nodded and turning slightly toward the sergeant who was leaving, said, "Do you have any idea when we'll be able to get our replacement Huey?"

"I am not 100 percent sure, but Sergeant Miller, who was just here, has to release it and I think it will be ready at 0900 tomorrow," he said. "It's likely you have one or two replacements going with you back to Evans."

Connelly nodded and started looking in the direction of the corporal.

"Are they replacement pilots?" he asked.

"No sir," the corporal said. "Two people slotted for your unit are supposed to be here in the morning from MACV, but I won't know for sure until the C-130 lands."

"So are we released until then?" Hooper asked.

"Yes, sir," he said again and sat at his desk. "We do have an O-club, of sorts, and the mess tent is almost always open, but I won't have your paperwork until morning."

Hooper picked up a large brass bolt paperweight that was placed on top of a stack of papers on the corner of the desk and nodded. "OK - see you in the morning," he said, and then, almost as an afterthought, he asked the corporal, "do you have any paper and an envelope? I'd like to write a letter or two."

The corporal picked up almost half an inch of paper and 10 envelopes and passed them to the pilot.

Without another word to the corporal, the two pilots walked silently back to their tent.

"I'd like to write a couple of letters and then hit the club," Hooper said. "Sound good?"

Connelly didn't say anything, but by now, Hooper knew the kid was short on conversation. They entered the tent again and Connelly flopped on his cot.

"Give me a nudge when you're ready to head out," he said and pulled a pillow under his head.

Hooper smiled but before he could say anything else to him, he noticed his eyes were shut. He watched as his breathing slowed naturally and in minutes, the soft sound of sleep filled the tent as Hooper wrote to his wife and his parents. When he had finished with the letters, he put the sealed envelopes on top of his duffle bag and found his way to his rack. A few minutes of sleep sounded like a good idea.

The two pilots didn't realize how tired and exhausted they had become during the past few months and both slept until it was late in the afternoon. Connelly woke first and for more than a minute, he had trouble remembering where he was. As panic started to set in, he noticed he was sweating again and then he remembered flying to Tam Ky with Hooper.

"Hey," Connelly said and tossed his pillow toward Hooper. "I think we missed lunch."

Hooper laughed to himself and stretched his six-foot frame until it nearly filled the entire length of the cot he was sleeping on.

"Now I really need a beer," he said and swung his feet toward the floor. "What do you say?"

Connelly stood and joined his bunkmate as they made their way out of the tent. He scratched his head and ran his fingers along the top of his scalp. He was hungry and thirsty. "Sure," he said. Connelly hadn't been inside an O-club since he'd left Washington, and even though it had only been a few months ago, that almost felt like a different lifetime.

"Let's see if we can grab something to eat before we get there," he said. "I'm starving."

The mess tent wasn't serving dinner yet, but the cooks and staff stationed at Tam Ky were used to transient pilots and crewman stopping in at all times of the day and night. The smell of slightly burned coffee was a constant reminder of the purpose of the tent and Connelly and Hooper convinced the duty sergeant to let them make a tray full of food. The two men sat and ate silently and Connelly thought it felt like they were a long way from Camp Evans. He knew they weren't going anywhere until tomorrow morning and sitting at the table with a cup of coffee in front of him and knowing nothing was going to change for the next twelve hours was a gift he'd gladly accept.

The two men poked at their food with feigned interest. They knew they needed to eat, but the quiet and unadulterated solitude allowed their minds to wander to a place or think of people far away from their current dinner table.

"Hey, look," Hooper said, breaking the silence. "There's Lopez."

Connelly moved his head in the direction of the chief and with a subtle nod, he indicated that he'd like to tell him something.

"We're definitely here for the night," he said. "Are you settled somewhere?"

For a minute, Lopez nodded his head toward each scrap of food on the two men's trays and then pushed his ball cap toward the back of his head. His jet-black hair escaped from under the brim of the cap and with a toothy grin, he smiled and responded.

"Yes, sir. I am just fine. What time are we supposed to meet and check out the new bird?"

"Why don't you plan for 0700," Hooper said. "We'll have to do an inspection and probably even a short test flight before we leave here."

Lopez nodded again at the officers and straightened his ball cap.

"Yes, sir. I'll be there," he said, and without another word he turned and walked from the tent.

"What do you say, Connelly?" Hooper asked. "Time to find that beer."

The two men returned their food trays and headed for the small tent that had a crude sign over the door indicating it was the Tam Ky Officers' Club. There was something strange about the door. It might have been built from a leftover wooden pallet and there was a small window placed at a funny angle in the top half. A dark green blanket had been cut and trimmed to fit the opening and it served to keep most of the light and noise from entering the single room. There was a second, smaller room attached to the back, but to Connelly, that appeared to be some sort of loading or working area.

Once inside, the two men noticed the temperature was at least 10-20 degrees cooler than the world outside. Long fluorescent lights hung from the ceiling and neon beer signs cast a gentle glow across a makeshift bar. There was one stand-up refrigerator at the end of the serving area with a glass door and Connelly could see row after row of cans of beer.

"How about two of those," he said to the sergeant standing with his back to them. The sergeant turned toward the voice and the first thing Connelly noticed were the cloth wings he wore above the pocket on the left side of his shirt. He too was an aviator.

"Kind of quiet in here, sergeant," Hooper said as he took his beer. "Is it always like this?"

"No, sir," the sergeant said and collected a dollar from Hooper for the beer. "It's usually busy later in the day and sometimes we even get a local visitor or two from the village - female visitors."

Hooper stared at the sergeant and started to twirl the wedding ring he wore on his left hand.

"Sometimes it helps," the sergeant said and turned his attention to Connelly.

Neither of them responded to the sergeant. They took their beer and made their way to a couple of empty stools at the other end of the bar, and for the next few hours, they sat there trading stories of home, places they'd like to see when they got back, and what they wanted to do with their lives. Neither of them talked about the Army or the next six months of their tours.

"I think I'd like to fly for one of the airlines," Connelly said. "California, close to San Diego."

"Not me," Hooper said. "Once this is over, I promised the wife I'd take a job with her dad's trucking company. They ship shit from all over the Midwest."

Connelly laughed. He knew Hooper had said "ship shit," but all he heard was "shit, shit" and after three or four beers, it was about the funniest thing he'd heard.

The door to the club opened and Connelly noticed the light was gone. He checked his watch and it was nearly 2100 hours. Hooper noticed too and stood from his stool.

"I'm heading back and get some sleep," he said. "Are you coming?"

"I'm going to have one more," Connelly said. "It might be a while before we get another chance."

Hooper nodded and put five dollars on the bar. "Give him one more, sarge and then kick him out," he said. The sergeant smiled and exchanged the money for another can of beer.

Connelly turned to watch Hooper leave and when he turned back to the bar he noticed the sergeant had made his way back to his end the dimly lit room.

"We can serve a few other things here," he said and turned his head toward the doorway that led to the storage area.

Connelly saw a thin, female face staring blankly in his direction. She didn't smile. She didn't speak. She didn't move, but Connelly knew exactly why she was there.

"What do you say?" the sergeant asked again. "It might be a long time before you see another female face."

Connelly took a long pull from his beer and moved in the direction of the girl. She was used to watching for the movement of men and she sensed his arrival. Connelly could've sworn her expression changed. She winced for a moment and then a smile spread across her thin face.

"Not tonight, sarge," he said and put the can of beer back on the bar. Leaning toward the woman, a girl really, he extended his hand and gave her a 10-dollar bill anyway. It was all the money he had in his pocket, and he didn't think he'd need it.

The girl twirled silently and in seconds was gone. Maybe it was the beer, maybe it was the way she moved, but when she turned to go, her long straight black hair reminded him of a pair of wings that were about to take flight. He remembered that he still wore his mother's bracelet, and he smiled to himself as he reached for his wrist.

8 – Leaving the Nest

November 1967

Thirty-seven days. When I first saw my orders at Fort Rucker, I thought there must have been some kind of mistake. "It was strange," I thought. "I'd only been in the Army for seven months and 30 days of leave was the most you could get in a year." But the orders were clear. I was supposed to clear Rucker and report to Fort Lewis, Washington and then on to Vietnam. I didn't have a specific destination or unit. According to the paper, that would come from the MACV.

Mom and dad didn't make it to graduation after all, and that didn't bother me now. I was going back to Massachusetts and try to forget about the Army for a while. I had plenty of pay, plenty of time, and a hope for the future.

The problem was that once I got home, everything was different. No matter where I went or who I saw, the clock in my head was ticking. Time was anything but a friend to me.

For most of the kids I grew up with, seven months wasn't that long, but for me, everything in my world was different. By the time I got back to the Berkshires, I was no longer the kid who worked on the farm, the kid who liked fixing cars and talking about what was going to happen during the winter. Everyone knew I was headed to Vietnam and they came by to say goodbye. The days were getting short as winter approached but at least I had my truck, and most afternoons I went for a drive along the river while Sandy was in school. About the time she got to the store and checked in with her parents, I made my way into town again.

"Mr. Miller," I said, nodding in the direction of her dad and taking off my cap. I saw Sandy standing near him when I entered the store. Her face wasn't turned in my direction and I had the impression she was intent on finding something in one of the post office boxes. When she heard my voice, she stopped looking and her hands settled near her waist. The smile that filled her face only made me more unsure of what to say next.

"I'm heading over to the farm, to see Mr. Grondan," I said. Mr. Miller stopped what he was doing and turned toward me.

"Do you want to ride with me? If that's all right?" I asked Sandy while still turned toward her dad.

Mr. Miller didn't smile, but his head did go up and down as if he were measuring the distance between the two of us, and his eyes paused for a heartbeat or two when he got to my hands. I was fumbling with my hat and trying to think of something to say.

"You look good, Russ," Mr. Miller said. "Mrs. Miller and I are proud of you. Make sure you and Sandy are back by supper."

"Yes, sir. Thank, you," I said and turned toward Sandy.

She moved to get her coat from behind the counter but didn't change the expression on her face. Not waiting for any other conversation, I pushed the door open for her and put my cap back on. By the time I reached for the door handle of my truck, I almost slipped and fell as it swung open toward the street. It might have been the near accident, or perhaps it was the fact that I was finally home and she was with me, for whatever reason, I started to laugh. For the first time in months, I was happy again.

We rode through town and listened to the radio and I caught myself looking at her every few seconds. She didn't say anything but her cheeks had that flush look to them and she tapped two or three of her fingers in rhythm to the music. I'd swear she was happy too. For nearly two weeks, we followed the same pattern until the thought of me leaving and heading to Vietnam almost felt like a dream or an old memory that might not come true. Even the events of boot camp and AIT school started to fade. It was only when I laid in my bed, late at night, and listened to the dull rolling sound of my parents snoring as they slept that I thought about how many days I had left. More than once, I watched the hands of my windup Timex clock move past midnight as I continued to wonder what it would be like, wondered what the next year would bring.

My family and friends gathered at our home on Thanksgiving for an early Christmas dinner before I finally had to leave for Fort Lewis. They wanted to give me gifts and let me have a little bit of what I was missing, but it didn't seem right. I kept getting present after present, and for the first time, I hated the holidays.

Knowing that I was heading to a warzone, my mom, dad, and Sandy all drove me to the airport in Connecticut. There wasn't a lot of conversation and everyone was preoccupied with the scenery between the hills of home and Bradley Field.

No one said much, but no one had to. My dad's only words to me were: "Keep on your toes and we'll see you after your tour ends."

Sandy took it the worst of all, I'd never seen her cry like that and she said she'd write, but I wasn't sure. I was going to be gone for at least a year. Her letters had tailed off when I went to boot camp, what would happen when I was half-way around the world? I was going to a warzone where you didn't get regular mail delivery.

She held my hand until they called for us to board and as the line formed, she squeezed one more time and pulled me toward her. All I could say was, "I'll see you." And without looking back, I boarded the plane.

~ ~ ~ ~ ~

A year ago, I had barely ever left Massachusetts, let alone the country and now I was flying from Connecticut to Chicago and then from O'Hare to Seattle. From there, I had orders to cross the Pacific.

I knew that Fort Lewis was south of Seattle and I thought I could take the bus to the base. When I arrived at the airport, I learned there were three buses that traveled to the post daily. I missed the first two, but the last bus was leaving at 8 p.m. and if I hustled, I could make it. Technically, I didn't have to check in at the base until Sunday night, but I didn't know anybody in Seattle and if I managed to report in before midnight, I'd save two days of leave.

The ride to the base was a little more than 40 miles and by the time the bus was loaded and everyone was seated it was nearly 9 p.m. I knew it wouldn't be more than an hour before we got there, but we had to stop twice in Tacoma to let off passengers and pick up a few soldiers who needed a ride for the last five miles or so. I checked my watch several times as we rolled toward the gates and it was nearly 10:30 when the driver set his brakes with a loud hiss, and he swung open the front door.

It wasn't clear why, but I felt like I was stepping off the bus and into the jungle. It might have been from seeing the trees outlined by the harsh yellow-white lights on the edge of the buildings, or the image of the faceless soldiers walking through the night air toward the fence in their worn and tired fatigues. Maybe it was the fact that I had been obsessing about the idea of traveling to a war. All I could seem to think about was the year to come.

I saw the lights from the processing center, and collected my bags and started for the stark brick building. It was late and in less than an hour it would be Saturday. I wanted to make sure I checked in before midnight and didn't lose another day of leave, but there were only a few clerks who had been unlucky enough to pull the second shift on a Friday night. Sergeant Collins was sitting at the desk closest to me and there were two large metal trays for the personnel papers of the soldiers who managed to sit here. After looking at him for a few minutes, I quickly came to understand the Fort was a place where soldiers both left for Vietnam and arrived home after their tours were completed.

After passing my papers to the clerk who might have been more at home in a high school typing class than an Army post, I took two short breaths and sat in the gray, metal folding chair next to his desk. The two large trays were within arm's reach. The one in the right-hand corner was marked INCOMING and it was nearly full, while the tray for OUTBOUND documents was almost empty. For a second, I was trying to decide if I was incoming or outbound.

I must have been staring at them for a while because I was startled when the gruff voice of the sergeant said, "there's a shitload of you leaving next week. In the meantime, you'll be assigned to work with facilities until your departure date."

The words didn't mean a whole lot to me at the time, and I nodded like I understood and waited for more instructions.

"Keep these in your barracks, you'll need them when you get to MACV," he said and returned my orders. He had magically pulled a new folder from his desk and with a sharpened yellow pencil, he copied my name on the little tab at the top.

"We'll keep your travel orders here, but officially, they need to be on your person until you are at your final destination. Right now, your flight orders are for a week from Monday. Report in with Sergeant Griggs Monday morning at 0700. He'll be in the mess hall," he said and with one hand, he returned my personnel jacket. With the other hand, he flipped my nearly empty file to the top of his OUTBOUND tray. He was through with me and had answered my question. I was leaving, not arriving.

The weekend passed quickly, and for the most part, I spent the time by myself in the barracks. I wrote to Sandy a few times, but the letters didn't sound right and I decided not to mail them. She had come with me to the airport when I left and said that she'd wait for me, but something told me things were different. All she wanted to talk about was her graduation and what she planned to do in the year that I'd be overseas. I remembered her talking to me about it, but as I sat in the barracks at Fort Lewis, I couldn't remember any of the details.

In the end, I spent most of my time reading the local Seattle newspaper and one of the Louis L'Amour novels my father had given me, "Hondo." Sandy and I watched the movie version of the book at the theater in downtown Williamsburg, so I knew the basic story, but it was still a good way to pass the time and get through the weekend. On Monday, we were woken up at 0530, and by 0630 I was standing in front of Sergeant Griggs ready for my temporary duty assignment. Apparently, I wasn't alone. There were three other PFCs with me and all of us waited for our instructions for the day.

"All right you dumb bastards," he said without looking directly at us. "You'll be here for just a few days. Try not to piss me off."

He didn't seem to care what we did as long as we didn't make more work for him.

"Follow Jenkins and he'll give you a job for the day,"

he said and with a small wave of his hand, we were off. I don't think he ever actually saw us, but that was fine with me.

My first day I was assigned to the mess hall. We were supposed to clean the kitchen after every meal and work the line passing out food, as needed. For me, that meant putting a slice or two of plain, white bread on each tray as the soldiers moved through the line. Breakfast and lunch passed without incident and I thought this might be fine until we shipped out for good. Around 3 p.m., I saw the cooks fire up the large grills in the back of the kitchen. The black iron grating on top of the grills glistened as the remains of countless other meals melted away under the heat. We were instructed to head to the freezer and help the cooks pull the beef for the meals.

"Monday night is always steak night," one of them said to me as we slid boxes across the frozen steel floor of the freezer.

"The fucking Army thinks these fuckers want a steak dinner," he continued. "Fuck no. They just want to go home."

We pulled the boxes from the freezer and slid them to the front of the grill area. The cook reached in and pulled a group of frost covered, frozen steaks. With a shiny, wood-handled spatula, he separated the steaks from one another and placed them on the grill with a sizzling thud.

The steaks were cooked and the dripping, steaming meat was placed in large stainless steel trays as we waited for the returning soldiers to enter the dining hall. Apparently, they were allowed to come early and get their meal before the rest of the soldiers, staff, and family members.

"Happens every week," one of the cooks muttered as we stood in the chow line and waited. "The last thing most of them want is another Army meal."

Sure enough. The line of soldiers coming for steak dinner was short. More than half of what we cooked went unclaimed, and those who did show up were disinterested, thin, and preoccupied. I avoided eye-contact with them and wondered if I would look like them in a year. I wondered if I would be here in a year.

If there was one thing I learned about the Army after seven months, it was that everything was subject to change. I was supposed to stay at Fort Lewis for a week, but on the third morning, after I reported in at the mess hall, Griggs pulled me and two others aside and told us our shipping date was moved up. He handed us a single sheet of paper, our new travel orders, and told us we were leaving that afternoon. There was room on the flight leaving at 1600 and the Army wanted our happy little asses on the flight.

I swallowed once or twice and mumbled, "OK."

For the first time in three days, Griggs acknowledged us. For once we were more than just names on a piece of paper, and he had this look on his face like he was trying to find the right thing to say - like he wanted to share something with us.

"Keep your fucking heads down and see you in a year," he said and pushed our orders into our hands.

We were dismissed for the day and told to pack our gear and get on the bus heading to the airfield.

Somewhere between the mess hall and the barracks it hit me, I really was leaving. I didn't walk any faster, but I didn't stop either.

I hadn't strictly settled into the barracks and packing was almost a formality. Fatigues were the uniform of the day and I didn't think it was necessary to shine my shoes or change my shirt, and it took me almost 30 minutes to strip my rack and pack my gear. I checked it twice and assured myself I was ready to go. Sitting on the bare end of my bunk, with my boots resting on my bag, I stared at the ceiling for a while and thought of Sandy. I hadn't heard from her at all, but I wasn't even sure how the mail would find its way to me. There were a few hours to go and then I'd have a new address and God knows how long the mail would take to get there. I was spending too much time thinking about her, but unless I was busy with some job or activity, the way she used to look when she was riding in the front of my truck was almost always the first thing to creep into my idle mind. I hoped that closing my eyes would help me avoid or, better yet, abandon these thoughts. In seconds, I dozed off, almost oblivious to the light and noise of the base.

A small scream almost leaped from my dreams as I felt a sharp pain in my foot. I realized I was asleep. "How long had it been?" I thought. "Shit, shit, shit," I said more to myself than anyone else and I noticed Rodriguez standing near my rack. "We gotta go," he said and moved toward the open barracks door. I scrambled to my feet and as I lifted my bag to my shoulders, I noticed the barracks clock. It was 1030 – we had enough time to get to the bus and our flight.

As the shuttle carrying us to the airfield got closer and closer, I saw a Boeing 707 sitting on the tarmac, its white paint shimmering in the midday sun. The engines weren't spinning, but a temporary staircase had been pushed to the side of the plane. After checking in with the duty sergeant, I formed up with about 50 other soldiers heading to MACV and we settled into a small circular group about 20 yards from the stairway to the plane. We'd been told we would be able to board in about 20 minutes, but for now, we were to stay together and wait for the signal. There wasn't any smoking allowed on the field, but by now most of us had picked up the habit and we were getting antsy standing out in the midday sun. Looking around, I noticed I wasn't the only one who kept checking the paperwork in their hands. Somebody said the plane was stopping in Guam because it couldn't carry enough fuel to make it all the way non-stop. He said the distance to Guam was further than the distance from New York to LA, but I didn't think that was possible.

"It's like going to Hawaii twice," he said. "I swear – one of the pilots at Rucker told me."

"That can't be right," I thought, and even though I knew it by heart, I checked the paperwork again. I was reminded that we'd leave here and 12 hours later we'd stop briefly in Guam for fuel and food, and from there, it was a straight shot into Cam Rahn Bay. Once I reported into the base I would be assigned to an in-country aviation unit. Where that assignment would be was still a mystery to me, but I was hoping it would be near Saigon. That was the largest base and I was certain they needed more than a few mechanics.

"Twice the distance to Hawaii," I thought. "Over the water?"

The plane was loaded and rolled off the runway a few minutes ahead of time and I settled into my seat, determined to sleep my way across the Pacific. Some of the other soldiers read, some talked about their wives and their girls, but I closed my eyes and tried to sleep. I was sure it wouldn't happen. Thankfully, I was wrong.

I woke once and had to find the makeshift bathroom that had been installed on the plane and by the time I returned to my seat, I knew there'd be no more sleep for me.

Luckily, I was close enough to the window and as the night sky started to fill with light, the humid pacific air and the bottom of the clouds blossomed with a deep and almost familiar gray color. I thought of the unpaved dirt roads that bordered nearly every farm at home. Each spring the farmers in our part of the state took loads of slate, gravel, and clay and filled the damaged sections of their roads. After their tractors pulled a set of iron tines back and forth across the roads, they became smooth and reliable for the rest of the year. I didn't know where these streets in the sky were leading us, but I hoped the pilots did. At the base of the last cloud, the front end of our plane dipped toward the sea and I thought we must be heading toward Guam. We started to make a sweeping turn and the airliner lined up toward a blinking yellow and white light. I didn't understand how the pilots, in the middle of the night, managed to find this small piece of land; It was nothing more than an atoll that had the good fortune of rising above the surface of the sea. But I was glad they did. Word passed through the plane that we'd be on the ground for less than 30 minutes.

We were allowed to get off the plane and stretch our legs in the hangar that bordered the field while the tankers pumped more jet fuel into the thirsty 707. I wondered if we were changing crews too or if the same pilots were going to bring us all the way to Vietnam.

It didn't seem like 30 minutes passed, but as soon as the tanker trucks pulled away from the plane we were herded back toward the rolling staircase and the front end of the plane. As I stepped inside the long steel and aluminum fuselage, I looked toward the window that framed the pilot's face, and I noticed him taking a long pull from a can of Coca-Cola. Finding a seat toward the rear of the plane, I hoped he wasn't too tired yet. After leaving the small island base, the drone of the plane's engines succeeded to lull me back to sleep and in a strange way, the next words I heard were "Welcome to the Republic of South Vietnam." I wasn't sure if I was dreaming or not, but then I felt the landing gear lock in place and the tires kissed the runway.

As the plane filled with American soldiers rolled to a stop, the seal on the door was broken and a moist overpowering heat washed through the cabin. It was the second week in December, and only a few minutes after 10 a.m., but the temperature on the tarmac was 101. For more than one reason, I started to sweat.

It took two days to process all the incoming servicemen, and each morning at 0700 I would join the other soldiers who'd entered this part of the world in last few days and we'd muster at the operations office. Permanent assignments to line units were handed out as soon as they became available. I wasn't given an assignment right away and I assumed that was because I was probably staying here at the base and working with the maintenance crew.

"It's kind of like being picked for a team," I said to the PFC who happened to be in front of me on the second day. We each nodded and kept moving forward in the direction of the company clerk's desk. He didn't respond, but his laugh sounded all too familiar. There were no more than five people in front of us in line when we heard a commotion. The duty NCO had arrived and he didn't look happy.

Standing with his back to the sun and an open hangar door, he spoke to the assembled group, "The following people are the lucky guys going to the 1st Cavalry Division. Get ready to leave for your units."

"Private Warriner – you're 2nd Battalion 20th Artillery," the sergeant announced in a mechanical manner.

At first, I didn't realize he was speaking to me. My thoughts were elsewhere – home, Sandy, I am not sure where, but I wasn't listening. When he mentioned the 1st Cavalry, I thought he was talking to someone else. "I'm aviation," I thought.

I didn't know what to say or who to see, but I thought he must have made a mistake. I was aviation. I was supposed to be at a base.

"Sergeant Brooks?" I asked with a voice that managed to irritate the older man.

"Private," Brooks said cutting me off. "That's what your orders say. Get your bags and get over there ready to go."

Over there was a C130 fueling up for the short run to An Khe and the home of the 2nd Battalion, 20th Artillery. Once there I'd be assigned to a specific unit or battery.

As the words swirled in my head, the temperature inside the hangar suddenly felt hotter than ever and I thought it must be a mix-up in the paperwork.

"It happened all the time," I told myself. But I wasn't going to ask Brooks again. Instead, I saw that there was a specialist loading the plane and I decided to ask him about the orders.

"I went to school to be a helicopter mechanic," I said. "Not the artillery or infantry."

The specialist stopped what he was doing, and for almost a full minute he looked me up and down, paying special attention to my new uniform and duffle bag. He was annoyed that he had to tell me anything. He said, "Don't worry. We're an Aerial Rocket Artillery unit. We fly B and C model Hueys. You'll see plenty of helicopters."

In a matter of seconds, I realized that in this war, mechanics fly as part of the crew – sometimes as a gunner, sometimes as a crew chief. If something happens to the ship, they're there to fix it.

Without any other choice, I got into the C130. There was nothing else to do but hop a short ride north to the next base. At An Khe, I learned there were three batteries within the 2nd Battalion 20th Artillery. There was an Alpha, Bravo, and Charlie battery, and I was assigned to the Charlie battery, which was located even further north, closer to the DMZ between North and South Vietnam. Our first stop was at a dirt field, a landing zone near Tam Ky. A crew from my new unit was already there and I was told they'd wait for me and give me a lift to my new home.

I ran from the plane and grabbed my gear that had been tossed onto the tarmac. With my bag in hand, I trotted toward the Huey parked furthest from the operations shack. There were two people standing near the front of the Huey and from what I could tell, one of them was a pilot and one was a sergeant. They didn't offer to help, but as I got closer the sergeant grabbed my bag and threw it into the back of the Huey. The sergeant didn't say anything to me, but he nodded in the direction of the pilot and they exchanged a glance as if they were ready to go. We'd be leaving soon, but I still had my orders stuffed inside my uniform shirt.

"Do you need these?" I asked as the sergeant made a quick circle around the Huey and untied the tail of the aircraft. "Fuck no. Clip in," he said and threw a flight helmet in my general direction.

In some ways, I couldn't believe what I was seeing. My eyes were riveted to the movements of the chief. He untied the main rotor and then announced, "clear and untied."

There were two pilots up front now and they started the engines. The turbines creaked and groaned as the metal fans inside the engine housing spooled up, gaining RPMs, and there was a loud whooshing sound when the fuel ignited and hot exhaust gasses were blown from the back of the green and black bird.

Within seconds, the main rotor started to spin and the pilots lowered their heads to check the gauges. Standing next to the canopy that surrounded the pilots, the crew chief slid the armor panels forward and jumped into the left side of the aircraft. The hardened steel plates were meant to protect the pilots from incoming fire. The chief hooked himself into his harness and slapping the steel fuselage one more time, he signaled to the pilots that everything was ready.

Not a word was spoken.

"How am I going to be able to do this?" I thought from the right side of the cargo bay. The crew chief watched me and moving closer he yelled, "Hang on - it looks like you're in for a treat."

The crew had gotten word that there were ground troops in the vicinity that were pinned down and taking fire from the enemy. On our way from Tam Ky, I was going to witness my first mission. We were going to see what we could do to help them. The Huey carried 48 rockets and two M60 machine guns. The chief would man one of them and I would try to stay out of the way.

On the way to Camp Evans, the pilots made three rocket runs - three passes over the tree tops, and I thought at any second we were going to clip them. I watched in wonder as the crew chief and pilots worked in concert. As the ship rolled and dove for the canopy, the chief and his M60 thumped a steady beat as the rockets streamed toward their target. Not once did I see anyone on the ground, but the crew understood where they were, that much was clear. When we landed at the base, my head was still buzzing with what I had seen.

Sergeant First Class Cole met the Huey and told me he'd help me get settled. He'd show me the ropes and then he would see what I'd learned in school. During the next few weeks, as the new man in the group, I absorbed as much as I could of the surroundings. I saw what it meant to be a member of the crew and worked with the maintenance group. But it wasn't long before Cole came to me and told me it was time to be assigned to a Huey. He said any fool could see that I knew how to use a wrench, now it was time to learn how to be a crew chief. For the next two to three weeks I'd be rotating through with the crews, flying as a gunner, but really, my job was to learn how to become a chief. No matter what Cole said to me, or the others, I had this nagging thought that I still had a lot to learn.

Specialist Kellogg, one of the long-time crew chiefs, came to me on the morning of December 10, 1967. It was one day until my birthday. I was going to be 20-years-old, and my teenage years were over. Kellogg told me I'd been slotted to be the crew chief for 054, one of the B model Hueys. It was an older ship, but a good one, and it used to be his, but in less than 30 days he'd be heading back to the world.

"Move your gear to the left side and set it up the way you'd like. It's yours," Kellogg said. "You've got a mission tonight and Hooper and Connelly will be the pilots."

Warrant Officer Thomas Hooper was a soft-spoken pilot from somewhere near Toledo and one of most seasoned pilots in the battery. Many considered him one of the best pilots. He'd fly as the aircraft commander and Warrant Officer Bobby Connelly would act as the co-pilot. I was glad my first flight as the official chief was with a veteran group, especially Hooper. He was a by-the-books regular and everyone said he was destined to command a group like ours. Not a single member of the crew was more than 24 years old.

The mission for the night was mortar patrol. The idea was that we would take off at close to 2100 hours and fly to a specific location. We'd circle that area for an hour or so waiting to see if the enemy would fire mortar rounds toward the American bases. If they did, the crew would swoop down and fire rockets at the mortar positions. At close to 2100 I untied the main rotor and told the pilots "clear and untied."

After checking for leaks or any other problems, I slid the armor plating that protected the pilot's backsides forward, locked it in place and jumped in. We were off, and I was the chief.

9 – Too Many Candles for the Cake

December 11, 1967

The day started like most of the other days at Camp Evans - I was hot, nervous, and I knew that sometime today I'd end up clipped into the back end of the Huey. Our unit was flying nearly every day, and on most of the previous missions, I flew with Hooper, Connelly, and Ed Gallagher.

Gallagher, a big redhead from somewhere near Indianapolis, had been their crew chief for more than six months, and he was supposed to be showing me the ropes, but what he seemed most interested in was counting the number of remaining days he had in the Army.

"You won't see my sorry-ass here a day longer than it needs to be," he said to me while we were counting the cases of MK24 flares stored in the ammo shed.

"If you're smart, you'd find a way to start the count now, Warriner," he said to me. "You got here about a month ago, so you're still over 300, but by New Year's day you'll be in the twos."

I didn't know what to say, but he was right. By the time the first of the year rolled around, I'd be looking at almost three months in. "Not too bad," I thought.

"I'm almost single digits now," he said. "Today's

my last flight with you and if you don't fuck it up too bad, I'll sign off and you're on your way."

We had a short recon flight scheduled for the morning, and after that, I'd officially be the chief.

I tried not to think about it as we locked up the shed and headed for the field. Mr. Hooper told me we were supposed to leave in about 30 minutes and Gallagher wanted to give the Huey one more look before he made the last flight. We got to the field and it didn't take long to see that things were in a scramble.

The Medic's jeep was there and he and the old man had binoculars in their hands. They were looking for one of the morning flights and as I watched Captain Walsh scratch the side of his head, I imagined he wasn't too happy about something.

"Let's steer clear of that mess," Gallagher said and moved closer toward the maintenance tent that stood at the far end of the field.

There were two other guys working on the tail rotor of a Huey parked near the maintenance shed. Gallagher spun his head back toward the captain's parked vehicle as if he were surprised by something and then turned back to the two men.

"What's going on?" Gallagher asked. "Looks like a bit of a shit storm."

"Word is - one of the pilots was hit by ground fire, a lucky shot through the side window, and we were the closest base," he said.

Gallagher didn't respond but in less than a minute the sound of a Huey at full throttle could be heard.

Even after only a few months here, I knew the

Huey was coming in faster than normal. It slid across the field into the dirt and turf. The pilot jumped from the moving aircraft and ran around the nose of the Huey to get to the co-pilot's door. I could see some sort of stain on the windshield and while it might have been a dirt or mud streak, I kind of knew it was blood. The copilot sat motionless, slumped forward in his seat.

"Shit - this isn't good," Gallagher said, more to himself than anyone else. The two men who had been working, stopped, and each stood quiet and motionless as they watched the medic pull the injured pilot from Huey. He was placed on a stretcher on the back of a jeep and Captain Walsh said something to the doc.

"Shit - now I know it ain't good," Gallagher said and pointed toward the jeep. The medic had a long blanket in his hands and he quickly covered the body from head to toe.

"Nothing we can do about that," Gallagher said. "Let's go find Hooper and get this over with."

We walked back toward our Huey and strangely enough, Hooper and Connelly had arrived as well.

Neither of them mentioned the Huey that had just landed, but I did see Hooper look twice at the shielding that was welded to his side of the aircraft.

In minutes, we were up and away and any thoughts I had about what we just witnessed dissapeared. I knew we were in the middle of the worst area of the fighting, but every time we took flight, I felt a bizarre sense of joy and excitement, a strange sense of peace. I hoped that didn't end, but Hooper's voice in my headset broke my train of thought.

"What do you think, chief?" Hooper asked. "Do you think he's ready?"

I knew Hooper was referring to me and I focused on Gallagher. For once, he didn't seem to be in joking mood. "Yeah - he'll be fine. You'll be fine. He'll take care of you," he said.

We made our run and Hooper and Connelly calibrated their instruments for a pass we'd have to fly later that night. There was going to be some kind of push and we had to drop flares to help the ground grunts. It sounded pretty easy.

We had a few hours to ourselves before the next flight and I thought I'd write to Sandy. Nobody in the battery knew it, but it was my birthday. I was 20-years-old, in the middle of Vietnam, and all I wanted to do was talk to her. She'd only written to me once since I reported to Evans, but I thought that was because we only received mail delivery about once a week.

But one of the pilots, Mr. Braxton, was given a handful of letters every time the mail bag made its way here. He'd yell and scream for a few minutes and then run off to his tent like his feet were on fire. I'd heard him say the letters were written by two or three girls from back home. If nothing else, I'd settle for one letter. I wanted to hear from her.

Sitting on the edge of the cot, I wrote to Sandy and told her about the monkey who'd managed to become our camp mascot. I told her about the food and how it all started to taste the same and I told her about the heat. The weather was always good for a paragraph or two. I never wrote to her about our missions, or the sleepless nights when I waited for the mortar attacks or seemingly random sniper fire. What could I say? What would it matter?

I didn't know what to say and didn't know how to connect with someone who was thousands of miles away. Each letter I wrote to her ended the same way.

"I know you must be busy with school and your studies, but your letters remind me of home. They remind me of you," I wrote. "In less than a year I'll be through here and then we can be together again."

I didn't want to sound desperate, and most of the time I didn't feel that way, but by the time I got to the end of the letter, an almost overwhelming feeling of angst would hit me. More than anything, I wanted to be in her part of the world.

"Hey Warriner!" came the booming voice of Ed Gallagher. "They'll be ready to leave in 30 minutes. You better get your ass over there."

He laughed as he saw me scramble to my feet and put the letter I'd been working on in my footlocker. Within seconds, I'd pulled the padlock closed and headed for the doorway.

"I am the crew chief," I reminded myself.

I double-checked the load of flares to make sure they were secure and wouldn't move as we made our way through the early evening sky. I untied the Huey, watched Hooper and Connelly work their way through their checklists, and we were off. I clipped into the harness and settled in for the 20-minute flight to the drop zone. The M60 in front of me was heavy, but the dense and strangely cool metal gave me a strange sense of comfort. I noticed that with each minute that passed, the sky became darker and darker until by the time Hooper's voice came over the intercom, it was hard to tell the difference between the tree line and the horizon.

"Chief – are you ready? We're almost there," he said. We were going to start flying an expanded circle over the drop zone. Every minute or so, I was to set the timer and then push a flare out of the Huey. The attached static chord open the chute and then a few seconds later the charge would go off and the flare would drop from the lower half of the MK24. The manmade signal would burn at about 4,000 degrees and gently swing as the chute found the currents of night air that spilled over the jungle hills.

"Ready," I said and pulled the first flare from the pile. I looked toward the pilots, waiting for the word that we were on station, and I noticed the shiny butt end of the AK47 that Mr. Connelly kept stored behind his seat. The rumor was that he'd pulled the Russian rifle from a landing zone about a month ago. It was now his good luck charm. He never flew without it.

"Here we go, Chief," Hooper said and started turning the Huey in a gentle right-hand arc. This is what I was meant to do, I thought to myself and reached for the top end of the flare. The dial was facing away from me, but I knew that I had to turn the handle about one-quarter of the way around and then push the flare out of the open cargo door.

I grabbed the handle and started to turn it away from me, but it was stuck. Then I started to second guess myself and hesitated. I wasn't sure I was turning it in the right direction, and I leaned forward to get a better look at the dial and moved it back toward the 12 O'clock position. I had to try again. It moved. The dial clicked forward and then without any warning there was an explosion. In an instant, the sun was inside the Huey and everything was bathed in a sharp, white light.

The top end of MK24 must have blown off. It felt like I'd been hit in the head by an oak log. The light was gone, and I couldn't see anything. There was a loud buzzing in my ear, but most of the pain went away if I moved my head forward. I tried to move – even an inch or two - but my chin snapped down toward my chest and for a second, everything was black. The pain was gone, but the buzzing was becoming louder. Finally, I recognized the sound. It was Hooper.

"Chief, Chief …. Holy shit," he said. I couldn't see much. There was something in my eyes, but the flare was still on the floor of the cargo bay. I kicked at it. It had to go out. The bottom would blow out any second and start burning. I missed, and the pain in my head returned as my leg flailed in the direction of the explosion. I kicked again and this time, the heel of my boot found what was left of the top end of the flare. It skidded toward the open door and the rushing air, and as it got closer, it picked up speed until it disappeared and slipped from the side of the helicopter. The static chord was still connected to the Huey, and even from where I was now sitting I could see that it had become tangled in the landing skids. It was swinging toward the ground, but it wasn't more than 10-feet below the belly of the Huey, a Huey loaded with flares and fuel.

"Chief," I heard Connelly's voice. "Hang in there were gonna put her in a crab and see if we can make it to the sea."

I put my hand to my forehead. There was something in my eyes and I wanted to wipe whatever it was away. I must have been bleeding. Even in the low light of the Huey, I could see dark drops falling to the floor.

As soon as I put any pressure on my forehead, the skin and the top half of my face moved as if it weren't attached to my skull. It was funny - there wasn't any real pain there, and the only discomfort I had was a dull, deep ache somewhere in the center of my head. I pulled on the bridge of my nose and the top section of my skull flopped forward and the blood that had been dropping to the floor now filled my eyes.

"This might be it," I thought. "My head is barely connected."

The wind from the doorway filled my lungs to the point where they were painful. And yet, even through the cloud of agony, I could feel the rapid beating of my heart, and the sharp ache in my chest almost matched the throbbing I felt in my skull. The last thing I remember about the flight was the nearly endless scream that left my lips and led me to darkness.

The next three hours were a jumble of images and sounds. I have no idea how, but I ended up at the hospital near Tam Ky that served the 1st Cav. I remembered where I was and what happened, but I wasn't sure how I'd been transferred from the Huey to the hospital. I recall being laid out on a table and a Navy doc tried to lift my helmet from my head. Every time he moved it, the pain jumped from the center of my skull and it became focused in my eye sockets. They couldn't get the helmet off without the skin covering the top half of my head sliding forward as if the blood that pooled between the bone and my face had become the slickest of lubricants. The nurse standing to my side held my hand and I heard the doc call for another medic.

"You take this side and I'll pull from the other side. Let's see if we can separate the helmet and pull it from the top of his head," he said.

Without a response, two thin hands with strong fingers pulled the helmet away from my ears and I felt the cool air of the room brush against the top of my head. My eyes were open again and I was aware the doc had placed one of his gloved hands near the crown of my forehead.

"Relax, Chief," he said. "You're pretty lucky. The force of the blast caused the edge of your helmet to peel away the skin near your hairline. We can stitch you back together in no time, maybe even give you a bit of a face lift," he said.

He was the only face I saw – I didn't want to move, and I didn't know what to say. The pain in my head was more than anything I'd ever felt and now tears were rolling down my cheeks. I wanted to turn away.

"We'll give you something to knock you out and take care of this mess," the doc said. "When you wake up, you still might have a headache, but you'll be good as new. I'd be willing to wager, maybe even better."

I saw him nod toward the nurse and felt a sting as

she inserted a syringe of something clear into my right arm. I wanted to ask what that was but by the time I started to turn my head back toward the doc, everything was black again, and then nothing.

I must have slept through the night because the next thing I knew, I was in a small rectangular room with 10 or 12 other beds. Each one was filled with a wounded soldier and the light from the coming day was starting to fill the space where we all slept. Each of us was struggling to will ourselves to better health.

I tried to lift my arm to my head, but row after row of gauze bandages surrounded my skull. My eyes were half-covered and looking up and through the bandages reminded me of the times we flew through the clouds, everything was hazy and almost shapeless.

"Well, hello there," came a female voice from the other side of the bay. "You've been asleep for a while. Do you want to try and sit up?" she asked. I nodded, or tried to nod, and touched my head again.

"Three days ... Warriner," she said, pulling the chart from the end of my bed. "Let's see if you can sit up and I'll find you some water."

In minutes, I was sitting almost upright in the bed, and after drinking two large glasses of water, I felt almost human. The nurse, Claire something from somewhere near Philadelphia, told me that being asleep for more than two days was actually a good thing. "Your body needs to heal and this will give it the time it needs," she said.

I stayed in bed for another hour or so, but it wasn't long before the water worked its way through me and I had to find the bathroom. For sure I wasn't going to lay there and pee in a pan while the nurse stood at the foot of my bed.

"Do you think I can go to the bathroom and sit in the hallway for a while?" I asked and pointed to a wheelchair that was parked near the far wall.

"I think that would be fine," she said. "It might be good for you get moving."

Sure enough, I felt better after knowing my bladder was still working and sitting in the hallway I could see the compound and feel the warm breeze coming through the windows. I was alone and there wasn't much to do but think, think about the mission, think about the fact that I was still among the living, think about home, and as the morning wore on, I thought about Sandy.

I wasn't sure what was going to happen next. Would I be shipped back to my unit, or somewhere else, possibly even a different base? "I've been wounded," I thought. "I might even get transferred to a stateside hospital."

My thoughts were interrupted when I saw a doctor in a Navy uniform walking in my direction. "There you are," he said. "I'm Dr. Lehigh and I'm the one who stitched you back together."

"Thank you, sir," was all I could manage to say.

"Let me take a look at my handiwork," he said and pulled my head closer to his face. He unwrapped most of the gauze and poked at the stitches as if my head were a slightly-too-ripe melon.

"Warriner - this looks good if I do say so myself," he said. "It's healing nicely."

I didn't say anything, but I was glad to hear that my face and head had been reconnected.

"I don't see why you can't be transferred back to your unit," he said. "We'll keep you here another day or so to make sure, but in about 10 days, the medic in your unit can remove the stitches and you can resume flight duty."

"Yes, sir," I said, somewhat disappointed by the prognosis.

"You're pretty lucky, son," he said. "Those two pilots practically flew here sideways to deliver you to us."

I knew he was right, and I was grateful for the way Hooper and Connelly got me here in one piece, but some dark area of my brain wished I was hurt just a little more.

As the doctor walked away, I saw the nurse named Claire standing in the hallway watching us.

"Do you think I could come back here after lunch and write to my parents? I asked. "I'd like to let them know I'm OK."

"Sure," she said. "Let's get you some lunch and then I'll see if I can find you some paper and a pen."

I spent the next 24 hours thinking about my unit. I'd been told that one of the Hueys in our group was coming to get me and I packed all the meager belongings I had into the small knapsack the hospital gave me. When they first carried me in, I was wearing my flight uniform, but during the time I'd been here, I now had a pair of fatigues with my rank sewn on the sleeves and my name stenciled over the shirt pocket. I guess I was ready to go. I wasn't going to stay or go anywhere else.

Without thinking about it, my hand traveled to

the u-shaped scar and stitches that ran along my hairline. It didn't hurt anymore. It felt like I needed to scratch it all the time. It didn't make any sense, but each time I scratched at the wound in my head, I thought of my mother.

"You can tell you're healing when it starts to itch," she used to tell us each time we came home with a scrape or cut.

It was late in the afternoon, and I was sitting in the hallway, a few seconds away from being asleep, when I heard a laugh and a familiar voice.

"Well, look who's here," Hooper said. "It looks like they've zipped you back together and you're as good as new," Connelly laughed and patted me on the shoulder.

"C'mon, let's go home," he said. I noticed he'd picked up the small duffle they'd given me at the hospital. It was good to see them, good to head home.

10 - The Valley of the Living

February 4, 1968

No one wakes up thinking this is the day I'm going to die. It doesn't seem natural. But for the men of Charlie Battery, every morning, as the sun crept over the surrounding hills and made its way into the canvas cracks and crevasses of the tents that acted as their temporary home, death was always a possibility. The danger associated with their world was a constant companion.

For Bobby Connelly, one of the youngest and most talented pilots of Aerial Rocket Artillery group, flying dangerous missions was the one component of his job where he felt most alive. While most of his friends considered a day without a mission to be a good day, Connelly dreaded those long stretches of down time. For him, those hours without action only deepened his ever-present sense of despair, to cover him with a blanket of melancholy the way the mist and rain often covered the trees and forest surrounding their home in the jungle. It wasn't lost on him that those actions which made him feel most alive might be the same set of circumstances that lead to his demise.

Every community, no matter how big or small, has a place where people can gather and hear the news of the day, even share gossip about the latest scandal or the trouble they face. For the men of Charlie Battery, that place in Vietnam was the small green communications shack next to company mess tent.

Technically, only the radioman, the officer in charge, and the aircrew that was designated as the hot-section were supposed to be inside the tent, but the enlisted men and officers from Camp Evans routinely rolled through as they made their way back to their bunks or their duty sections. Morning, noon, and night – the questions were usually the same. What's the weather like? Is there anything hot going on? For Bobby Connelly, it was another ordinary day, a day to fly.

"Hey Sparky, any news from the world?" Connelly asked as he opened the door and stepped into the dimly lit electronic domain of the radio operators. There weren't any windows or other doors in the 10-foot by 12-foot rectangular space that electronically connected Connelly's unit to headquarters, and even with eyes accustomed to adjusting to the dark, it took Connelly a minute to see anything in the eerie glow of the radios. The 20-year-old corporal, who more resembled someone who should still be sitting in his living room watching his parent's new color television, now sat in front of a large intricate panel of knobs, needles, and buttons. He didn't move or look back at Connelly, but even with a bulky pair of earphones half-hanging off his head, he managed to speak with the warrant officer standing behind him.

"There's a shit storm brewing in the valley about halfway between here and Hue, sir," he said. "A Ranger unit is trying to take hill 861-Lima, the one that overlooks the approach to the city. They're pinned down about halfway to the top and they've requested fire support."

Connelly didn't respond immediately. He took a sip of the bitter black coffee he'd brought with him from breakfast and wondered if they'd take the mission. They had been flying every day for more than a month, and for the next four hours, he and his crew were now designated as the hot section. If need be, they'd be in the air in two minutes or less. Their crew chief, Sergeant Mike Anderson, a 21-year-old long-limbed, blond-haired kid from the lakes region of Minnesota was temporarily assigned to their four-man crew. Their regular ship was in the middle of its 100-hour airworthiness inspection, and Anderson had already prepped their Huey for flight. He'd been in-country for nearly 11 months and it was only a short run from the shack to the airfield.

"Verify their position and ask for an estimate of the enemy," said Captain Walsh, the officer in charge. Walsh and copilot Billy Braxton, a warrant officer from the hills of North Carolina, flew the lead helicopter in the section, and if Charlie Battery took the mission, they'd be the first to leave the ground.

Connelly and Warrant Officer Thomas Hooper were assigned to the second ship in the section, and Connelly would fly as copilot, sometimes referred to as the 'Peter-Pilot.'

The duty officer for the day started writing something on the clipboard in front of him. Connelly had a nagging feeling they would be getting orders for a mission. He turned back toward the door and as he made his way into the dull morning light, he tossed the contents of his coffee cup on the dew covered rocks and sand next to the tent.

"Hey, Hooper – you still in there?" Connelly yelled in the direction of the mess tent. "We might have to go. Do you have your gear?" Instinctively, Connelly turned his head once more to the sky and tried to determine what it would be like once they were airborne.

Connelly and Hooper had been flying together for more than five months and Captain Walsh didn't want to split them up, but he knew Connelly was ready to fly as an aircraft commander. He was a natural pilot, and as all the good ones did, he had a sixth sense for guiding the powerful Huey through the air and bringing it back to the isolated base in one piece.

~~~~~~

There was a dull gray blanket of clouds covering most of the base and earlier that morning, before breakfast, the two pilots talked about the weather during their meandering walk from the latrines to the mess tent. It wasn't raining, but the air was saturated and if they stayed outside for more than a few minutes, droplets formed on their clothes and before you knew it, they were soaked to the skin. Both pilots estimated the ceiling to be about 500 or 600 feet off the deck.

"Warriner has to inspect our bird," Hooper said, referring to their normal crew chief and the Huey they ordinarily flew. "It needs a 100-hour inspection, and the old man won't let him go. We've got a new one today."

Hooper had been flying the Hueys long enough to know that no two aircraft acted or flew the same. Each one was a complicated combination of more than a million parts, and as intricate as it was, those parts worked in unison to bring them to the fight and bring them home again.

"And a new chief?" Connelly asked. "What about a gunner?"

"We've got Anderson's bird for the day, and I heard that Freeman was riding with us as a gunner," Hooper said. "I saw him last night and he said he needs some hours to qualify for flight pay."

Master Sergeant David Freeman was the most senior man in Charlie Battery. The 38-year-old career soldier from Maine had spent more than half his life in the Army, and the rumor was this would be his last tour of duty. As a cook, he'd fed the men of the 1st Cavalry as the Army rebuilt Europe. He'd fought an unnamed war on the Korean peninsula, and now every indication was that his country was determined to follow the same tragic and violent path here in Vietnam.

Freeman was an imposing man – a little more than 6 feet tall and most of the 200 pounds of muscle he packed on his frame still occupied the same place as when he entered the service. His skin was the color of a starless northern night and for a man from Maine, that was unusual. The Army had officially ended its practice of segregation, but more often than not, Freeman still found himself in the company of only black soldiers. His quiet, confident, often imposing demeanor earned him the respect of officers and enlisted alike, but still, he served from the kitchen.

After Freeman had been at the base in Vietnam for a little more than two weeks, he requested to qualify with the M60. It only took him a few hours at the range to shoot as an expert. The cook was one of the best shots in the battery. With two decades of service behind him and most of those in a mess tent, he'd fired nearly every handgun and rifle the Army had. The M60, a 25-pound light machine gun, was not that different. With his new qualification in hand, he requested time in the air as a door gunner.

If there is one thing cooks in the service know about, it's the Army manual. They seem to live by the never-ending list of rules and regulations. They hear every piece of gossip and news in the mess hall, and Freeman knew that anyone who flew as an aircrew member for at least four hours a month qualified for aviation pay. Even for a man with his time in uniform, this meant an extra $50 a month. For the last six months, his name regularly appeared on the list of qualified aircrew members.

The morning sky was filled with the harsh sound of an electronic alarm, indicating they had a live fire mission. "Shit … here we go," Connelly muttered more to himself than anyone near him, and he started jogging in the direction of the flight line.

Without a word to the other three members of the crew, Connelly opened the door on the right side of the Huey. Grabbing a handle, he pulled himself up and into his seat. He felt the buckles of the web harness on his shoulders, and within seconds he started to clip himself in. He pulled on his helmet and made sure the small rectangular navigation kneeboard on his right leg was secure. When Tom Hooper climbed aboard, he had a clipboard in his hand and there were two loose sheets of paper trying desperately to free themselves from the grip of the metal spring that held their orders in place.

Hooper placed the board with the orders and the weather report on a hook behind his seat and to his left. Both pilots started through their checklists to get the helicopter into the air, but they stopped momentarily when Sergeant Freeman jumped into the right side of the cargo bay. The Huey actually bounced a little as the bulk of the cook, his weapon, and an extra box of ammo settled on the deck.

"Hey – did you feel that?" Connelly asked through the headset. A small grin appeared on his face as he flipped the switches powering the electronics. "Sarge – you forgot something," he said, pointing back toward the large cook who was trying to store his gear. "Your apron."

Freeman gave him a look as if he didn't understand or didn't care. He'd been in the mess tent helping one of the younger cooks when the alarm went off, and he'd nearly forgotten the extra box of ammo he always stored by the coolers. "I can never have too much of this," he said as he left the tent and ran toward the airfield.

As the three men worked to ready the chopper for flight, Chief Anderson was moving from one side of the helicopter to the other looking for anything that was out of order or might be a cause for concern. As the pilots worked to light off the engine, Anderson was especially mindful to look for leaks coming from the dark green skin of the ship. Leaks meant fire, and fire meant death.

As he made his way around the front of the aircraft, he took the safeties off the 48 missile pods that hung like ripening fruit on both sides of the fuselage.

"Here we go," Hooper yelled into the morning air.

They both felt the deep thud as the jet fuel ignited and the turbine engine started to spool up. The main rotor picked up speed and now a high-pitched whine came from the powerful engine housed above their heads. It started to vibrate through the Huey's metal airframe, but as the speed of the turbine increased, the vibrations magically smoothed themselves out. The gauges in front of their eyes came to life, and the lights surrounding the instrument panel became brighter as the electrical system was switched from the batteries to the power generated by the engine.

"Coming through," Anderson responded, scanning the area and the aircraft for anything that was out of the ordinary. After several slow revolutions of the main rotor, he made the decision they were ready to go. He shut each pilot's door and slid two steel protective plates forward, locking them under the cockpit seats. When the second thump reached their ears, Hooper and Connelly knew it was time to pull pitch and lift off.

"Whoo hoo!" Hooper said and nodded toward Connelly. At the same time, he gave Anderson a thumbs-up signal, and the crew chief jumped into the left side of the ship and clipped himself into his safety harness. In a smooth motion, the helicopter raised itself about six feet from the ground and leaned forward as if it were a hound looking for its prey. The power of the jet-turbine picked them up and pushed each pilot's backside further into their seats. The crew and their aircraft transitioned to forward flight.

Connelly watched Walsh and Braxton lift off in their helicopter ahead of them and as both birds slid over the treetops surrounding their jungle home, he heard the commander's voice in his ears.

"I'm going to circle the base and head one-three-zero degrees for about 10 or 12 klicks. Watch for ground fire."

Hooper and Connelly didn't respond. Both pilots knew where they were going and Hooper didn't like to spend any extra time on the radio. The rumor was that the VC could hear every word they said, and most of the pilots believed they had translators to help them find the aircrews. Connelly thought about his mom and as a child, she often spoke to him in both Spanish and English – he didn't see why the VC regulars couldn't speak English and Vietnamese. Hooper clicked his mic twice indicating the message was received and understood.

"We've got to hug the deck," Hooper said, pointing to the hanging base of the clouds. "We'll never find them if we climb into the soup." Connelly didn't say anything. He took a few seconds to turn away from his instruments and look toward the space behind their seats. The two enlisted men were arranging their extra ammo and slowly swinging back and forth in the open space on either side of the aircraft. Neither one liked to sit on the bench seat in the back. As the helicopter picked up speed, the treetops rushed by the open doors and the lush green foliage became a single steady streak of color. Within minutes, the base was lost amongst the mist and the jungle, and only an expanse of thick trees could be seen from either side. An almost palpable organic smell blanketed both the men and their gear. Connelly didn't know if it was the smell of life or death.

~ ~ ~ ~ ~ ~

The radio crackled and came to life in their headsets again and the orders from ops came in about their mission. "Rendezvous 2 klicks south, southeast of LZ-23 and Rangers know you're on the way."

Glancing toward Hooper and then back to his kneepad, Connelly tried to determine exactly where they would rendezvous. His thoughts were interrupted by the voice of Billy Braxton.

"Heads up. We just took some small-arms fire. Must be the last hooch we passed. Some piss ant farmer raised a rifle," he said.

Hooper and Connelly nodded. Not to anyone in particular, but they both knew they'd probably take fire the rest of the way.

Connelly turned back toward Anderson and Freeman and tapped the headsets on his ears. "Chief – if you see any roads or hooches, let off a blast or two to keep Charlie in his cave," he said over the intercom. Connelly saw Sergeant Freeman stretch his fingers and pull on the arming handle of the M60. Both men nodded as Connelly turned back toward the front of the ship. They were ready.

In bursts of three or four rounds, the gunners took turns firing from the sides of the Huey. The ammunition was loaded with tracers, and every fifth round an orange-white streak sailed from the end of the American guns. It seemed to work. Both birds continued to hear occasional fire directed at them but the paths, huts, and roads were strangely empty. If someone was still taking aim, they were doing it from behind a large piece of cover. The shots were random and only occasionally did they hear a metallic clink as a round tried to pierce the skin of the Huey.

"Up ahead. See the rise. I think that's the valley," came a voice over the radio. Hooper and Connelly scanned the area ahead of them and nodded to each other in confirmation. Hooper clicked the mic twice in response.

"Guidon 6, this is Blue Max 68, request you pop smoke," Walsh said trying to communicate with the stricken Rangers. Connelly and Hooper didn't add to the conversation. They listened, maintained their position and hoped there would be a quick response.

"Let's hold here and look for smoke," Walsh said over the radio. Almost involuntarily, Connelly pulled in a deep breath and leaned a little closer to the windshield separating him from the 50-foot drop to the top of the trees.

"Shit – we've already been hit twice and I see a lot of fire headed in our direction. They know we're here," Walsh said. The words had barely left his lips when another message came over the radio.

"Blue Max 68 – our smoke's away. Charlie's climbing fast and they're about 50 meters west of us. We'll hold em off. Blast the bastards."

The Ranger company knew that once they started

sending smoke, it would be a race to see who would get to them first.

"There's the smoke. My two-o'clock about halfway up the hill, on the left," said Walsh.

Connelly and Hooper turned their heads in the direction of the lead chopper and sure enough, there was a small cloud of pinkish, purple smoke rising through the trees. The rest of the dark green treetops were eerily connected to the gray mist drooping from the clouds, but in this one spot, there was a dull neon quality to the color escaping from the trees.

"That's some welcome sign," Hooper said. "We see the smoke."

"We're getting hit pretty good – we're only gonna get one chance at this. I'm sending in a marking pair," Walsh said.

Captain Walsh sent a pair of missiles to the spot where he thought the enemy was last seen.

A voice filled with desperation came to them from the jungle floor. "Let 'em all fly. That's the spot."

"Unload everything on them in one run. Give us 30 seconds and then follow us in – we'll clear the way," said Walsh.

Hooper touched his nose and turned for a second toward Connelly. They too had started to draw more and more ground fire as they circled the highlands that led to the valley.

"They know we're here and they'll be waiting," Hooper said. He tapped his head twice and then touched the picture of his wife wedged into the metal crease next to his altimeter. Connelly watched as Hooper drew his hand back and touched his lips. Both men pulled the straps on their flight harnesses and made sure their flight helmets were buckled.

Connelly turned back toward the gunners and gave them a thumbs-up, indicating they were nearly ready to make their run.

"We're going in straight and hot and bank left at the end of the valley," Hooper said over the intercom. Anderson knew that meant his door would be facing the ground and the Aircraft Commander would have the best view of the action. Connelly mouthed the words, "here we go," and as he turned back toward the front of the aircraft he tapped the stock of the AK-47 strapped to the backside of his seat. He'd picked it up in a hot LZ about a month ago and now he never flew without it.

"I'm not ending up in a fight with the .38 they issued us at MACV," he said when Hooper first asked him why he strapped the automatic rifle and spare clips to his seat.

Both helicopters were south of the valley and they made a slow, almost lazy circle to the left as they got ready for their rocket run. As they lined up once more on the valley, Walsh's voice again came over the radio.

"Stay back and to our left. You come in straight behind us and you'll get hit for sure."

Connelly clicked the mic twice and tried to see Hooper, but he was turned toward the window next to him. Neither one said a word. They both knew the lead ship would draw the fire, but the enemy would work out a firing solution for their Huey by the time they started their run. There'd be no surprise when they dove for the treetops. Bobby instinctively put his gloved right hand on the top of his helmet and made one last adjustment before they started their run. As he did, the thick silver bracelet his mother had given him before he left for boot camp slid up his forearm, and for a second he saw the intricate outline of an eagle that had so often fascinated him as a child.

~ ~ ~ ~ ~

For as long as he could remember, his mother had worn the bracelet, and when he once asked her why she wore it every day, she replied: "It reminds me who I am and where I've come from." To his then 13-year-old mind, that made no sense, but he knew better than to ask again. They didn't speak about it again until the day before he left for boot camp and she gave it to him

"This will help you while you're gone, Bobby," she said when she removed the bracelet from her thin, brown wrist. At first, he was surprised to see her take off the intricate artwork, but before he could say anything she spoke again.

"The spirit of our family, of the eagle that resides in each us, goes back generations. That power will protect you and bring you home to us."

Connelly understood only a few things about his mother's family. His dad once told him that his grandparents came into the country from Mexico, but his mother was orphaned as a young girl, something about a car accident. Ultimately, after she left the hospital, she lived in a foster home in the eastern part of Washington. They didn't talk about it often, and he didn't know why, but he wasn't sure if the story was entirely true. He knew his parents met at the lakefront resort where they lived and worked, but beyond that, his mother's immediate family was as much a mystery as the bracelet on her arm.

He'd only misplaced it once, and for the short time that his right wrist remained bare, his heart raced and his body became covered with a light coating of sweat and fear. And yet, as the panic and desperation filled his mind, he couldn't help but notice how exhilarated and alive he felt as the adrenaline generated by the experience filled his body.

~~~~~

The final unit exercise for the Warrant Officer pilots graduating from aviation training was to march in front of the command structure from Fort Rucker and receive their wings and orders. In unison, they pivoted their heads slightly to one side as they passed a seated row of generals, politicians, and other dignitaries. For exactly five seconds, 52 eyes shifted to the right and they were focused on the podium and the commanding officer of Fort Rucker. They smartly saluted the two-star general, stopped their forward momentum and crisply stood at attention.

General McKernan, a 56-year-old veteran credited with piloting 31 bombing missions over Europe and commanding an aviation unit during the Korean conflict, returned their salute and barked an order instructing them to stand at parade-rest. He then gave a brief speech commending them for their work and welcomed them to ranks of Army aviators. Each new pilot was then called forward and after pinning a set of wings to their chest, they were given a copy of their travel orders. Connelly wasn't in a hurry to look at his. He knew the packet would contain instructions on where and when he was to report, but in the end, the only thing that mattered was that he would be assigned to an aviation group in Vietnam.

His gear was packed and like most of the men in his training company, he'd leave Alabama that afternoon. He wasn't sure he'd ever see it again.

Each of the soldiers in his unit was leaving for combat. They all received 30 days leave at graduation and were told to get their affairs in order before they left the country. The Army provided each of them with an example of a soldier's last will and testament, and there were forms to fill out concerning who should be notified in case he was killed or declared missing-in-action. For the first time in his life, he thought about the fact that he might not live forever. It was sobering. Connelly flew across the country to his home outside of San Diego, but he only spent three days there before he decided to travel to Fort Lewis, in Washington, and wait for his flight to Vietnam.

Like many men who left their homes for Vietnam, Connelly's father had served during World War II, and now his son wore his country's uniform. "My dad was on a destroyer during the war," he said one night in Officers' Club. After a few more beers he added, "he was a machinist's mate and part of the ship's anti-aircraft crew, but that's about all I know."

Connelly and his dad were close, but neither of them would be considered talkers. They were comfortable with each other and comfortable spending time together with few words passing between them. Sometimes, on fishing trips on the lake, nothing more than a nod or a simple grunt would be exchanged, and yet each knew what the other wanted or was thinking.

On the last day at home with his father and mother, Bobby told them, "There's no sense waiting here. The sooner I report in, the sooner I can come home for good." That afternoon he packed his duffle bag, knowing that his dad would take him to the train station and from there he'd begin the journey to Fort Lewis.

He stood on the porch of his small lakefront home as Jimmy Connelly put the bag into the backseat of the family sedan. Bobby was standing with his face toward the fading sunlight when his mother approached him.

"Bobby, keep that with you," his mother said, pointing to the bracelet on his wrist. "For so many years it connected me to my family, now it will link you to us." She had trouble saying the last few words and as Bobby watched his mother speak, he noticed her dark, olive-colored eyes were filled with tears. Her hand instinctively went to his cheek. Turning his back to her and moving toward his father and the car, he mumbled, "OK."

It took Connelly nearly 24 hours to reach his destination, and when he finally found the right building that contained the clerks and staff who processed incoming soldiers, there was little time left in the work day. The clerk who accepted his paperwork, a sergeant named Landry, was more interested in cleaning his desk and leaving for the day than making sure Connelly knew where he'd be bunking and where he had to report in the morning.

"Sir, you're temporarily assigned to the 16th Combat Aviation Brigade while you're here at Lewis, but when you get to Nam, you'll be reassigned," Sergeant Landry said. He stamped and signed the forms in front of him with the accuracy and speed of someone who'd given these same instructions to hundreds of pilots. Connelly watched in amazement. To him, the weary sergeant barely glanced at the paperwork, let alone read them.

"The 16th is based down at the airfield and the temporary officers' quarters are located on the next road over from here, sir," he said, pointing toward the front of the building.

"Check in there and they'll make sure you get a ride to the field in the morning," he said, giving Connelly the manila folder that contained a copy of his service record and his orders.

Three hours later he was collapsed on his rack when there was a knock at the door and an unknown face pushed its way into the room.

"Hey, newbie … Connelly. I'm heading to the O-Club. You want to go?"

Connelly wasn't much of a drinker. He'd only had two or three drinks in his whole life, but he'd slept most of the way to the base, and sitting in his room staring at the walls and ceiling wasn't going to help.

"Sure – hang on," he said and stood up quickly. He was still wearing his uniform, so he grabbed his hat and wallet and followed the sound of fading footsteps.

At the main entrance to the building, he saw another pilot sitting in a jeep tapping his hand lightly on the black steering wheel. As he approached, the airman stuck out his hand and said, "I'm Danny Quinn, hop in."

Quinn, like Connelly, was a Huey pilot and had graduated from Fort Rucker a few weeks before Connelly. He was from Maine and had spent nearly all of his 30 days leave at home before coming to Fort Lewis.

"I processed in yesterday," he said as they walked into the dark air-conditioned club. "It's like everything else in the Army – hurry up and wait."

The two newly pressed pilots sat on stools near the end of the bar and for the next hour or so, Connelly nursed a drink as they watched people come and go. Each time the door to the outside world opened, Connelly noticed the sunlight was fading until, and about the time he finished his drink, there wasn't any difference between the level of light inside the bar and the outside world.

"Do you mind if I sit here?" a woman asked and took a seat on the stool next to Connelly. It was the last seat in the bar and no matter where he turned, Danny Quinn was nowhere to be found. While Connelly nursed his one drink, Quinn managed to guzzle three whiskeys and was now loudly playing pool with two other pilots. Connelly only wanted to leave, but he wasn't sure how to get back to barracks or what to do about Quinn.

"I'm Betty Hatcher," the voice next to him said, and as if by magic, a hand appeared in front of his chest. Connelly turned to face the woman, intending to shake her hand, and he was surprised by the pain that radiated from her face. He held her hand for a second or two, but even after he let go, he kept staring at her somewhat swollen features. She had red-rimmed eyes and he noticed the loose, almost sloppy way her lipstick covered only her top lip.

There was a partially filled drink glass in front of her, and as he looked once more in her direction, she raised the glass. The sweat and condensation on the outside of the cheap tumbler pressed roughly against her bottom lip, and he knew at once what happened to the lipstick.

"Nice to meet you, ma'am," Connelly said, and he made a motion like he was going to stand up.

Pulling a cigarette from her purse, Betty scanned the room and then looked once more at Connelly. "See you around," she said and motioned to the bartender that she wanted another drink.

Within minutes Connelly was alone outside the bar and trying to decide the quickest way back to the barracks. He loosened his uniform tie and started walking east in the hope that it would be the right direction. There were only a few lights along the street, and once he was outside the glare of the officers' club, the darkness surrounded him and reminded him of the back roads near his home by the lake. In a way, it was comforting.

The gravel under the soles of his shoes made a crunching sound, and for 15 minutes or more, that was the only sound Connelly heard until a set of headlights washed over him and most of the road. He could tell the vehicle was not following a steady line, as the lights moved first from one side of the road and then to the other. The engine didn't sound like it belonged to the jeep that had carried him to the bar, but perhaps worst of all, the vehicle was slowing down. It was a light-colored Chevrolet Impala. Connelly knew his cars and from the size of the fins and location of the taillights, he thought it might be a model from 1961. It pulled into the path in front of him and stopped without any warning.

The window on the driver's side was already rolled down and there was a pause before a woman's voice, thick from the effects of alcohol, made its way back to him.

"Do you need a ride?"

Connelly stopped moving forward. Standing close to the rear wheel on the driver's side of the car, he placed his hand on the car's fender and leaned toward the open window.

"Betty? Are you all right?" he asked, trying to focus on the interior of the car. "Where are you heading?"

Betty leaned out of the window. Her eyes focused again on Connelly, and as they contemplated one another, a knowing smile spread across her face.

"Bobby!" she said. "It's you."

"Why don't I drive you home?" Connelly said, and no sooner had the words drifted toward the car than he knew she'd say yes.

Betty said she lived on Capital Drive in one of the homes for officers and their families, and it was no more than a 10-minute drive from where he was standing by the side of the road. She slid across the bench seat in the front of the car, and as Bobby opened the door and got behind the wheel, she moved back across the seat, a little closer to the young aviator.

True to her word, in no time, the car rolled into the

small carport next to her house. Connelly noticed the lawn looked like it hadn't been cut in weeks, and unlike many of the houses they passed on the way, there weren't any children's toys in the yard.

"Made it," Connelly said and removed the keys from the ignition. "Hang on, I'll open the door."

Connelly tried the lock on the front door and found the house was already open. He turned back toward his passenger and held the door for her.

"Always a gentleman," she said. Somewhere between the carport and the front steps to the house, she'd pulled off her shoes and now stood in the tall grass smiling at Connelly.

"Feels good. C'mon in," she said and walked up the steps, past Connelly, and through the open doorway and into the darkened living room.

"No thanks, ma'am," he said. "I should be going."

Bobby knew he should get back to his room, but she was a mess and, she acted as if she was hurt. Not physically, but there was something in her eyes, something in the way she kept turning in his direction.

"Crap, crap, crap …." Bobby heard her struggling with the furniture in her own home.

There was a fumbling sound, like someone was taking quick short steps trying to balance themselves, and he saw her attempting to turn on one of the lights in the small living room. There was a crash as the end table turned over and the lamp hit the floor. Connelly went inside and found a light at the other end of the room. He turned it on and saw Betty lying next to the broken table. She was resting with her back to the couch. Bobby moved to her side and sat on the floor with her.

"Why don't we call it a night," Connelly said to her and smiled as she sat up and leaned into his shoulder. "You'll feel better in the morning."

"Not yet. Just stay here for a minute," she said and pushed the hair away from her face.

Connelly noticed the portrait of a pilot, a young man who wore the insignia of an aviator and a bright yellow patch with a black ribbon and horse's head that meant he was assigned to the 1st Cavalry. Even with less than 12 months in the service, Connelly knew it was the type of portrait the Army routinely sent to the newspapers when you were missing or killed in action. He moved away and noticed the wedding picture sitting on the bookshelf at the end of the room. The pilot's face was young and full of life, full of promise. He was dressed in a plain black tuxedo, and with Betty holding his hand, the two of them smiled as if they had their entire lives in front of them.

"Are you married?" he asked and nodded toward the service picture.

Betty didn't respond at first and then drew in a deep breath as if she were trying to draw some amount of strength before speaking.

"You act like him," she said. "He left three years ago. He told me it was for 12 months and then he was coming right home. He promised me."

Connelly looked at her hands; for at least a minute, she tapped her thumb against her bare knee in some rhythm known only to her. He started to think about the Morse code lessons they all had to endure at Fort Rucker.

"Three short, three long, three short," he thought.

His mind was racing at the speed of light, moving from one idea to the next.

"What happened, where is he?" Connelly asked.

For a moment, she gathered herself and drew another deep breath. "He's still there. His first tour was extended – 18 months, and then he signed up for a second tour. He didn't even ask, didn't even talk to me."

Betty lost all the strength she had, and as the last words passed over her lips, she slumped toward the pilot who now occupied her empty home. Tears that had been held back all night now dropped in regular intervals toward her arm, and silently she sobbed. Bobby reached down toward this woman, but he wasn't sure what to do and trying to find some way to comfort her, he put his hand on her leg. The moment he touched her, a message passed between them. It was as if he had a strange, almost unnatural ability to communicate with her. She nodded almost imperceptibly and rested her head on his shoulder.

"We make quite a pair," Betty said and tried to sit a little straighter against the couch. "I can't seem to get out of my own way and you're about to head over there too. Look at us."

Slowly the sobs coming from her turned to chuckling, and as Bobby realized that she was no longer crying, he joined her and started laughing too.

Betty reached down and pushed herself closer to Bobby. "When are you leaving?" she asked.

"Day after tomorrow, well, technically tomorrow I guess," he said.

Every logical instinct he had was telling him that he should leave, that he should find a way out of the house and get back to the barracks, but at the same time, he wanted to stay. She wanted him to stay, he knew that, and the attraction of spending time, any time, with a woman kept him seated on the floor. His thoughts were in overdrive and he reminded himself that he might not be back - comfort, any type of comfort at this point, was not a bad thing.

With one hand, he wiped a tear away from her cheek. Connelly was surprised at how small and thin her hands were as she reached up and held his hand on her cheek. She was warm, and after pressing his hand to her lips, she moved it toward her blouse.

"It's all right," she whispered and started pulling him closer. The two lost and lonely souls found each other's eyes and for nearly a minute, they didn't say a word. Bobby noticed that her breathing had become deeper, and in some way she seemed more focused and alert than she had been at any time during the past few hours. He told himself that she was now sober. Their bodies moved together and finally, without looking away, she spoke to him again: "It's OK."

Bobby gave up any pretense he had about leaving and his lips found hers. It was well after midnight, but now neither one felt the least bit tired. Betty fumbled with her clothes and pulled Bobby toward the couch behind her. He reached for the cushioned furniture and attempted to put his arm around the squirming woman underneath him.

"Ugh," she said and moved away quickly as if she were in pain. "Your arm, take your watch off," she said.

Bobby didn't bother to explain that the pain came

from his bracelet. He'd scratched her shoulder when, with one hand pulling at his pants, he'd tried to embrace her.

"The light," he said as he half stood and put the rest of his clothes next to the small wooden table in the living room. He removed the bracelet and placed it on top of the table, knowing it might hurt her again.

"I want to see you. I want you to see me," Betty said, her voice now thick and slow.

Bobby didn't argue. He didn't say anything, he moved and joined her on the couch.

It had been so long since anyone held Betty the way this young pilot now clung to her, and she welcomed the feeling. She'd been married to Richard Hatcher for nearly four years, and she'd been thrilled by the way they connected when they were alone, when they were first married, but for so long now she thought that part of her life was over.

With almost no experience and a lifetime of anticipation built up, Bobby showed no restraint in his lovemaking. In a matter of minutes, his world changed in front of his eyes, and as he let out an uncontrollable exclamation of pleasure, he slipped and fell from the couch. With one knee on the floor and one still firmly planted on a pillow, he turned his head away from Betty.

"Whoa …," she said as she pulled him back to the couch. Within seconds both of them were giggling like young children, and as the laughter slowed, she once more touched the corners of his dark eyes.

"I have an idea," she said and stood up. Taking him by the hand, she led him toward her back bedroom as if it were the most natural thing to do. Bobby simply followed.

For the next two hours, Bobby learned a little patience and Betty instructed him as best she could. Sore, sated, and feeling as if the world was still a pleasant place to live in, the two young lovers fell asleep and slept soundly.

Sometime before 5 a.m., Betty moved one of her legs and brushed up against Bobby. It startled him, and when he saw the lights from the living room, he realized what time it was and he remembered he had to report to the airfield in a little less than two hours. As he tried to extricate himself from the bed, Betty stirred again and then propped herself up on her elbows.

"It's OK. I know you have to go," she said. The sadness had returned to her face. "I'll remember you – try to think of me."

Bobby nodded but didn't respond as he moved away from the bed looking for his clothes. He dressed in seconds, and without any other conversation he let himself out of the house and started moving toward the road. He knew that if he double-timed it toward the barracks he'd have enough time to get dressed and report in. He was almost halfway there when he realized he'd left his bracelet, the one thing he had from his mother, on the small coffee table in Betty's living room. He turned and started running back toward the house.

The back door was still unlocked and he tried to let himself in without making a single sound. He'd made it to the edge of the living room when he realized Betty was standing right behind him. He could tell that she had a small bathrobe on, but nothing else.

"You came back?" she asked, reaching for his arm.

"Sorry. I didn't want to wake you, but I left something here," he said. Betty saw him reach for the bracelet.

"It must be important to you," she said. Bobby nodded, but he didn't say anything. Placing the bracelet in his pants pocket, he turned to head back to the door.

"Bobby, you keep that with you. I don't know how or why, but those wings'll bring you home."

Without warning, the words of his mother rang in his ears and resonated in his soul. He looked again at the bracelet and thought of what she told him when he left home. "This will remind you of us and your place here in the hills," she said and slipped it over his wrist. "Its spirit, these wings, will bring you back to us."

When most of the other recruits mailed everything they owned back home from boot camp, Connelly hid the bracelet on the bottom of the tray in his footlocker, and without any real explanation, it had gone unnoticed. Now, he never flew without it.

~ ~ ~ ~ ~

Braxton's voice came to them again through their headsets. "We're taking heavy fire – the Rangers are holed just above the smoke. Hit the bastards right below them"

As the last word came to them, Connelly and Hooper saw the lead ship sway to the left as it was hit. The stricken Huey righted itself, and as soon as their flight path became straight and level, the rockets on both sides of the fuselage streaked toward the land below. There was a black and then a gray trail that followed their route to the target.

"Hooo chi mamma," came Braxton's voice again. "We're through. Meet you on the other side of the puddle."

Hooper and Connelly couldn't help but smile at their friend's southern drawl. "Roger that," Hooper said and nodded one more time to Connelly.

The helicopter pivoted slightly forward as if the old horse was standing a little higher on her hind legs. Hooper moved the throttle full forward and Connelly kept his hands close to the flight controls in case something happened to Hooper. His feet were barely touching the rudders and he could feel Hooper using the cyclic and collective to guide them down and pick up speed.

"I see the strike," Connelly said, referring to missiles that came from Walsh and Braxton's Huey.

"Heads on a swivel," he said and turned one last time toward the back of their aircraft. Sergeant Freeman's face was covered in sweat, but he already had his M60 extended out of the fuselage and pointed ahead of them. The flames from the tracer rounds streaked ahead and marked the path to the valley.

On the other side, Hooper's side, Chief Anderson had his weapon out too and was pointing it down and toward the rear of the aircraft.

"By the time we fly by, every shithead with a rifle will think they can take a shot at us," he said. "Not at me, brother boy!"

He'd been in-country for nearly a year and was due to start training his replacement next month. He lifted his head slightly and nodded in the direction of the Warrant Officer. A simple shrug of his shoulders told Connelly he was ready.

"Take cover – we're rolling hot," said Hooper to the troops on the ground. They didn't wait for a response.

Both M60s started their steady, rhythmic beat as the gunners tried to protect the ship from all directions.

"Twenty seconds to target," said Hooper. Connelly focused on the jungle to his right and no sooner had he heard these words than he saw a log shaped rocket tube resting on a man's shoulder and pointing up in their general direction.

"RPG - 2 O'clock," he said into his headset. Almost on command, the tracers and rounds from Sergeant Freeman's gun moved to the general direction of the enemy on the ground.

"Let 'em go," Hooper said, rolling the ship slightly to the left. Connelly focused on the area ahead of them and pressed the firing switch – first the left side of the chopper and then the right, almost simultaneously. Because they had started with a roll to the left, the force of the rockets straightened the ship back toward level flight.

"Outta here – birds away," Connelly said and turned once again to his left to watch the missiles find their mark. The words were still hanging in the thick, wet air when the windshield located to the right of him exploded into the back of his helmet. He felt some of the glass and steel on his neck, but his face and head were turned away from the blast.

Having been hit on the right side, Hooper instinctively rolled the Huey to the left and got on the radio. "We've been hit," Hooper said, hoping Walsh and Braxton would hear him. "Bobby - are you all right?"

Connelly nodded toward his friend, but he noticed the firing from the M60 behind him had stopped. The shell of the rocket-propelled grenade had entered the helicopter about half a foot above the open cargo door on the right. It exploded no more than three feet from Sergeant Freeman as it pierced the fuselage and headed toward the clouds. More than half of Freeman's skull, and the skin and brains connected to it, left with exploding shell. His battle harness was the only thing keeping his lifeless form inside the Huey.

There was barely a quarter of a mile between one side of the valley and the other, and as Hooper struggled to find a safe path out of the constant stream of small-arms fire, Connelly moved slightly forward and to the left in his seat so his face was out of the blast of air coming through the broken windshield. At least half of the instruments in front of him stopped working, but he saw the needle on the oil pressure gauge was dipping toward zero, and the temperature gauge of the turbine was almost into the red zone.

"We gotta get out of here. She won't last much longer," Connelly said. He pointed toward the body of Sergeant Freeman and shook his head. The back half of Connelly's neck was hot and there was a steady stream of sweat rolling down his back. He wasn't nervous yet, but he knew their time was short.

"Mayday – mayday. This is Blue Max 68-papa. We're making an emergency landing, and our gunner's been hit," Hooper said, his voice picking up pace as the radio transmission left the stricken Huey.

"There - at the end of the valley - there's a small lake or paddy," Connelly said. "Let's head over that way and then turn toward the sea."

Hooper moved his head as if in agreement and when he lowered his chin, the left side of the helicopter exploded as another missile slid along the riveted steel skin. It wasn't a direct hit, but it was close enough to blow open a four-foot hole above Hooper's left shoulder. In less than a second, he lost consciousness. The force of the explosion thrust him forward and there was a sickening crunch as his chin hit his chest. To Connelly, even in the noise and confusion, he thought the sound of Hooper's neck snapping sounded like somebody stomping on a dry tree branch. The helicopter rolled through the air and Connelly saw the green canopy of the trees through his side of the windshield. He had to fly.

He managed to get his hand on the flight controls and steadied the stricken ship. Strangely, the tail rotor pedals were working and he thought he could fly them to the ground. There was water ahead and he knew if he could get them past it, he could auto-rotate. He had one chance. The engine was almost out.

Connelly remembered the one other time he landed without an engine. He was near home, and flying with his dad over the hills of Escondido after a day of taking some tourists fishing. The engine in their Cessna floatplane became eerily quiet when he crossed the last ridgeline before the lake and their home. Without explanation or warning, the engine stopped turning. Bobby was focused on flying the plane and finding the dock in front of their house and didn't realize they were in trouble. From the pilot's seat, Jimmy Connelly didn't panic. He focused his attention on his only son and said, "Look for a place to set down, I'll see if I can figure out what happened. You can do this." The two salesmen in the back were asleep, but when the engine stopped, both their heads popped up and each one was making more than a little noise. Bobby set the plane down without a problem, and as they were coasting toward the shore, Jimmy flipped the master switch back on and restarted the engine.

"You never know, Bobby, you've got to be ready," said Jimmy Connelly, smiling toward his only child.

His dad's words were ringing in his ears as he watched the altitude spin away and he counted down, "300, 200, 100, 50 ... pull, pull, pull."

The helicopter was not more than 100 yards beyond the end of the rice paddy, and from 30 feet, the 8,500 pounds of now dead weight dropped like the stone it had become. Connelly pulled on the collective with everything he had, but without any power or hydraulics, there'd be no cushioning the landing. The right landing skid hit first and collapsed. The cabin rolled to the right and the main rotor dug into the soft earth. The engine shrieked as the overheated turbine, now trying to spin without any oil, seized to a stop. It masked the sound of the open cargo door crushing Chief Anderson as it cut through his shoulder harness and then flung him from Huey.

As the stricken craft rolled one last time, Bobby saw the lifeless, nearly decapitated body of the crew chief hit the land. The Huey stopped rolling and Connelly was hanging from his harness. The landing skids were angled toward the sky and the main rotor was buried in the foreign soil. Ammo boxes, shell casings, oil and other fluids from the crew were all mixed together in what was left of their aircraft. Connelly heard only his breath inside the dying machine, and he didn't feel any real pain, but he couldn't move his left hand to get to out of the safety buckles.

More to himself than anyone else he said, "One second." Without another word, another thought, Bobby put his head down – he had to rest. He'd made it. He closed his eyes and thought that if this was the end, he hoped it would be quick. The thought trailed away and the world around him went black.

~ ~ ~ ~ ~

Drops of blood from the wound on his left shoulder pooled in a crease of his uniform shirt until the government issued fabric became a wick of thick human liquid and a drop fell toward his cheek. The second drop hit Connelly in the middle of a closed eyelid and instinctively he blinked. Both eyes opened to a new world.

The Huey was half upside down. The seat next to him was empty, but as Connelly looked through the broken and twisted front end, he thought he saw Tom Hooper standing next to the downed aircraft.

"C'mon, Bobby," Hooper said to his wounded friend and he motioned for him to move away from the wreck. "C'mon. It's safe here."

Connelly tried to move, but the left side of his body was pinned against the harness and he couldn't get out of the intricate web that his bindings had become.

He shook his head as if to say no and closed his eyes again. Once more the pain went away as the comforting blackness wrapped its arms around him. "Hang on," he said to himself.

Connelly remained suspended and half upside down in his safety harness for more than 20 minutes before he stirred again, and that only happened because his left leg, coated in blood, slipped from behind the instrument panel and hit a six-inch triangular shard of broken windshield. The pain traveled in an instant from his leg to his brain and as a gruff, primitive scream left his lips, he strained once again against the belts holding him in place. Looking around, he recognized the smell of burning plastic and fabric. There was hazy smoke everywhere. He had to go. He waited for one more second, hoping the radios might still work, but the only sound to reach him was hissing and ticking as the metal casing surrounding the turbine cooled. Everything he saw was dead.

He tried to turn toward the left side of his body, but his neck and back felt as if each vertebra had a sharp knife connected to the bone, and each turn or twist of his body pushed the serrated edges a little further toward his spine.

His left arm and hand were numb and no matter what he did, he couldn't reach the release buckle near his flight suit pocket. He realized he'd have to use his right hand and twist his torso toward the buckle. He tried to draw a deep breath and brace himself for the pain.

Blood and sweat dripped and fell to his face as he grimaced and involuntarily tightened the muscles in his abdomen. A quiet grunt filled what was left of the cockpit and he turned in his harness. His right hand found the metal latch, and with a quick flick of his thumb, he opened the safety release. The pain was immediate, and as he fell forward, his face hit the dirt. He screamed. With half of his body nothing more than dead weight, he watched the tree line for almost two minutes, but he couldn't see Hooper or the others. When Connelly turned back toward the wreckage, he saw them. Anderson and Hooper's eyes were still open but the life had left them.

The confusion of the last few minutes left him and he was filled with an almost unbearable feeling of grief. He couldn't move. He lay in the mud for more than five minutes wondering if this too was his fate. He'd all but decided to stay there with them when the first round hit the now dead chopper, and Connelly winced. He didn't want to get shot. Within seconds, another volley followed, and this time the rounds were moving toward his damaged left leg.

Knowing the only escape was straight ahead, away from the rice paddy, he remembered that beyond the open wetland there was a short scrubby brush that gave way to jungle palms. If he could get into the trees, he'd find shelter. When they were coming out of their run, they had seen the edge of Highway One about one or two klicks to the east. If he could get to the road, he'd have a chance for a dustoff, but right now he had to get to the trees.

With his right arm, he pulled himself forward and was rewarded with another reminder of his wounds. As he raised his head to pull himself away from the chopper and his dead friends, he saw the dull green banana clip of his AK-47 two feet to his right. He grabbed the clip and used the butt end of the magazine to push himself forward again. This time he kept his head a few inches off the ground and tried to find any other parts or wreckage from their Huey. A few feet away he hit the lottery. It was the AK itself, half in the mud waiting for him. Its barrel was stuck in the wet earth and for a second Connelly remembered the way fallen soldiers' graves were sometimes marked.

"Hot damn," he whispered to himself, and for the first time in an hour, he forgot the pain.

With the AK strapped to his back and an almost familiar sense of pride, he crawled for 45 minutes through the dark and fertile mud until he reached the edge of the field. Along the way he picked up more than his share of insects, and for the last 20 minutes his left arm and shoulder had started to burn and sing with pain as if it were coming back to life. His leg was still dead weight, but now he had hope. He pulled himself into the thicket and rested behind the first large tree he found. He needed water, but more than anything he wanted to be ready for the rescue flights. He knew they'd come; he hoped they'd come. Using the rifle as a crutch, he pushed himself into a half standing position. It was then that he heard the first chopper. "Whoop, whoop," the rotor of the incoming Huey sliced through the air and sent Connelly a message. "We're coming."

He waited, knowing he had one chance. They were low and moving fast. He heard them again and turned his neck and shoulders toward the noise. The pain filled his eyes with water, but there they were. Coming for them.

"Hang on, hang on, hang on," he told himself and when they were no more than 50 yards away, he stepped, hopped, and pushed himself out of the jungle. Frantic, he put his rifle in his right hand and pushed the barrel down toward the ground to balance himself. His mud-covered face now turned toward the helicopters and he tried his best to wave with his left hand, but he couldn't lift it above his waist.

The pilots and gunners in the search helicopters were looking for four downed airmen, and when they saw this mud covered man step from the jungle with an AK-47, they identified him as another crazy local with a rifle.

"Let him have it," the pilot radioed to the crew, and as he dipped the Huey forward, he released two missiles in the Connelly's direction. The gunners joined in and sent a 30-second burst toward the single man.

Connelly saw the first helicopter dip in his direction and pick up speed. He'd been on the other end so many times before and knew this wasn't a pickup.

"Shhhit," he said and used his one good leg to dive back toward the trees. He hit the lower left side of the trunk about the same time the first missile exploded 20 yards to his right. The tree knocked the air from his lungs and one of his ribs cracked as he rolled back behind his new fortress. The concussion from the blast hit him next, and like a one-two punch in the ring, that was all it took. Bobby Connelly found the darkness again.

He didn't move for almost four hours and when he first tried to open his eyes it was nearly impossible. The blood and sweat from his wounds had pooled in his eye sockets, and over time the glue-like mixture dried and hardened to form a crusty seal. He used the rough backside of his right arm to scrape away the material in his eyes and tried to figure out how long he'd been out. He didn't have much time to think about it, but he did notice most of the daylight was gone.

From somewhere ahead of him he heard a click-click sound as if someone was methodically snapping their tongue, and that was followed by a rolling crunching noise. His body ached and felt as if a sack of stones had been dropped repeatedly along his left side. But being able to feel the pain was a strange gift.

"Ugh," he said and tried to stand on both legs. The Pain intensified and raced from his leg, but that was good. It meant he was still alive. He pulled the AK from the mud and scrutinized the surrounding woods trying to get a fix on the sound. As he stepped around the tree, he saw an old man in dull brown pants and sandals leading an emaciated ox. The beast appeared to be barely alive. Its eyes were red and rimmed with white spots of foam-like puss, and with each step he took, Connelly could hear it exhale as if its breath were the only way to complain. There was a small cart attached to the animal, and sitting in the back there were two young children with passive stone-like expressions, staring straight at him.

"Stop," Connelly hissed and raised the AK in their general direction. The old man clicked again and reached for the yoke around the animal's shoulders. The children kept staring as their cart slid to a stop and settled in the muddy earth.

The old man rubbed the top of his forehead but didn't speak. Connelly knew if he let them go, they'd tell the first VC soldier they ran across about him. He tried to swallow, but the inside of his mouth and throat felt like the dry desert sand near his California home. A soft scratchy cough left his lips and the old man raised his head. Holding his palms up and out, he reached toward the wagon and pulled out a small cloth covered canteen from under the seat.

"Shit," Bobby muttered to himself. "Stop," he said and raised the rifle again. The old man stood his ground and for a second and tried to find the children.

Bobby walked and wobbled slowly toward the man and nodded in the direction of the canteen. "Open," he said hoping he'd understand. He motioned with the rifle and said it again. "Open." The old man twisted the top off and reached across to the American flyer.

Bobby transferred the rifle to his left hand and stepped back after grabbing the small round container. He wasn't sure if it was water so he turned it back toward his wrist and poured a little of the liquid on his left sleeve. There was no smell when he rubbed it against his lips. "It must be water," he thought, as he heard the liquid slosh against the metal canister. He knew it wasn't full, but he needed to drink something. Connelly drained the container in two loud gulps and kept his eyes on the people in front of him.

As he lowered the flask, one of the children, the youngest, pointed toward his wrist and said, "Chim, chim." There was a low almost ancient tone to the words and Bobby didn't know what it meant, but the old man now acted nervously. He moved back and forth with a speed he hadn't shown before.

"Yankee ... bird," he said, and pointed at the mud-covered silver bracelet. Bobby knew he couldn't let them go, but he couldn't bring himself to shoot them. "Killing someone who was about to take your life," he thought. "That might be OK, but these people..." He moved his rifle away and said, "Go ... Di Di... Mau." It was the only Vietnamese phrase he knew. The old man didn't waste any time. He turned the cart and left without another word. Bobby stood there - the pain and agony of the day overwhelmed him. His eyes filled with tears and his face felt flush. There weren't any sounds, only a crushing and complete sense of sadness. He knew he'd probably die soon, but at least he'd done one good deed before checking out.

For the next hour, Connelly continued to make his way toward Highway One - crawling, walking, and limping in a generally eastern direction. The road was the only landmark the crews all knew, the only place where you might get picked up by one of the search flights. Connelly had a small survival mirror in his flight vest, and he wondered if he could signal the medevacs looking for them. The Huey pilots in the 1st CAV were supposed to get survival radios, but he'd heard that the flyboys and jet jocks got them first. Moving in the dark proved to be painful and slow.

Bobby had abandoned his flight helmet at the crash site and now the mosquitos and other flying insects were feasting on his exposed flesh. The seeping wounds were like a beacon to them. The left side of his body had become somewhat functional, but his left arm and foot felt useless - it was as if they were asleep. Every five minutes or so, there'd be a flash of pain as if that part of his body was coming back to life, but as soon as the agony reverberated through him, it began to fade away. It came and went in waves, and both limbs remained useless. The switch had been turned off. Thinking the end might come quick, he put his survival knife into his left hand and wrapped a length of parachute cord around the knife and his palm. He still could hear the steady ticking noise from his flight watch, and he noticed it was now 2:30 a.m. Smiling, he thought about how long he'd managed to stay away from those who were hunting for him. Planning to rest for a few minutes, he rolled himself into a group of low, thick bushes and trying to cover his head, he pulled his vest up until his face was mostly covered. Once again the darkness settled on him and he lost touch with this world.

He slept for three more hours and as the sun tried to find his side of the planet, a VC patrol entered the general area where he was resting. At first, they didn't see the American, but when they stopped for a water break, they heard him. His left lung was starting to fill with fluid, and as he struggled to breathe, a gurgling sound left his mouth with each exhale. The soldier closest to him raised a hand to warn the others and in a strange side-to-side, silent motion, he circled around the bushes. He nearly tripped over Connelly's extended leg before he saw him. There were swarms of bugs near a wound on his thigh, and every few seconds the limb would twitch as if the muscles themselves were fighting the bugs who hoped to feast on him. Motioning to the others to join him, he got ready to approach the injured American.

"Mau! Mau!" the VC soldier yelled and struck the bottom of his boot with his rifle butt. For Bobby Connelly, the pain was instant and horrific. "Argh," he screamed and started coughing droplets of blood and globs of yellow-green phlegm. "This is it," he thought.

He leaned forward and pushed himself into a sitting position, and as he did so, he swung the AK up and in the direction of his attackers. By his count, there were at least five of them. "Argh," he screamed again and pulled the trigger, but nothing happened. The chamber of the rifle had long since filled with mud, and as a weapon, it was useless. The VC patrol didn't know that, and as the American raised the Russian rifle again, they moved out of his line of sight. When they did, he saw the cart, the old man, and the children. He tried to throw the rifle in their direction, but as he raised his right arm, the soldier closest to him hit him in the head with the back end of his own rifle, and Connelly's world became a swirl of colors and pain. He didn't pass out, but he couldn't move.

Two soldiers reached in quickly and pulled him to

his feet. As they did, he noticed one of them was wearing an Army issue flight vest. Over the right breast pocket, he saw dried blood and Anderson's name. For the second time in a two-minute span he screamed.

There was some sort of argument or discussion in the group as they held Connelly, but it ended when one of the largest soldiers cut a Y-shaped branch from a nearby tree and they propped it under his left arm. As they lashed the wounded limb to the crutch, his flight gear was ripped from him and anything that happened to be in his pockets was split amongst them. They were nearly done when the old man pointed in his direction and said, "Chim, chim"

They pushed his right sleeve back and as he fought against them, they took his mother's gift. They controlled him now.

The soldiers and the old man separated. Connelly saw the cart continue on toward the east and Highway One, while he was pushed toward the west.

"Hey! Where are we going?" he asked and tried to lift his head a little higher. "Hey!" he continued. The soldier wearing Anderson's vest turned toward him but didn't respond. Bobby knew there wasn't much between the backside of the valley and Laos, and heading in that direction wasn't good. There were rumors about camps over there. The black ops boys sometimes said too much when they were drinking and most of them said they'd rather end it themselves than head into Laos as a prisoner.

"Hey! Hey," he tried again. "Where?"

After a few seconds, VC Anderson turned again and scowled at him.

"Nhà, nhà," he said and pointed to the west. "Home."

Book III – The Only Road Home

11 - Cages for the Dead

February - March 1968

The group of soldiers who captured Connelly knew they had a flyer, knew they had someone who understood how the wire-guided-missiles worked, and they knew they needed to keep him alive until they reached their camp that was two klicks west of the border between Laos and Vietnam. After stripping Connelly of any possession that might have some value, his wrists and ankles were bound together with long, coarsely-braided pieces of hemp. He was forced to squat on the ground with his head lowered as if he weren't worthy enough to look at the men who held him prisoner. After a short, guttural conversation, the largest of the soldiers approached him with a stout pole that appeared to be about eight feet long.

"No, no, no," Connelly stammered, thinking the man was going to beat him as if he were some type of trussed-up animal waiting for slaughter.

The soldier's expression didn't change nor did he move any slower as he continued his determined and steady progress in the direction of the injured soldier. Instead, he nodded at the VC soldier standing closest to the wounded American. Connelly was pushed from his seated, squatting position until he rolled backward. Like a stricken turtle, his hands and feet were in the air. Once he was no longer capable of moving, the two soldiers acted quickly and in unison. They slid the pole into the narrow space between his ankles and his wrists and both soldier's hoisted the airmen off the ground as if his carcass were the catch of the day.

Connelly's body swung and bobbed in a gentle rhythm as the two soldiers carrying him found their cadence and the group moved slowly in the direction of the setting sun. With every bounce or bump on the trail, Connelly experienced a new and deepening level of pain. And with each sharp reminder of his wounds, he let out a louder and louder exclamation. Finally, a gag was placed in his mouth and he was blindfolded with what smelled like a towel that had been recently used to clean horse stalls. It didn't take long for him to lose his sense of time and his mind raced with thoughts about where they were headed. Through the night and into the next morning the band of soldiers and their prized prisoner continued westward. Thankfully, for Connelly, he spent most of that time in an unconscious state.

The soldiers carrying him changed positions every hour or so and as one stepped in to shoulder the burden, one would step away. In this manner, the group was able to keep moving with little or no real breaks until they crossed the border.

When they were finally able to see the entrance to the camp where they would stop, Connelly was unceremoniously dropped to the ground. Pain and nausea forced him awake, and two men removed the pole that had been his carriage. They didn't say a word to each other, but with a simple nod and half-grunt they understood it was time to pull him to his feet. The largest of the men took charge. As he pulled a knife from his webbed belt, he grunted in the direction of the towers and pointed toward two soldiers standing next to a rocky hillside. The forest itself looked as if it were crawling its way up the hill, as if it were trying to completely cover the boulder-strewn land, but after 100 feet or so, the dense jungle gave way to the power and steepness of this foreign world and the trees thinned. But in that first 100 feet of the hillside, the North Vietnamese dug into the land and created a base and a series of tunnels. The rock, soil, and wet clay they removed became one more layer of protection and camouflage for a temporary prison camp.

Important prisoners were often brought here, away from the fighting and they were interrogated before a final decision was made about their life. Most of the prisoners who had the misfortune to see this camp never saw home again. Connelly felt the sun on his head and even after traveling through the night, his compass told him they were no longer in Vietnam. He saw the entrance to the camp and knew he had only one chance left - he started to run for the trees.

He managed to take five steps before he felt his neck snap forward and he crashed to the ground. His world became a swirling mass of colors. In seconds, the world he now lived in became a blanket of black comfort, almost nothing. He felt two strong hands on his shoulders, each fist grabbing a handful of his uniform shirt and Bobby Connelly was dragged back toward the entrance to the cave. More than anything, he hoped to retreat into the blackness again, but the pain throughout his body woke him and he realized he was weeping. He was still alive, still a prisoner.

Connelly was pulled along the floor, it was actually more like a dirt pathway, until the tunnel opened up into a small, round room with a few candles, a desk, and a chair. There was an officer in a clean uniform seated at the desk and at first, he ignored the American prisoner. Connelly tried to stand, but one of the soldiers positioned near the officer pushed him to the ground and the back end of a rifle was thrust into Connelly's neck.

"I wonder if that's my AK," he thought to himself and focused on his breathing.

Without any warning, the room was filled with language, his language.

"Mr. Connelly. Do not move," the officer said in a deep and resonant voice that reminded him of the French actors he sometimes saw in the movies.

Connelly assumed they had read his name on his uniform shirt, but he didn't respond.

"I have a few questions about your Huey and your unit," the officer said. "But that can wait."

Connelly still remained silent but he heard the man unscrew something, then he realized the officer was taking a drink. Connelly had not had anything to eat or drink since before they left for the mission and his stomach reacted to the sounds. He was thirstier than he'd ever been in his life.

"Connelly 3 065 924," Connelly said and like the turtles he used to see along the shoreline near his home, he pulled his head toward his shoulders. He expected the rifle to come crashing again toward him. But, his statement was met with silence and then finally a simple response.

"We shall see, Mr. Connelly. Maybe tomorrow," the officer said and that point there were two hands on his shoulders and two at his ankles.

He tried to kick and wriggle free, to resist in any way he could, but the pain and surprisingly, the fear, came roaring back through his body as the soldiers carried him deeper into the tunnels. He saw another room, similar to the first, and it reminded him of the inside of a small dome, and there was some type of doorway, a gate of wooden bars, about halfway up one wall. Connelly saw there were eight doors in total and they formed a crude semi-circle around the room. The guards headed directly for one of them.

The soldier closest to his head reached forward and opened the crude doorways, and then without a word amongst them, they pushed Connelly into what appeared to be a six or seven-foot hole. There was a rough, wet board along the bottom and as soon as his shoulders passed through the opening, the guards pushed him by the bottoms of his feet until his body filled the space. As the door swung shut and locked into place, Connelly realized his wrists and ankles were still tied together. Again, he was surrounded by darkness, but he was fully aware of what happened, of where he might be kept until he was no longer useful. For more than a minute he remained composed and he tried to control his breathing and his heart rate - he remained a soldier. But ultimately, one of the base emotions that connects all humans together took over and fear filled him. He screamed and no matter how hard he tried to stop, he continued to scream until his voice gave out. As the last raspy sound left his throat, his captors placed a cloth over the bars, and the darkness was now complete.

All Bobby Connelly experienced was fear and pain and more than once during the next hour or so, he wished the pain would carry him away to what he now thought of as the other side. He didn't care if he passed out or died. He simply wanted the sweet and complete blackness to come again and take him away.

For the next two days, Connelly was pulled from the hole every few hours. Four guards stood, two at each end of his body and the officer in the room asked him one fundamental question, "Where's your base?" Each time Connelly heard the question, he thought back to the week he'd spent at Fort Rucker learning about what to do if he were captured.

"You won't be alone and you won't be forgotten," he was told. "We will come for you."

With each trip to and from the hole in the hill, he found those simple lessons harder and harder to believe. He had lost track of the number of times he was pulled from his coffin-like perch, but each time he was questioned, he simply repeated his name and service number. The guards and the officer questioning him recognized the routine and no sooner had he given them the last digit of his service number than he was struck again. Most of the time, they focused on his wounded leg or torso. Twice Connelly thought he heard a crack as his body tried to absorb the punishment, but the pain was now constant and being struck only served to keep the pain at a perpetual level. The worst part of the interrogation process for him was the moment he realized it was over, and he was going back. He was almost thrown headfirst into the hole that had become his home.

Fear and the earth swallowed what was left of him and Bobby came to understand there are things worse than death. He lost any real sense of time and was tortured to the point where his body and mind nearly gave up. After his first day as a prisoner in the new camp, the guards provided him with a small cup of water and made a motion like he was supposed to eat three brown and black marble-sized balls of rice.

Finally, during one of the trips from his cell, he decided to say something, anything to keep them from pushing him back into his version of hell.

The guards were still at his feet when he heard a now familiar question, "where's your base?"

Instead of repeating his name and service number, he tried to draw a breath, but the pain in his chest made even that almost impossible. His mind was racing with thoughts and in a low tone, he started to respond. In his head, he heard himself yell, "Connelly, you stupid bastard!" but, the sound or words that filled the dimly lit space were incoherent to anyone but him. Connelly managed to turn his head back toward the officer in the room and he acted as if he were puzzled by the noise coming from the American, and then Connelly saw his lips move slightly. He was smiling. Bobby Connelly screamed as he felt his body moving forward, moving back toward his door.

But, Connelly said something and his captors knew that was the beginning they were waiting for. For the first time, he was left alone for nearly eight hours and allowed to sleep and heal. At some point during unexpected reprieve, Bobby Connelly knews this too and he convinced himself it would be better if they finished him off. He even decided that taking one of them with him would be better than living through the torture.

In the cramped space that was meant to break him he tried to flex his arms and legs, to see if he had any strength left. Each time his muscles contracted, the pain increased, and he could not bend his knees or move more than 10 inches in any direction, but he could push against the side of the dirt walls. Counting or trying to recite from memory the songs his mother taught him became the only way he maintained a sense of rationality. The tunnel he was placed in was filled with rancid, humid air and he had long since stopped worrying about the fact that he was lying in dried pools of his own waste.

At some point, the impossible happened and Connelly fell asleep. Instead of being trapped in a tunnel in Vietnam, like the child he had been only a few years ago, Bobby Connelly dreamt of home, of his house by the lake and he heard his mother's voice. As a young boy, he often asked for the light to be left on in his room. He didn't feel comfortable in the darkness and he always wanted the lights to remain on.

"Bobby," his mother said. "Light or dark, the

world is the same." Whether it was a memory or a dream, he thought he felt his mother's hand on the side of his face.

"When the sun rests for the day, the world rests too," she said. Her voice had a calming effect and in his dream, he turned toward her face. The eagle on her bracelet seemed to almost glimmer and shine as the light from the moon danced off her wrist. Bobby reached, with a sleepy hand, to try and touch the eagle's head.

"This bird has been the symbol of our family for more generations than you or I can count," she said. "When I was a little girl, my grandfather told me that eagles and men shared a common bond. We were spirits that traveled together and wherever I went, whatever I did, as long as I carried the spirit with me, I would be safe. I would be home."

The words were still in his ears when he woke abruptly from his fitful sleep, and the light of the room filled his eyes. Once again, he saw the crude rope that still bound his wrists. The movements, the beatings, the dirt and sludge from his cage caused the rope to burn marks into his arms. He had a bracelet of his own and the more he looked at his wrists, the more he was sure the red marks on his right arm, the wounds of his captivity, resembled the marks of an eagle. Where he once wore his mother's bracelet during each flight, there was now a scar, a wound with three different abrasions that appeared to be the result of a talon. He has been marked by the eagle of his dreams. It was as if the eagle were trying to lift him from the cage he was in and carry him home.

In that moment Bobby decided, the next time he is pulled from the cells, he is going to launch himself at the officer.

"With any kind of luck, I'll be able to crush his skull before they shoot me," he thought and smiled at the marks on his wrist. He knew he was nearing the end.

Connelly hears the door start to swing open and braces himself. He starts to count. It calms him, but he is not pulled immediately from the cell.

"Mr. Connelly. Today you are leaving," the officer said. "We are done here."

They pull him again, feet first, from his hole and as soon as he is free, he sees a stretcher and some clothes. They looked like tan pajamas. His restraints remain on and using what looks like an American Bowie knife, the guards cut his clothes from his body. A pair of rough hands pours a bucket of water over him and finally, the rope that kept him in place for nearly a week is removed, his hands and legs are free.

The guards and the officer do not speak to him, but instead, they push him in the direction of the larger room and from there toward the doorway leading back to the forest. He is stopped at the entrance and Bobby Connelly's hands are confined by ancient-looking, iron shackles.

Magically, there is a small truck there with a canvas back. He and two guards are unceremoniously put into the back and the vehicle lumbers away from the hill. Even in the early morning light, Bobby understands the direction their bouncing vehicle is traveling. They are heading north and east, back toward Vietnam.

12 - My Brother's Keeper

March - April 1968

The day Hooper and Bobby Connelly went missing never seemed to end. We flew an ever expanding search pattern hoping to find some sign of the aircraft and some indication the crew was alive, but the only thing I saw underneath us was the unbounded layer of treetops. The wind had picked up and as we flew over the jungle canopy, the moving trees made it appear as if we were riding above an ocean of green waves. The current of air had a rhythm and measure all its own and we were simply conveyed by the forces that moved through the trees.

"Chief, you see anything?" McCarthy, one of the other pilots in out unit, asked me from the front end of the Huey.

"Nothing but trees," I said. We'd been airborne for more than four hours and I hadn't seen any smoke, any activity, or anybody on the ground. I imagined that the world below us had become vacant, void of any humanity.

CW2 McCarthy had more than 11 months in-country and I thought I heard the other crew chiefs say he was due to rotate out in a few days.

"We're almost out of fuel and daylight," McCarthy said. "We're going to make one more pass and head back to Evans."

I didn't know what to say. I should've been with them and now I'd be heading back without them, again.

"Roger that," I said and lifted my chin toward the open door. A drop of sweat rolled into my eyes and as I tried to wipe them, the scar, on the top of my head, began to itch. I hoped I'd see something, some reason to stay. Ten minutes later, without another word from anyone, our Huey turned away from the sun and headed back to the base. We were done for the day.

The night passed slowly and without any real sleep. I'd doze off for a few minutes and the next thing I knew, I'd smell smoke or see the flash from the explosion that I assumed hit my Huey. I'd seen the aircraft that Braxton and Walsh flew back to the base, and they said the guns were training on them as Hooper and Connelly left the valley. In seconds, I'd be awake again, covered in a cold sweat and filled with a deepening sense of dread about my friends. It was hard to breathe and I felt like someone had placed a pail of water on my chest. After three or four rounds of this, I decided enough was enough and I sat up. What was the point?

About 0600 I heard a Huey land at the field. It was sleek, different from the aircraft assigned to our group. It didn't have any rocket pods hanging from the side and there were only three people aboard – it looked like a newer model, probably from Headquarters. There was some sort of extra piece of black baffling up near the turbine exhaust area. The main rotor was still spinning and the turbine spit a steady stream of exhaust gas into the morning sky. I saw the company clerk ride over in his jeep and pick up three large duffle bags from the cargo area. As soon as they were loaded into the back of the jeep, he lifted two similar bags from the empty front seat of his vehicle and swung them toward the open door and the waiting hands of the crew chief. "It must be one of the mail runs," I thought.

We didn't get mail that often and I followed the jeep toward the CO's tent and the admin office. I stopped to see if any of the other crew chiefs were in the mess tent, to let them know we had mail call, but the tables and chairs were empty. Either they were already on their way to the admin or they were still flying. I took a short swig of bitter, lukewarm coffee and kept walking.

They must have been still in the air looking for the missing aircraft and crew; the company clerk was the only one in the admin office and his desk was covered with piles of envelopes and packages. There were two large stacks, one for official mail and the other for personal items.

I stared at him and didn't say a word as he finished unloading the three bags. I hated it when someone kept talking to me as I was trying to turn a wrench or figure out how to replace a part. The last thing I wanted to do was annoy him. When the bags were empty, folded, and placed on the shelf next to his desk, he turned in my direction.

"Yeah. You want your mail?" he asked.

"If there's any - thanks," I said.

The company clerk rummaged through a pile of

small white envelopes. I could see the red and blue stripes along the edges that indicated they were airmail letters from somewhere else in the world and that only made me more anxious. I started to lean in his direction and I tried to see if there was something for me, something with my name on it.

"Here we go," he said. "Two for Warriner." As he passed them over in my direction, he turned once again toward the pile of official packages, his job for the morning.

The letters were light and weighed almost nothing but I could tell from the handwriting on the front of the envelopes that one was from my mother and one was from Sandy. Despite the cool morning air, I felt sweat beginning to form on the lower part of my back. More than anything I wanted to open her letter, but I managed to wait until I made it back to my rack.

It was unusually short, but I'll never forget the way her words sucked the breath from my lungs. There were only three short paragraphs. The first one was the usual "I hope you are doing well and taking of yourself," kind of stuff, and the second started to make me think there was something wrong. She started to tell me how hard it was for her with me away for so long. I don't remember the exact words, but I won't forget the way she ended the letter. The way she made it clear that things were over between us. I was here, and I was alone.

… Russ, with all the danger there, I think you should focus on staying safe and getting through this war in one piece. I'll never forget you. My parents have enrolled me at

Springfield College and I truly think it would be best for you if I was not a distraction. It may be best for me too. Please don't write, but more than anything – stay safe.

Sandy

There it was. I read the end of the letter over and over again, but no matter how often I read it, or what I tried to tell myself, I kept coming up with the same answer. It was over. I didn't even open the letter from my mother. I grabbed my gear and headed back toward the airfield. I wanted to scream - I wanted to run from this place - but where would I go?

Despite the increasing demands placed on our unit because of the Tet Offensive, the CO was able to find a way for us to spend the next two days searching for the missing Huey. I am certain he told the brass we were doing some type of other mission, when in fact, we were still hoping to find our missing friends. But with each hour that passed, the mood and the morale of the unit darkened. Finally, I was in the comm shack when the word came down, the search was officially over. We were needed elsewhere and the Army couldn't afford to have us flying off with only hope in our hearts.

Seven days after they went missing, an American ground unit trying to push their way north, near the outskirts of Hue, came across the burned and stripped carcass of the aircraft.

It was partially rolled over on its right side and there were three bodies near the scarred and battered fuselage. We were told they had been dead since the crash, but we were given the task of going to pick them up and bring them back. It was a short, silent flight, and when we finally arrived, there was broken glass, smashed equipment, and nearly a ton of tangled wire and metal, but there was no sign of Bobby Connelly.

"He might be alive," I thought and proceeded to help the medics put Hooper, Anderson, and big Sergeant Freeman into the body bags we carried with us. My lifeless friends were stacked in the cargo bay, one on the bench and two on the deck and as soon as I clipped back into the safety harness, I moved my hand in a circular fashion and tapped Captain Walsh on the shoulder. We were ready to lift off. They were going home. I kept thinking either I should be in a bag with them, or if I had been there in the first place, I could have kept the bastards away from the Huey.

"This isn't going to happen again," I swore to myself. "If my bird flies, so do I."

The company medics met us as the Huey settled once again at Camp Evans. They knew about our cargo and were ready to prepare them for transport back to the south and eventually to the States. As each of my friends left the Huey one last time, I tapped their hooded heads and promised them I would not forget what had happened. I would not let another Huey go down without me, without a fight. I removed my flight helmet and turned away from the jeep to wipe away the tears that I felt on my cheeks.

The crew chief's tent was empty and as I settled down on my rack, I saw Sandy's last letter. After everything that happened in the last week, more than anything, I wanted to see her, to talk to her, to hold her again and smell the lavender perfume she used to wear. I decided to continue to write to her even though in my heart I knew it was over. I hung on to the idea that I was misreading her letters.

~~~~~

The day we brought Hooper, Anderson, and Freeman back to the base, I sent another letter to Sandy, I didn't know it at the time, but it would be the last time I wrote to her. The language wasn't complicated and I tried not to sound desperate or like I was begging. I asked her to wait for me, I hoped and half-expected to get a letter back from her within a month. The mail came and went, but I never heard from her. Three months passed from the time I dropped the letter into the company clerk's basket for outgoing mail. My parents, my grandmother, and even my brother George managed to write to me, but Sandy remained silent. Nothing.

I didn't have much of a chance to think about it. From the time we lost Hooper and Bobby Connelly, my unit flew almost non-stop in support of the ground boys. About four weeks after we found the missing Huey, an official list came out with all the men who died or were missing from the 1st Cavalry. Anderson, Freeman, and Hooper's names were all there, but Bobby Connelly's name was nowhere to be found. I looked three or four times, ran my finger up and down the list of names, but he wasn't there. He wasn't MIA or killed in action. I didn't understand.

The next day, I was flying with Captain Walsh and Mr. Braxton, and I had the chance to ask them, "What happened to Mr. Connelly's name?"

Braxton nodded at me and then glanced at Walsh who lifted his head from the instruments before Braxton said anything.

"We heard last week that his name is going on the POW list," Braxton said. "As far as we know, chief, he's alive, but he's been taken somewhere up north."

The desperation of the day he went missing came rushing back. He was alive, but Bobby Connelly was stuck in some prison and I was here.

"It's all my fault," I thought and turned back to the M60 resting on my thighs.

Now with each day that went by, each day when we had a mission, I thought of Bobby Connelly and the others. I thought about their last flight and tried to place myself with them in the back of the Huey. In my version of their flight, we ran out of ammo and rockets, but we came home. Too bad my version wasn't reality.

Good or bad, the fighting near our base intensified and I had little time to do anything but fly and maintain my new aircraft. I'd been officially transferred to Captain Walsh's crew and I was determined to keep them safe and our Huey in the air.

We were adding hours to the flight log at a near record rate and as the end of March approached, our Huey was almost at the 100-hour mark again and it needed another airworthiness inspection. A few days ago, I had replaced the hydraulic pump after noticing the pressure was dropping during the last few flights, and I suggested to Mr. Braxton that we take the Huey for a short test flight to see if the pressure would hold. He was always happy to get in the Huey. He rounded up Captain Walsh and we flew for about 90 minutes, a short run toward the coast and back.

After we landed, I scanned through the logbooks and noticed that before the flight our inspection total was 99.6 hours.

"Shit – 90 more minutes puts us over 100 hours," I thought. I was doing the calculations again when Braxton came running in my direction.

"Hurry up with that, Warriner," he said. "Captain said there's something going on in the A Shau valley and we'll need to lift off in about an hour."

I gazed, trying not to look directly at him, and closed the maintenance log. The entry for the test flight could wait until we finished the mission.

"I'll have her fueled and armored in about 20 minutes, Sir," I said, and turned my back to him before he had a chance to ask me about the logbooks.

The mission to the A Shau valley sounded like any other mission we'd flown during the last few months. An infantry unit was pinned down by a growing number of VC and it was our job to get there and clear a path for them, to help them either move forward or retreat back to their firebase.

"Same ole shit," I thought. I yelled, "clear and untied," and listened as the pilots started the turbines. Without looking at them or the base we were leaving, I jumped aboard the nearly hovering Huey. Just another mission.

The run to the valley lasted no more than 30 minutes and by the time we got close, I could see the smoke and hear the mortar shells from the firefight below. The deep rumbling, thump of the deadly shells hitting the earth sounded almost like a summer thunderstorm.

"There's our boys," Braxton said, pointing to the right side of the aircraft.

"There's supposed to be some type of field at the end of the valley," Walsh said over the intercom. "We're going to see if we can use the rockets to clear a path to the field."

I nodded and understood.

"If we get there in one piece, you'll need to make sure everything's clear in the field," he said.

I patted the M60 like it was my favorite puppy and nodded.

Walsh and Braxton knew how to fly that Huey and as if we were on one of the ski trails in Vermont, we slalomed from one side of the valley to the other. Each time the nose passed the centerline they lit off the missiles. Sure enough, the rockets created a line, a path in the forest that led to the open end of the valley. The problem was that after the first run, the VC also understood how the game was being played. They started sending ground fire in our direction and it wasn't long before I heard rounds hitting the side of the fuselage.

"Not today," I said and let them have a piece of the M60.

We swung through the valley at least three or four, maybe even five more times. My M60 pounding out a steady tempo that I hoped would keep the VC hidden behind whatever rock they could find.

"We're there," Walsh said. Up ahead I saw an open plain that reminded me of one of Mr. Grondan's empty pastures. But it wasn't vacant, and I saw a buffalo, or cow, or some beast pulling a small wagon near the tree line. There was a farmer sitting up front and he had some kind of rifle slung across his lap. He heard us coming and turned to follow the sound.

"Oh no, you don't," I said to myself and felt rounds start to leave the M60. I don't remember thinking about my weapon. It was strangely connected to my thoughts and it simply started firing.

The shells hit the ground about 10 feet behind the wagon and then followed a straight line toward the animal pulling the cart. I missed the farmer, but the animal nearly exploded as three shells hit him in the throat. His head almost came off as he slumped into the tall grass at his feet. The Huey swung around again and I switched canisters.

As soon as we were lined up again, I started firing. This time, the shells made a progression toward the back half of the wagon, toward the large wheels and the farmer himself. He had his rifle raised in our direction and when the shells from my weapon hit his cart, he tumbled backward, directly into my line of fire.

"Got him," I said over the intercom, but I saw we were circling for one more pass.

The farmer was bleeding on one side, but he was standing again. His rifle was raised in our direction and I could see the flash from his muzzle. I fired again.

The shells marched in a steady progression toward

the spot he was defending and in less than a second, they cut into and across his torso. The rifle became airborne and the farmer fell to his knees. My M60 stopped firing and it too became still. I was out of ammo.

"We're out of rockets, Chief," Walsh said over the intercom, and the Huey started a climb back toward the sun. "Nice job – you got him."

With the empty brass shells pooling around my feet, I told Walsh I was out of M60 Ammo too, but I didn't feel like celebrating. Most of the time I fired my weapon, the jungle canopy always provided a visual shield for the enemy. I'd never seen them up close like this. I'd never seen one of them fall and know that I was the one who ended their life. I knew I had to do it, but I didn't want to think about it. My only thought was to get us back in one piece.

When we landed at Evans, Captain Walsh came into the back of the cargo bay and started counting the holes in the fuselage.

"Holy shit, Chief," he said. "We look like a piece of big green Swiss cheese."

He took a ball of twine and started connecting the holes. Looking at the way the metal flared around each hole, he figured out where the shells entered and where they left the fuselage. By the time he was done, the back of the Huey resembled some strange version of a spider's web. The most amazing thing was that not a single round nicked an electrical or hydraulic line. The fuel tanks and the main rotor had been spared and everybody on board that day came through it without a scratch.

"You must be our lucky charm," Braxton said,

without thinking.

I didn't smile. It only reminded me that any of the luck I had was left on the ground when Hooper and Connelly took off.

When we finally secured the aircraft for the night, I knew I had one more thing to do before I hit the rack. I'd been thinking about it for days and this mission sealed it. Captain Walsh had asked me earlier in the week if I'd ever thought about extending my tour.

"You've learned the ropes quickly," he said. "The Army's not a bad career. There's a push on for crew chiefs to extend. There might even be a bonus and a promotion for you. You should think about."

I had. If nothing else, I knew I was part of the unit, part of the Army, in a strange way, even part of this stinking land.

"I've thought about it, Captain," I said after knocking on the door to the Officers' tent. "I want to extend for six-months."

He had a funny habit of putting his index finger and thumb together and touching his top two teeth when he was trying to make a decision He didn't say anything, but his fingers tapped his teeth for a minute. In the end, the only thing he did was nod in my direction and he turned toward his desk. There were a set of papers on top with my name on them.

"Sign here, Warriner," he said and extended his hand toward me. In the last light of the day, I took the papers from him and pulled a pen from my service shirt. I signed on the bottom and that was that. I was going to be here for at least another year.

Captain Walsh took the papers from me and shook my hand. Before I could say anything to him, he pulled a small manila envelope from the top of his desk. He opened it and poured the contents into his hand. There were Sergeant's stripes for my shirt sleeve and gold chevrons for my collar.

"Put these on, Warriner," he said. "You've earned them."

13 - The Man in the Mirror

February 1970

The heavy metal door to Bobby Connelly's cell had two marks on the outside. One, a simple hand-painted black X, was about chest high and placed inches above the small sliding door that served as the portal through which Connelly's food pail was passed. The other, his cell number, 462, was stamped about six inches from the spot where the metal door formed a seal with the stained concrete floor. At some point in time, the floor and the door must have been the same color, but it had been decades since either one had seen any real care or maintenance. The hallway that served as an entryway to the row of isolated cells had a dark path running down the center of the floor from the dirt, grime, and blood that attached itself to the guards' boots.

The food for the prisoners who were kept in isolation arrived at odd intervals and some days not at all. It had been two years since Connelly was hauled, without regard for his wounds, from the transport truck that carried him from Laos to the prison in the center of Hanoi.

Connelly remembered climbing a set of stairs and being pushed and pulled down at least two hallways until his guards arrived at the door to his cell. It was an ancient, metal looking thing with the number 462 stamped near the concrete floor. Dazed, but still trying to fight against the two men forcing him to move forward, he started to speak for the first time in days.

"Hey, hey, hey! Where am I?" he asked. "Where are the other Americans?"

The guards were amused and annoyed by his protests and muttered something to each other in Vietnamese as their small hands tightened their grip and launched him into the dark and empty space.

Connelly lost his balance and tumbled headfirst into the space that was to be his new home. The cell was nearly square and each wall was no more than eight feet long. The ceiling, if you could call it that, was about 10 feet above Connelly's head and was crudely constructed with rusted, wire mesh. Through the center, the thin barrier above his head was stronger and bordered with steel bands.

What Connelly didn't know when he was first thrown into the enclosure, was that the X on his door meant he was to be isolated, kept away from most of the other prisoners or guards. He was an important asset.

It didn't take long for Bobby Connelly to understand that his cell was going to be lit 24 hours a day and the guards would walk overhead. Some of the nastier guards would spit or urinate through the grating as they made comments to each other. Connelly didn't understand their language, but he was sure they were laughing and disgusted with the American curled up beneath their feet.

The single blanket given to him provided no comfort

and certainly no protection from these random attacks and more than once, Bobby's screams woke him as he realized the wet and rancid smell that filled his lungs was coming from his bunk.

Bobby soon lost all sense of time and the days began to string together into one long ribbon of pain, anguish, and despair. He was not allowed to sleep according to any schedule nor was he given the opportunity to shut his eyes for more than 30 minutes before he was jostled back to a semi-alert state. After days, weeks, or months of this, his mind started to retreat and he lived almost exclusively in the world between his ears.

The one thing he knew or thought he knew, was that he must have some value for his captors. They hadn't killed him yet, and they certainly had their chances. Connelly became accustomed to the pattern of his interrogations. He was pulled from his cell and brought to a large, bright room about halfway down the hallway. There was one chair in the center of the room and more often than not, two officers were waiting for him.

In his head, he'd started to call them Martin and Lewis after the famous comedy team from back home. Martin was serious all the time and probably would have killed him if he'd been given the choice and the other one, Lewis, was smiling all the time like Bobby Connelly was his long lost friend.

"Robert Connelly," Martin said on one recent occasion. "We have learned quite a bit about you and your unit, it's time you verified a few things."

Connelly tried not to glare at the man. He'd seen him almost every week since he'd been put into this prison, but for the life of him, he wasn't sure if that was six months, eight months, or eight weeks. It had been a while, though.

"Warrant Officer Robert Connelly, from Escondido, California – a member of the famed 1st Cavalry and a Huey pilot," he said.

"Apparently, we are better at keeping track of you than your own U.S. Army," he said and pulled a letter-sized photograph from the manila folder he was carrying. Bobby knew this trick and didn't want to look at anything the man brought with him.

"Nhin! Look!" Lewis said and pulled Connelly's chin in the direction of the photograph.

Connelly struggled again and tried to force his face away from the guard, away from whatever he was holding. Without moving his head, he turned his eyes toward the folder and the photograph. He saw two pages from a newspaper, the front page and one of the inner pages. Someone was holding the paper and their fingers were curled near the top of the page, but they didn't block the area that contained the date: Monday, December 29, 1969.

As soon as that date registered in his mind, Bobby Connelly' heart started to pound and he was sure the guards could hear it thumping in the center or his chest. He felt as if he were suddenly wearing a weighted vest, a vest that carried the burden of his circumstances but also a vest that tightened against his chest with each passing second, each heartbeat. His breaths became shorter and the temperature in the room rose as he moved closer toward the picture. From the front page, he knew the paper was the San Francisco Chronicle but he still didn't understand why they were showing him the photo.

"Your country doesn't know about you. Your family doesn't know," Martin said. His voice was crisp and his English was clipped, almost forceful.

"To them, you're gone. You're missing," he said.

Bobby Connelly then saw the second page of the paper. There was a picture of a downed aircraft, it might have been an F4 Phantom, and beneath the picture, the heading for the article read: "A Record Number of U.S. Soldiers Listed as Missing."

To make its point, the story included a catalog of the major battles and campaigns of the year followed by an alphabetical listing of those still recorded as missing in action. Bobby Connelly saw his name: Connelly, Robert F. – US Army – MIA: 04 FEB 68. There he was - for all the world to see - just ahead of those names beginning with the letter D.

To Bobby, the nightmare had become a reality. He'd been a prisoner for more than two years – two years he screamed to himself. Connelly lost control and felt only anger and rage. He tried to spring forward and grab the photograph, but after two years without food, regular sleep, or any real activity, he was a weaker version of himself. The officer holding the photo laughed at the lunging prisoner, stepped quickly to one side and struck Connelly on the back of the head. He collapsed on the floor and as the air left his chest, he heard the officer ask him one more question.

"Are you ready to tell us about your unit?" he asked. "Maybe then you will be a prisoner."

Bobby Connelly heard the words, thought of the time he'd already spent in the prison, he thought of his mother and father at home and for the first time, he didn't see a way out. He started to sob as if he were still a small child. No matter what he told himself, or how he tried to control his body and emotions, he couldn't stop. With the pain, despair, and suffering of the last two years coming out of him with each spasm, he knew it was over.

"Yes," he said and exhaled deeply. Once more Bobby Connelly curled himself into a protective fetal position, holding the top of his head. "Yes," he said again, this time, louder.

For the first time, his words were met with silence. Still sobbing, he waited for a response from the two men.

"Good," Lewis said and Connelly felt a hand on his shoulder. He heard the man walk away and realized a second door has opened. Connelly pivoted his head toward the sound and saw a bathroom and the base of a sink.

"You wash up and take a seat," Lewis said. The hands that sought to hurt him a few minutes ago, lifted him as if he were another bag of grain or rice from the floor and turned him toward the open doorway.

Connelly looked once more in the direction of his interrogators and saw they were prepared for this outcome. There was a small pad of paper, pencils, and some type of electronic recorder on the table in the center of the room. Two chairs were moved into the space so they might be able to document this conversation.

Bobby Connelly took two steps into the bathroom and for almost a minute, he stared at the faucets as if he was unsure how to operate them. It wasn't the faucets that gave him pause – it was the rectangular piece of stainless steel above the sink. The polished metal surface was there to act as a mirror. He saw a face staring back at him, but it wasn't his face. It was the face of an old man – more like the face of his father or worse yet, the face of Henry Jackson, a few months before he died.

Connelly's skin was dark and mottled and his eyes were placed deeply within two nearly gray and black recesses. His beard had grown, but not evenly, and as he raised his arms to touch his cheeks, he noticed the back of his hands. The skin there was similarly dark and dirty, but it was also loose like he had shrunken on the inside and his skin didn't have the time to catch up. He settled himself and stopped sobbing. His chest had finally finished heaving and his breathing became regular again.

Bobby approached the sink as if it wasn't really there and turned both faucets. Almost immediately, the water started to run into the washbasin. For a minute, he stared in the direction of the falling water, but something deeper inside him instructed him to move. From the other side of the room, it must have appeared as if the prisoner was bowing to the water flowing in front of him.

He bent at the waist and pushed his hands and arms forward. His head met the crude washbowl he created with his hands and like a man deep in prayer, he closed his eyes and his face entered the cool, pool of water he was holding. Bobby Connelly didn't remember anything ever feeling so good. Every time he lowered his head, his hands pushed cups of clear water toward his eyes, nose, and mouth. It strengthened him.

One of the guards, Martin, watched as the prisoner a few feet in front of him washed in the water and from the noises he was making, he too understood things would be different with Bobby Connelly. He walked into the small bathroom and pulled the prisoner away from the sink. For a second, Bobby Connelly resisted, but soon he couldn't fight any longer and any defiance left in him was fleeting as he let the guard guide him back toward the table and chair. With water still dripping from his beard, he slumped into the seat and lifted his head toward his captors.

For the next four hours, with little interruption, Bobby Connelly talked about flying and the Aerial Rocket Artillery. The guards knew what unit he was attached to and the type of aircraft they flew, and the one thing they were most interested in were the details behind their operational plans. How many men? How many pilots? How far north? How far west? The questions were unassuming, direct, and asked in such a way that he was expected to answer with more than a simple yes or no. He was asked to explain.

Bobby Connelly had not given his captors much in the way of information for two years, and now in less than four hours, he told them stories about rocket runs, sorties to support the ground troops, missions to search for missing soldiers, and the training they often did on the hillsides surrounding their base. He knew he had to talk, but he also knew he didn't have to tell them the whole truth. With each story, with each detail, he managed to mix the truth with more than a little fantasy - numbers, quantities, duration, even time itself became a fable of sorts for Bobby Connelly. It didn't seem to matter to his guards and for Connelly, that was good enough for him.

The conversations lasted until late in the afternoon and probably as a gesture of good faith and as a way to encourage the pilot to keep talking, the guards announced that he would be allowed to go into the yard with the other prisoners before the evening meal. He would still be separated, but he would get to see them, to finally understand that he was not alone. More importantly for the guards, Bobby Connelly would understand that if he continued to cooperate, he might be transferred to the general prison population.

The guards took him from the interrogation room and brought him to the end of the hallway that bordered his cell. There was an ordinary looking door in the center of the wall and when the guard pushed it open, Bobby could see sunlight and the sky. He stopped moving, and like a person who through some miracle is given the gift of sight, he stood motionless and watched the clouds overhead. They were moving left to right and to Bobby, they were the best sight he'd ever seen. His entire being drew them in.

The doorway led to a pen, a small wire-encased enclosure with its own door or gate leading to an open compound. There were prisoners gathered in small groups throughout the yard. For Bobby Connelly, it was the first time he had seen a face with similar, western features since the day his Huey had crashed. He stared straight ahead and stepped into the confined space.

"You have five minutes," Martin said from the

doorway. "No talking."

Standing with his back to the building, Connelly didn't respond, but he didn't move either. He'd heard the guard and understood perfectly that he was not to interact with the other men in any way. For now, that was OK, he wasn't alone. Standing, without speaking, he moved both of his arms hoping the group nearest to him would see the movement and they'd turn in his direction. They did.

As their faces became clear and their eyes connected with him, an alarm went off in his head.

"They're going to know why I am in this cage, why they let me out," he thought. He started to shake his head, trying to signal them. "No," he thought and mouthed the word.

The men in the group started to move in his general direction but continued their conversation as if he weren't there.

"We see you," came a snippet of conversation. "Don't move - Don't look at us," came another burst directed at him. "We won't forget you," came the last bit of conversation and the men started to move away from him. Bobby Connelly wanted to run in their direction, to shake the wire walls that kept him separated, and above all else, to join them. He didn't know what else to do and stood frozen in place. His chin dropped toward his chest.

The guard came back through the door and reached for Connelly's arm. He wanted him to come back into the building. As Bobby turned, he tried once more to see the men who had been so close. He stumbled and almost fell to the ground, but managed to catch himself. As he did and started to stand again, he saw two large birds circling near the entrance to the yard. They made a low sweeping pass within 20 yards of the main gate. They picked up speed as they descended and passed over the yard, and without any hesitation or real effort, they climbed into the early evening sky and were gone. But they had been there. Bobby had seen them – and now he had a dangerous thought - he thought of home.

14 - Final days

March 1973

When Bobby Connelly's Huey crashed into a small field somewhere northwest of the city of Hue, and he managed to avoid capture, he often thought he might only live for five more days, or at most, five weeks. He was injured, dehydrated, and sure that his captors would have no use for him. More than once he told himself this was the end and as he lost consciousness, he never expected to see the light of this world again. Carried from the jungle to the prison camp in Laos, he never once thought he might spend the next five years as a prisoner of the North Vietnamese Army. With tears falling silently toward the filthy mattress beneath him and his wrists and ankles shackled to the corners of his steel cot, he started counting backward again. His breathing became faster as the months passed in his head and he realized he been in captivity for more than 60 months.

"How many days?" he thought and tried to do the multiplication.

Connelly shook his head in an effort to clear the tears and think through the math problem.

His eyes were closed and in his head, he saw a

small piece of white paper with numbers on it. During the past five years, Connelly learned to create images as a way of solving problems or thinking about the world he'd left behind. On the paper, in his own handwriting, he saw the multiplication problem, 365 X 5 = 1,825. Seeing the total didn't make it any easier.

Bobby Connelly screamed and tried in vain to pull against the chains that bound him to the steel frame. He wasn't always confined to his bed in this way, but if there was some type of infraction or the guards wanted him away from the rest of the prisoners, Connelly would be isolated in his cell for hours at a time, sometimes days.

Once, perhaps two or three years ago, he was in the yard and heard that some of the prisoners were taken to a hotel somewhere in the city. They were filming a statement about the war and the treatment of the prisoners. One of the men, a sergeant who'd been held longer than Connelly, told him the prisoners were allowed to shower, eat a real meal in a restaurant that served western food and those who were filmed were given a new set of uniforms.

"You only have to read from some stupid script," he said. "Nobody believes it's the truth and you get out of here, at least for a day."

Connelly stared at the sergeant, his mouth open but at a loss for words. He didn't know if this was the truth or one of the rumors that ran through the prison. Every few weeks there was a new one. He remembered rumors about the Russians coming to run the camp, prisoners were taken as human shields to other camps in the north, prisoners exposed to drugs and disease, even a rumor that some of the more valued prisoners were flown out of the country and taken to camps or labs in Russia.

After listening to the sergeant, the idea that he might be able to get a free meal and a shower was all that occupied his mind. Finally, as he and the other prisoners were being led back to their cells, he decided to ask. There were three guards that usually herded the men back into their cells at the end of each afternoon, and one of them, the oldest of the group, rarely screamed or yelled at them as they made their way into the building. Bobby Connelly decided he would he be the one to ask.

He turned the corner toward his cell and lowered his head in an effort to avoid looking the man in the eyes.

"Film?" he asked. "Do you make films in town?

The guard lifted his arm and stopped Bobby Connelly in his tracks. He cocked his head to one side as if to indicate that he hadn't heard the prisoner. Bobby thought it must be the English, but even after more than two years, his Vietnamese was limited to statements about food, the bathroom, and sleep. Bobby Connelly decided to ask again and never heard a second guard approach him from behind.

"Make film?" he asked again, speaking slower and a little louder. Pointing at his own chest he continued, "I will make a film."

The second guard, much younger and carrying a club in both hands, close to his chest, saw Bobby Connelly make a gesture toward himself and then point at the old guard in front of him. He didn't need to see anymore. Using his baton, and he struck Connelly with precipitous and brutal force in the back of the legs. The guards all understood that if you hit the prisoners, especially the tall Americans, in the lower half of their body, they would drop like their legs were made of thin twigs. Bobby Connelly fell to his knees and put his arm out to brace himself. The guard struck again, this time connecting with the spot where his skull and spine connected. He pitched forward, unconscious and unaware that his head was about to strike the floor.

The guards pulled him into his cell and shackled him to the bed. It would be hours before Connelly managed to open his eyes again. He wasn't sure how long he'd been out, or whether it was even day or night. The light was on over his cell and he heard the steady pace of the guard walking overhead.

The magnitude of the dull, deep agony in his head was offset by the sharp, stinging pain he felt in his legs and moving, any movement, on his bed only made the pain and discomfort worse. Two guards must have heard him moving and they approached his cell from opposite ends of the overhead walkway. They stood silent for a moment and snickered as they pointed toward the former American pilot beneath them.

One, a heavyset man with a pronounced limp said something to the other guard and pulled money from his pocket. Laughing, he pointed at his watch and made a motion like he was going to urinate on the prisoner. Bobby saw everything and understood all-too-well what they were about to do. He tried to turn his head away from the men, but with his restraints tightly bound to his arms and legs, he could not move more than a few inches. Bobby Connelly closed his eyes and waited for them, knowing they were using him for some form of amusement the way cruel children sometimes abuse helpless, captured animals.

But the guard didn't hit him as he watered the cell below him. Each, in turn, did urinate, but not with the intent of covering the prisoner. Instead, they sprayed both sides of the bedframe and laughed as Bobby Connelly wriggled and squirmed. Once he realized he wasn't their direct target, Connelly opened his eyes and he saw one of the guards pointing at his watch. He said something to the other man on the walkway, but Connelly didn't understand his meaning. Each guard smiled and Bobby thought they must have been talking about him, but he had no idea what game they were playing.

Hours passed and the two guards continued walking overhead without saying much to one another or the prisoners beneath them. Connelly tried to get some sleep but his mind was racing. Most of the time when he was shackled to his bed, he tried to sleep and let his mind escape from this reality. He figured, the longer he slept, the faster the time would go. Sleep, darkness, and dreams of home and his life before the crash were better companions than the reality he was forced to face. Today he was not that lucky. His body and mind remained focused and alert and time became an element of torture.

Connelly tried to calculate the correct day, month and year, but after so many sleepless days and nights, he was never sure of the exact date. His mind raced back to his home and he thought again of his father. He tried to remember the days they spent together on the lake. The time they worked on the machinery and labored to repair the cabins where the tourists and fishing groups stayed when they came for a week or a few days. He wondered if he would ever see them again in this life.

"Do what you need to do to protect yourself and the other men who are stationed with you," Jimmy Connelly said to him one of the last times they were together. He didn't talk about his time in the service much, especially to his son, but as the number of days before his departure grew smaller and smaller, Bobby remembered their conversations were often short, nearly cryptic, and focused on his enlistment.

"I manned the anti-aircraft guns on the ship when we went to general quarters," he said. "I couldn't let the zeroes hit us, and they always dove right for the main stack."

Bobby remembered his father, stopped talking, and he turned his attention for a while toward the sky, imagining he could once again see the planes that filled his dreams.

"Do what you have to and come home," he said.

The words were still ringing in his ears when he realized he was still bound to the bed. It had been hours since he'd last been released and now his bladder was reminding him of how many minutes had passed. He turned his head toward the overhead light and he noticed both of the guards had stopped moving and were looking down at him. The older one grabbed at his crotch and made a motion like he was going to urinate again. He laughed in the direction of the other guard and pointed to his watch.

The younger guard was not smiling and it became clear to Bobby Connelly how this game would be played. They were betting on when his body would let go and he'd piss all over himself.

"Arrgh!" Connelly said and pulled his legs and hands toward his chest. This only caused the guards to laugh more and they both placed their batons in front of their pants as if they were giant penises. They waved them back and forth and made noises as if they were letting air out their bodies.

Connelly closed his eyes and tried not to think about the increasing pain and pressure in his abdomen.

"Sleep, sleep. I hope I can sleep," he thought.

The two guards saw him close his eyes and starting spitting in his direction. Bobby Connelly felt the drops of liquid hit his arms, legs, and chest, but he refused to allow them to win. He refused to give in. Minutes passed and the guards started to become agitated at the lack of response. The globs of liquid became larger and Bobby remained still and refused to move or open his eyes.

The agony was almost too much and Bobby thought, "I'll squeeze out just a little to get rid of the discomfort." He tried to start and stop, but his body worked on instinct and betrayed the idea. He couldn't stop.

"Arrrre you happy?" he said as loud as he could, his voice ringing off the cell walls.

The guards noticed right away that they had won and started laughing again. Bobby watched as money changed hands and they left him there in the mess he'd made. He closed his eyes and turned his head toward the wall. For what might have been the thousandth time since his captivity, he thought about dying.

"It might be better than this - it's got to better than this," he thought.

With the pain in his abdomen gone, and his teary eyes swollen like small, overripe melons, his body collapsed and he slept.

He slept soundly for nearly an hour before the dreams started again. For the last month or more, the dreams were always the same. He was shackled to his bed and somehow he knew the prison was abandoned - no guards, no other prisoners, no other sounds. Strangely enough, in his dreams the bars, doors, and steel mesh that kept him from connecting with the outside world were removed. He was strapped to his bed, nearly naked, and alone.

In his dream, he could tell it was almost daylight and as the air warmed and daylight filtered in, he started to see the birds. They were large birds of prey, not eagles, not falcons, not anything he recognized but he knew they were deadly. Their talons and beaks were black and from the looks, they were razor sharp. Their wingspan was nearly three-feet across and the feathers that covered their massive chests and wings reminded Bobby of the bark that covered the redwoods back home. It appeared tough, strong, and almost impenetrable.

The birds circled as the air warmed and some deeper part of him knew that when they reached a certain height, they would dive for him. He was nothing more than another meal.

"Get out, get out," Bobby started to yell and the

birds turned their heads in his direction. The one who was leading looked directly at his eyes and it might have been a second or two before the creature turned to continue his climb toward the sun. The bird screamed, and the other birds responded as if they understood the instruction and started to dive toward the prisoner.

In his dream, he knew this was the end. They would tear strips of flesh from his body, feed on his organs, and pluck the eyes from his head. He started to yell again and heard the birds scream as they attacked their prey.

The nightmare always ended the same way. Bobby Connelly awoke to the sound of his own voice screaming. He was both bird and prisoner, both awake and asleep. This time he also heard a sound coming from the doorway.

The giant, ancient door opened and two North Vietnamese officers stepped into his cell. One was carrying a small package and the other, an official looking folder. One of the guards who had been walking above his cell entered after the officers and walked over to his bed. He removed the shackles from Bobby Connelly's wrists and ankles and stepped back into the hallway. He didn't look at the prisoner or acknowledge him in any way.

"The United States and the People's Republic of Vietnam have agreed to cease hostilities," the officer said as he read from the first page in his folder. Bobby Connelly tried to sit up.

"All existing prisoners of war will be released and repatriated to the United States of America," he said.

Bobby Connelly heard the words and saw the document, but he wasn't sure this was the truth. He started to stand, but his legs gave way, and he sat on his bed.

"You are leaving," the officer said. "Wash, get dressed and join the other prisoners. We are leaving for the airport within the hour."

"Home," Bobby Connelly said. "I'm going home."

15 - Watching the Count

March 1973

Everything in the Army is done according to the clock. Service time is counted and stored and your pay or rank may change based on the time you've spent in the field or on the job. The length of time you spend at a duty station or post is defined by the calendar. Even something as ordinary as a housing assignment is given to a soldier based on their length of service. I learned that it wasn't always whoever did the best job or completed the work in the most efficient manner who was promoted. As far as I was concerned, it was all about surviving to live or fight another day, and after five years with stripes of one kind or another on my shoulder, that was one thing I was pretty good at - simply surviving.

Most of the crew chiefs were not looking to extend their tours, especially those stationed near the border, so when I told Captain Walsh I wanted to stay, he showed me where to sign. I kept hearing this nagging voice telling me I needed to fly. I managed to stay in the air and away from the rest of the world for almost 18 months, and from the day Bobby Connelly, Hooper, Anderson, and Freeman were lost, my crew stayed intact, but that didn't make it any better.

"See," I thought to myself each time we landed. "I should have been there."

The week after I signed my extension papers, I managed to get a four-minute call home. It wasn't exactly a call with a pay phone, but I connected to the old black phone on the kitchen table. I heard my mother's voice. I remember telling her that I wouldn't be home as soon as they expected, but I was safe and would be home at the end of the summer, in the fall at the latest. What I didn't tell her, or my dad was that I finally figured out a way to sleep for more than a few hours.

Apparently, the Army had a special relationship with the big breweries and there were always cases of beer in the club or near the mess tent, and as a crew chief, it was pretty easy to store stacks of the 12-ounce cans under my rack. When I wasn't flying at night, I was drinking. I thought it was the smart thing to do – a way to get some sleep - it certainly seemed to help. The dreams and images of the missions and men I flew with stopped visiting me, but even with the beer, at least once a week, I woke up with a scream buried in my throat. I wasn't sure if anyone heard me, or if I even screamed, but the one thing that was certain is that each time it happened, my sleep for the night was over.

I hadn't heard anything more from Sandy and finally in one of my mother's weekly letters she told me she was engaged to some banker from Springfield. The college guy had worked in her branch office for a while and it wasn't long before he met Sandy. He was 4-F and wouldn't be heading over here to join me. He had a future. I guess that made the difference. They were going to be married in a few months and move away from Williamsburg.

"Huh," I thought to myself and read the letter one more time. I was surprised at how little the news seemed to matter to me now. When I wrote back to my mom, I don't think I even mentioned it.

About six months before I was scheduled to leave Vietnam, our unit started to take delivery of the Army's new Cobra gunships. They were mean and nasty things and I swear when we saw them flying through the sky, they resembled some giant lethal insect or prehistoric beast, all nose and teeth and ready to take a bite out of anything that got in the way. They were sophisticated killing machines and most of the time, the pilots flew without a crew chief. I felt like an old-timer, but I'd take the Huey every day of the week and twice on Sundays over the Cobra. The hell we created in the Huey was far more personal – we were certainly more connected to the troops on the ground.

At the end of my tour, I found out the Army was going to give me 30 days leave and additional travel time to get to my new unit. I was heading back to Fort Rucker as an instructor. I thought it'd be good to be the one giving the orders for a change. Tom Chambers, one of the other chiefs in the unit, was getting out of the Army altogether, and he asked me to head to Clearwater, Florida with him for a week before I went home. I had to go home. It seems my dad purchased a new forest green, Gran Torino for me, and it was sitting in the driveway in Williamsburg. They'd sent me pictures and said the dealer had even delivered it to the house. My dad had been driving it for almost three months, and my parents said if I didn't want it, they'd keep it for themselves. It looked like a great ride and I'd never had a new car, but Florida and a week on the beach sounded too good.

We got to Tom's house during the first week of May in 1969 and what he didn't tell me was that he had a sister, Gloria. She was younger, and from the first, I knew she was a wild thing. As we got out of the cab in front of their house, she came running from the screen door, a cigarette in hand and her large chest bouncing in the early morning sun. They lived about two miles from the beach and it wasn't long before the three of us were knee deep in the sand, beer, and the morning tide. After a day or so on the beach, Tom said he was heading to Tampa to see if there was any work at the airport for mechanics.

"I'll keep him busy," Gloria said and smiled in my direction. I wasn't sure what she meant, but I liked the way she walked toward me.

"We can spend the afternoon on the beach," she said and smiled. "Tonight, we can even have a bonfire."

We packed up some of the remaining beer and stopped at the store for enough food to get us through the day and Gloria smiled again at me as she picked up some sun-tan lotion.

"I may need some help with this," she said as she plopped it into our shopping bag.

That day might have been one of the best days of my life, from what I remember. We drank the beer, ate sandwiches and for a while, I forgot about the rest of the world and the past 18 months. As the sun started to set, Gloria turned to me and asked me if I'd like to move a little closer to the dunes and start a small bonfire. Whether it was the beer, the sun, or the way she barely fit into her clothes, I couldn't think of a better way to spend the night.

When the moon started to rise over the Gulf of Mexico, Gloria pushed herself a bit closer on the blanket and picked up my hand. I thought at the time I'd never seen such small and delicate hands. Mine were more like large clumps of misshapen pieces of clay compared to hers. I thought about the times I'd seen the moon on a night flight in Vietnam. It never looked like the half-shaded, yellow and white globe that was rising right out of the ocean.

"Tommy said you were a sergeant," Gloria said. "Are you getting out too?"

"Not yet," I said. "I've got to report to Rucker in 25 days or so and finish my enlistment. But, I've been thinking about signing up again. I think I can get a bonus."

She pulled her hand away for a minute and laughed. "They'll pay you to stay in?"

"Sure," I said. "It might not be forever, but I might be able to get enough for a down payment on a place, or possibly set it aside for when I get out."

She took my hand again and we both found another beer. For the next hour or so we sat almost silent, consumed with our own thoughts as we finished the last of the beer. I tried to stand when it was gone and was surprised by the way I almost instantly lost my balance. I started to laugh and reached for something solid to stop the fall, but all I found was Gloria. Our lips and bodies came together and I tasted cigarettes and beer. Strange as it was, it was the best taste in the world and I lost myself in her arms and legs.

Within two days, I'd decided she was the one for me, and I suggested that we get married and move with me to Alabama.

"We just have to go home and pick up my car," I said. "I'd like to see my folks for a few days and then we can drive to the base."

I don't remember much about the two days we were in Massachusetts, but it was strange to spend the night with Gloria in my old room. I didn't sleep well and more than once she caught me standing at the edge of the open bedroom window looking at the fields and pastures as chilly night air filled my lungs.

"Come to bed," she said. "It's freezing." She made noises as if her teeth were chattering and pulled me away from the window. I'd been thinking about the men in my unit who were lost and half wondered if this is what I'd survived for.

By the time we'd been at Rucker for a year, she and I managed to come up with an almost daily routine. Each afternoon before dinner, we'd have a beer or two while we waited for our food to cook and by the time we sat down, we'd often bicker or fight about some petty detail from the house. It could be anything from the way the bed was made to the dirty socks still on the bathroom floor. It didn't seem to matter – almost anything could become a trigger to ramp up our anger.

"I'm heading to the club," I said and almost ran through the screen door to the carport. In minutes, I had the car parked and I was in my usual spot at the far end of the bar. I didn't always spend the whole night drinking. More than once, I sat there alone nursing a beer and listening to the conversations floating around me. I recognized the tone, phrases, and the voices, soldier's voices and that made me feel comfortable. I understood the lingo, the emotions, but more importantly, I thought they understood me.

The days, weeks, and months all started to roll together. I reenlisted when I found out Gloria was pregnant and that caused a three-day battle royale.

"You've got to be fucking kidding me," she said and shut herself in our bedroom. Her muffled sobs stopped for a second and after drawing a deep breath I heard her scream, "What exactly am I supposed to do?"

"I'll take care of you and the baby," I said in a tone that made them sound like the burden they had become for me.

At the end of June 1971, I was transferred to Hunter Air Field in Savannah. I hadn't been promoted, but I hadn't been drummed out either. A few of my buddies found out that reenlisting was not an option or if they did stay in, they were going to have to take a reduction in rank. I asked the CO about another tour overseas, but he didn't seem to want any part of that conversation. He turned away from me and said no.

"We're trying to draw down and get the fuck out of there, Warriner," he said. "Why the hell would you want to go back?"

I didn't answer. I didn't know, but it was one way out of this mess.

"You're going to Hunter and I'm putting you in charge of one of the Huey maintenance units," he said and handed me a packet of forms.

"You'll also be on call for one of the honor details," he said.

I stared at him and tilted my head to one side as I tried to figure out what that meant.

"There is a military cemetery at Hunter and you'll be in charge of the enlisted detail," he said. "It's extra money and important work."

And now, nearly two years later, I'd become accustomed to the routine at Hunter, but it hadn't gotten any easier. Gloria and I still fought all the time and when we were not yelling at each other, I was still in a foul mood. The maintenance crew was all right, but I was bored with the work and I wanted to fly again. Vietnam didn't seem to be an option, but I heard the 1st Cav needed crew chiefs in Korea for units that were flying near the DMZ.

"I could transfer there," I thought, and after another knockdown, drag out fight with Gloria, I decided to ask.

"Sir, do you know if there are any openings for Korea?" I asked the CO. "I'm due to re-up next month and I was thinking about asking for a flying job."

Captain Jackson, the Maintenance CO, watched me and rubbed his chin as if he were trying to decide something.

"How much longer do you have on this

enlistment?" he asked.

"I think about six months," I said. "But I am planning to sign up for two more years at the end of this one," I said.

The Captain again turned his gaze away from me, and when the mirrored sunglasses covering his eyes finally turned again toward me, he said, "I'll tell you what, you commit for four more and I think I can get you to Korea."

As he finished speaking to me, I saw a black speck on the horizon. It was the Huey we'd been working on for the last week or more. It had gone for a short test flight and from the looks of it, everything was working fine.

"Sir, when do I have to let you know?" I asked the Captain and turned in the direction of the returning Huey.

"If we're going to do this, I think you should decide by today or tomorrow at the latest," he said.

"It'll be a flying job?" I asked and started to move in the direction of the landing area.

"Yes, Chief," he said. "Let me know."

I nodded and returned my attention to the Huey. It was now 50 feet over the end of the airfield and heading for the concrete apron that was connected to the Maintenance Hangar. Inside the hangar, I saw the Captain get into his jeep and pull away from the building before the Huey touched down.

"Hey, Gonzalez," I said in as loud a voice as I could manage. "Get out there and help them tie down the Huey as soon as they cut the engines."

The wind had picked up and every few seconds a gust of 20 miles-per-hour, or more, sprayed dust and sand across the concrete and asphalt-covered field. Gonzalez had been in the Army for almost six years and recently transferred to aviation from the infantry. I was trying to make him into a halfway decent mechanic. He gave me a thumbs up and started jogging to the area where the Hueys tied down.

For about a minute, the wind died down completely and the Huey settled into its normal spot. The main fuselage was about 25 yards from the big hangar doors and the tail was parallel to the building. Gonzales stopped about 10 yards from the Huey, with tie-downs in his hand and waited for the two pilots to turn in his direction. They were still talking to one another and didn't see him.

The Huey had been in for work on the tail rotor system. A few of the pilots had been complaining that at times no matter how hard they pushed on the pedals, the Huey didn't seem to respond. They had to compensate in the air by reducing power to change the direction of the aircraft's tail and nose.

"Gonzalez! Get back here until they're finished," I said, but with the main rotor still spinning and the turbine producing power he didn't hear me. He stood there, as if his feet were permanently part of the pavement, and watched.

A gust of wind hit the tail section and started to turn the aircraft. The pilots, feeling the wind hit the flat sided Huey with a dull thud, tried to compensate by pushing on the tail rotor control pedals. Nothing happened and then a second, more powerful gust hit the Huey. The tail swung violently toward Gonzalez and before he could move, the tail rotor cleanly decapitated the former infantry sergeant.

I screamed, but couldn't move. Gonzalez's body collapsed like someone or something had taken his legs out from under him. His head hit the tarmac, bounced, and then rolled as the waves of air from the rotor washed over his face. His eyes were closed.

~~~~~

Later that night, after the paperwork about the accident was completed, I decided to go to the club on the way home. I called Gloria and told her there had been an emergency, and I wouldn't be home until later. She said something about the kids or dinner, but I hung up before it got too far. I found the keys to my car and drove toward the club in silence, accompanied only by the images from the day.

The Officers' Club and the Enlisted Club were side by side, connected by an internal wall in the same building, and I saw Captain Jackson's car parked in front of the entrance to the Officers' door. Normally I would not step foot into officer country, but there were hardly any cars in the lot and I didn't need to see him for long.

It took 20 or 30 seconds for my eyes to adjust to the dimly lit room, but I saw Captain Jackson sitting alone at a table near the pool tables.

"Captain," I said, standing somewhat at attention next to his table.

"Warriner, what are you doing here?" he said. "I heard about Gonzales and thought you'd be home by now."

"No sir," I said, trying not to draw attention to myself. "I saw your car and wanted to let you know, I'd like the transfer to Korea. I'd like the chief's job."

He glared at me and didn't utter a word.

"Are you sure – four years and two of those are away from home," he said.

"Yes, sir," I said. "When will I go?

"Probably within thirty days," he said.

"Ok, thank you, sir," I said and walked next door to my side of the building.

After eight cool cans of Budweiser, I was falling asleep at the end of the bar, and I noticed the local news was coming on. They were saying something about Vietnam, but I couldn't make out the details.

"Hey, turn that up," I said, hoping each word was clear.

The announcer continued to explain that the first load of prisoners from Vietnam landed at Andrews Air Base this morning. I thought of the men I knew. I thought of Bobby Connelly and tried to focus on the television. In twos and threes - thin, gaunt, and sometimes sad looking men got off the plane. Most needed some assistance on the stairs and the majority wore uniforms that appeared to be one or two sizes too large. I studied the uniforms looking for Army Warrant Officers. I looked for the wings.

Some families rushed the men as they stepped on

American soil for the first time in years, others scanned the crowd hoping to see someone there to greet them.

The picture on the television started to become blurry, wavy, and I realized that tears had filled my eyes as I hunched forward holding my shoulders. Officers, enlisted soldiers, and sailors - people came and went, but I couldn't see him. I didn't know if he made it out alive. I didn't know if he made it home.

Epilogue

On most days, the English classrooms at Thornton Academy in Saco, Maine are filled with noisy and chaotic high school students. It's a place where homework is being finished or collected, gossip is traded about students and teachers, and there seems to be a constant buzz about the latest viral video or social media post. Today was different. In one of the classrooms, a group of 28 juniors and seniors were going to connect with a man who was sent to war three decades before they were even born. They were going to speak with a former soldier and helicopter crew chief who might be able to explain to them what it was like to live in a time when students, not much older than they were, faced seemingly impossible choices. The choices he and others made at that time changed their lives forever. He wanted to teach them about that and share something of his experiences.

Russ Warriner, an author, a decorated Vietnam Veteran, and a former resident of Old Orchard Beach, Maine was going to try to explain what it was like to be 17 or 18 years old and be faced with the choice of entering the draft pool (and in all likelihood being assigned to the infantry) or enlisting in the service. In either case, it was more than likely that Warriner would end up serving his country in Vietnam. He was going to speak to the class about the decisions he and his generation made, and what happened when the men and women who served returned home.

It was almost time to connect with the 68-year-old

veteran living in Florida, and the teacher fiddled with the controls on the large TV screen that consumed a large portion of the back wall of the classroom. He connected cables and switches from the screen to his laptop, shut off half the lights in the room, and assured the restless students that he knew what he was doing and he'd be ready in a minute. As if on cue, the screen of the laptop was projected to the television screen and a blinking green symbol flashed, indicating an Internet call was coming in. Warriner was nothing if not prompt.

When the teacher accepted the call, a man with a rugged, stoic face filled the screen. His eyes were searching for some indication the two groups could see each other. He was searching for his students. It had been at least 40 years since he last wore his country's uniform, but in many ways, he still carried himself as a soldier. He was trim and his full head of graying hair was cut short and neat. The mustache he now sported was not the bushy or unruly sort, but rather it was more of the neatly trimmed pencil thin variety worn by someone who spent time each day making sure his appearance passed his own version of an inspection. For Warriner, everything was in order. He now occasionally wore eyeglasses (a concession to age), but the polo shirt he chose for today's lesson had logos on it that were connected with veterans' groups and the creases on his khaki colored pants were regulation sharp. He smiled, looking for a familiar face and said, "hello." His voice was deep and throaty and yet there was a soft quality to his words and demeanor. It was an odd combination for a man who had seen so much.

The class and Warriner exchanged greetings and the

former staff sergeant told them a little bit about the talk he was going to give.

"If I get a little emotional about some of this, I apologize," he said. "Your teacher probably told you a little bit about these events, but sometimes they still affect me. I'd like to tell you how it started, how I got there and then if we have time, a story or two about the men who served with me."

For the next hour, the students sat silently in the room and listened as this veteran, living in a retirement community in Florida with his fourth wife, explained how someone who was about two years older than they were now ended up fighting for his country, his friends, and his life.

Warriner was born to working-class parents in the town of Williamsburg, Mass. He went to the local trade school and had ideas of working after graduation as a mechanic on heavy equipment of some sort, perhaps even the railroad. But by the time he left school (1966), the country was at war in Vietnam and "things were heating up."

"I knew I had a high draft number," he said. "My brother was already in the service, so I went to see what I could do."

The local recruiter for the Army told him he could work on tanks or other heavy equipment, but that was considered hazardous duty. If he worked on helicopters, there was a good chance would be assigned to a unit at one of the airbases. He told the young Warriner that he'd be away from the front lines. "That sounded good to me," he said. "He told me it would be safer."

Warriner took the necessary exams and passed the physical that would allow him to enter the aviation section of the Army. His basic training took place at Fort Gordon, Georgia, and then he was sent to Fort Rucker, Alabama. There he earned the Army's certification as an aviation mechanic specializing in helicopters, and in September 1967 he was given orders to report to the Military Assistance Command in Vietnam (MACV). The next stop for the 19-year-old Warriner was an air base in Saigon, and from there he would be assigned to an aerial unit of the 1st Cavalry, most likely in the north. Within a week he was transferred from the large airfield in Saigon and told to hitch a ride to one of the forward bases. He'd been assigned to an aerial rocket artillery battery. There he would learn his craft.

Almost four months later, on Dec. 11, 1967, his birthday, he completed his training at Camp Evans, a 3-acre clear patch of dirt carved out of the jungle near the city of Hue. He'd been training as a door-gunner and learning what it took to keep the UH-1C helicopters in the air, and now he was awarded the designation of crew chief and assigned to a specific helicopter and a group of pilots. He was a 20-year-old crew chief and door gunner, a proud member of the 1st Cavalry, 20th Aerial Rocket Artillery, 2nd Battalion, Charlie Battery. He and his unit were assigned to fight in one of the most dangerous areas of South Vietnam, only 10-15 miles from the border of Laos and North Vietnam.

Warriner's Huey crew regularly flew wire-guided missile missions throughout the jungle in support of troops who were fighting on the ground. "When a Ranger or Marine unit got pinned down, they'd call us and we'd send in missiles to try and keep the enemy away so they could get away or finish the job," he said. As a crew chief, Warriner made sure all of the mechanical equipment worked properly in the air, and from the cargo bay in the back, he would man the M60 machine gun and protect his ship as it sailed through the humid night sky.

"There were open doors on both sides and depending on the which way we banked, I would clip into the left or right doorframe," he said. "I wanted to be on the side that was facing the ground."

There were only three men in his crew - two pilots and a crew chief - and the chief had to make sure the Huey got them to the fight and brought them home. Warriner said that after 100 hours of flight time, he would routinely take his "bird" out of service for an airworthiness inspection, and in the early days of February 1968, he had to do just that.

The Tet offensive started late in January 1968 and Warriner's unit was given orders almost around the clock to fly support missions. When his crew was designated as the "hot section" (the next section to fly) they had to be in the air within two minutes after receiving their orders.

"We were flying all the time," he said. "As one (helicopter) was landing, another one was taking off."

On Feb. 4, Warriner took his aircraft out of service and the two pilots he normally flew with were temporarily assigned to another helicopter. They were both good pilots, and as a crew, they had become closer than blood relatives.

If needed, they would fly with another crew chief

while Warriner inspected their ship. He'd fly with them again when they returned to the base and his inspection was finished.

Warriner told the students that he had begun his work and after removing the metal inspection plates from his aircraft, the horns surrounding the base sounded. The piercing alarm signified an alert, a new mission, and the sound penetrated to the bone. The turbine engine on one of the replacement helicopters immediately spooled up and, with a screwdriver in his hand, Warriner watched his friends take off without him.

Warrant Officers Thomas Hooper and Robert Connelly (the pilots Warriner normally flew with) navigated away from the base, joining another Huey from their unit. As a flight of two, they took off to support an Army Ranger unit that was trying to take a hill near Hue. Enemy soldiers surrounded the Rangers, and as they called for help it became clear they had no means of escape. The two Hueys were going to try to fire some missiles into the area and clear a path for them. They needed to give the Rangers a way out.

"They had been gone for about an hour when the mission horns sounded again," Warriner said. "But this time, the battery commander came running and he said he was flying. That wasn't a good sign."

Warriner's two friends and the replacement aircraft they were commanding had taken fire from the enemy. The crew was now missing.

"I should have been with them," he said. "But I might not be talking to you today if I had."

Because the battle raged on, Warriner and the men

in Charlie Battery were not able to find Connelly and Hooper, and it wasn't until several days later that they located the missing Huey. "It was resting on its side," Warriner said quietly and removed his glasses.

"Hooper and the crew chief and the extra gunner were found at the crash site, dead, but Connelly was missing," Warriner said. His voice trailed off as he explained what happened to his crew.

According to Warriner, the infantry units fighting in the area found tracks leading away from the downed aircraft and they thought Connelly was alive and probably had been captured and taken as a prisoner of war.

"They got him, and he was taken north," Warriner said. "To the Hanoi Hilton."

Warriner explained that Bobby Connelly, the pilot who survived and was captured by the North Vietnamese Army, spent the remainder of the war in Hanoi as a prisoner and was only released when the peace treaty between the United States and Vietnam was signed in 1973.

"It would be 44 years before I saw him again," Warriner said. "But I never forgot him."

Warriner left the Army after serving for more than nine years, with an extended tour of duty in Vietnam and one more in Korea.

"I felt like I had to fly. That was my job," he said. Warriner tried the best he could to deal with the memories and demons he carried with him. But often he was unable to cope with the guilt and stress.

"After a while, I just tried to push everyone away,"

he said. "But that didn't help either."

After dealing with the effects of Post-Traumatic Stress Disorder (PTSD) for more than 30 years, Warriner wanted to find a way to honor all of the men and women who served their country. Living in Maine, and retired, he petitioned Gov. Paul LePage and asked him to declare the third Saturday in September POW/MIA day in the state of Maine, a day dedicated to the memory of all service personnel who were taken prisoner or listed as Missing in Action, no matter when conflict or war occurred. To his surprise, LePage agreed, and he signed a proclamation stating the day would be marked on the official calendar for the state.

With the document in hand and a community willing to help, Warriner worked for a year to organize a POW/MIA event to be held at the minor league baseball park in Old Orchard Beach. Dignitaries, speakers, and veterans of all ages were invited to the first of what he hoped would become an annual event. Warriner wanted to dedicate the weekend's activities to someone who served with him or served during his time in Vietnam. He immediately thought of his friend Bobby Connelly.

During the summer of 2012, Warriner found out that Connelly was living in California with his wife and three children, who were all born after he returned home from Vietnam. From a friend of a friend, Warriner got Connelly's home phone number and decided to call him.

"It was emotional," Warriner said. "But we talked for hours. I couldn't believe it was him on the phone."

Warriner asked his friend if it would be OK to dedicate the event to him, and would he consider coming to Maine to speak about veterans.

Connelly, who had never publicly spoken about his time in captivity, agreed to come to the event and talk about his time in the Army and his time as a prisoner of war. Thursday, Sept. 20, 2012, Warriner and four other men from his unit in Vietnam waited at the Portland, Maine airport to finally see their friend and fellow soldier again. All of the men who waited at the bottom of the escalator for arriving flights strained for a glimpse of their friend. Each man was now in his 60s and they lived throughout the United States, but for one brief moment, they were together again. They hugged, cried, and laughed about each other - they were young men again, young men who would do anything to bring their friends home.

Warriner explained to the students that he has since moved to Florida for health reasons, but he still stays in touch with Connelly and many of the other men who served with him.

"It helps me," he said, and then after a short pause he added, "I think it helps them too."

The allotted time for the talk was quickly drawing to a close and the teacher, who had been silent for nearly an hour, interrupted and told the students they would have to wrap up their conversation, but wondered if there were any last minute questions or comments.

Sitting at his kitchen table 1,500 miles away, Warriner nodded in the direction of the class and said he'd try to answer as best he could.

A thin, 16-year-old girl with bright eyes and a serious expression was sitting near the edge of the class and she quickly raised her hand.

"Go ahead Abby," the teacher said.

Abby sat a little straighter and tilted her head more toward the center of the room so Warriner could see her on his screen in Florida.

"I wanted to thank you for your service," she said. Within seconds, Warriner's eyes filled with nearly five decades of emotion and he turned in the direction of the young girl.

"Your story is amazing," she said and now noticed the reaction her words had caused. Her eyes filled with tears too.

"Thank you," she said. Warriner watched her and scratched the place where his hairline connected to his forehead. He turned again toward the teacher and simply said, "You're welcome." Seconds later an electronic bell sounded and it was time for the class to move on. The lesson was over.

ABOUT THE AUTHOR

David Arenstam was born in the foothills of the Berkshires in Massachusetts, raised by the sea in Plymouth but spent most of his adult life raising a family along the shores of the Saco river in Maine. Always creative at heart, Arenstam owned and operated a small data processing and software firm for nearly 20 years, but it was only after selling the business that he found his real passion and voice in teaching and writing.

Never one to sit still or stop learning, Arenstam has studied mathematics, literature, education, writing, and many forms of technology. Teaching and writing now fill his days, and he often tells his students, "the world just might be the greatest classroom you'll ever enter - take a minute and look around. You'll be surprised at what you see and the lessons you'll learn."

He is a proud and dedicated faculty member at Thornton Academy, an independent high school in Saco, Maine, and as a freelance writer, he contributes regularly to local newspapers, magazines, and online media companies covering current events, Maine lifestyles and writing human interest articles. As a lifelong student, his thirst for education continues, recently receiving a master's degree in journalism from Harvard University.

Made in the USA
Columbia, SC
01 May 2017